The
Poppy Field Diary

Carey
Richard

Bonhoeffer Publishing

Copyright © 2014 Bonhoeffer Publishing
Cover Design by BespokeBookCovers
Cover Poppy Image by Joaquim Alves Gaspar

All rights reserved

This book is a work of fiction

Cataloging-in-Publication Data on file with the Library of Congress

ISBN: 978-0-9899692-3-9

Printed in India

bonhoefferpublishing.com

Table of Contents

To
True Love

Prologue
September 2001

The day the Taliban assassinated Ahmad Shah Massoud, I crossed the Khyber Pass from Pakistan in a fever. I do not remember much about that day. Two nights later, my husband and I followed the shortwave radio reports of the attack on the Americans. As their shining city burned, I listened wearily to the distant shouts of "*Allahu Akbar*" from the village in the valley below my cabin. The staccato of automatic weapons sang a familiar anthem to the greatness of our tribes as bold tracer bullets etched the dark night—the shooting stars of zealous fools.

My husband stood on the sill, his sturdy shoulders filling the door frame. I never dreamed there would be a time when I would loathe him. I never dreamed I would curse him and rail upon him and defy him. I never dreamed my oldest son would become a legend in the resistance or that I would stare into the muzzle of a Kalashnikov and wish for the flash of a hasty round. I never dreamed I would dine with the Kabul elite or feel indebted to my enemy. I never dreamed love was violent and cruel. I did not know passion and jealousy were unmerciful, like the roar and flame of war. I did not know forgiveness was such a weary journey.

I thought my life would be romantic. I thought I would squander idyllic seasons in my medieval valley, among my books, surrounded by my children and my grandchildren. My life did not follow the course of my dreams.

I was wrong to dream. I was wrong about many things. But most of all, I was wrong about love.

Chapter 1

Seed—

Summer 1962

In the valley above my village lies an uncultivated field of poppies. And in that field, I scattered the seed of my naïveté. The summers in those days were as fresh as my mother's myrrh-scented hair. I would bury my face in the long sweetgrass and breathe in the deep, musty earth and cry without knowing why. Those daydreams have haunted me through the journey of my lamentations. I have tried to summon the virgin tears sown in such deep longing, but they will not return to me. It seems there is only one innocent season.

I once thought my field was a place of innocence, but it was only a gullible dream. Like the ground fog that rolled down from the mountains to consecrate my field in an elegant cloak, my innocence diffused. Those early mists gave a sense of mystical quiet, but they never lasted long. The harsh summer sun burned them away and baked the ground in merciless fury.

I wish I could have remained innocent. I wish my heart could have been kept in a careful swaddle, locked away in a secret garden, and guarded by benevolent fairies. I wish my heart could have been a simple heart, like the mongoloid child who lived in a nearby village—trusting and joyful and guileless. But my heart did not stay innocent.

I suppose no one is truly innocent, but some were like my mother. Some were beautiful. Little remained after war and greed and bloodguilt fury ran roughshod down our terraced slopes. Nothing beautiful endured. I wish I had understood, in those unfeigned days, the value of her elegant heart. But how can a selfish young girl understand grace?

I loved everything about her. Proud and erect and tall, she was exquisite. Her flawless porcelain skin glowed translucent in the clear sun of morning. Sometimes I would hold her hand up to the light that shone strong and bright through our window and marvel at the warm pink glow of the web of skin between her fingers. Her hair, long and straight and black, glistened in that sun like an oiled whetstone. I loved to help her wash it.

I would stand on the rickety bench in the courtyard and perch a wooden bucket on the top of my head. Sitting on the short milking stool, she would smile up at me. Her hair, flowing down over her face, was so long it would pool into the pan on the ground between her feet. I would tilt forward and release a steady stream of soft rainwater over the back of her head, and her hair would sparkle from the sheen of the cascading stream. She would soap and rinse it twice; then standing, she would wring out clear streams of water and squeeze her fist down her long rope of hair. She would finish by snapping a smooth wooden rod along the dangling mane, scattering a thousand droplets that shimmered like jewels on their brief journey across the courtyard.

It was magical. I would set my empty bucket down and watch in reverence. In my most desperate dream, I dared to hope that someday I would be beautiful like her. She told me I was pretty, and I suppose that at the time I was pretty, but I was not beautiful.

I learned of love within that careful cocoon. It was all I knew. In my innocence, I did not know there could be counterfeit love. I only knew of trust, of patience, of kindness, of fidelity, of hope. But for the love of a father, there was no affection lacking in my life.

Mother's marriage was a love match. In our land, a girl's family selects the man she will marry, and the decision is more of a financial matter than a heart matter. The dowry negotiations involve the extended family of uncles, aunts, and cousins. The haggling is tedious. When the family reaches an agreement, the bride has the right of refusal, but she rarely exercises that right. Tyrannical fathers intimidate their young, illiterate daughters beyond their wits. The rule of the men is the rule of law, and they rule without mercy.

I never knew my father. I only knew his fading black-and-white photo propped against the wall above our mantel. I would stare at it for hours, memorizing every detail of his lean, rugged frame. He was a foreigner, and my mother had suffered because of him. But she said he was her only love and worthy of her suffering. She said she had no regrets.

I had many. I regretted that I had never touched him, that I had never inhaled the warm musk of his jacket or felt the tickle of his mustache on my cheek or heard him call my name. I regretted that I had never known his love. Every little girl first loves her father and I suppose that every little girl is eventually disappointed. The young man of her fascination grows old and stern and possessive. Most young girls do not remember a vigorous young father but an aging tyrant. But my father was forever etched in my memory, young and lean and strong. He peered down from that mantel with a flirtatious, whimsical smile. He never disappointed me.

He was French and had come up through the Khyber Pass from Pakistan before the Russians raped my land, before those barbarians planted their mines and strafed the hills and roared up the valleys in their deafening tanks. He came in the time before the mujahideen and the Taliban, in those days when my field and my mountains and my people were noble.

Mother said he spoke Persian with hardly an accent, but she preferred when he spoke French. It was the language of his heart, she said, and though she scarcely understood a word, she would insist he speak it to her as they shared their evening tea in the fading sunset. I understood very little French, but I understood the language of the heart. She murmured that language to me as she put me to bed in my tiny loft above the kitchen. She spoke that language when she called me her little lamb and kissed me softly on my forehead. And in that gentle language, she was most fluent.

That my mother had managed a marriage to a foreigner was a testament to her remarkable intelligence. Matrimony outside the clan is frowned upon in my country, and most of my friends married their cousins. She never told me how she negotiated the marriage, but from my aunt I learned that the dowry my father offered had convinced our family. He paid them with local red gold.

Part of the dowry agreement entitled my mother to the rights of the property outside our village where my poppy field lay. In that field, my father built a small cabin. The little cabin was nothing like an Afghan village house. Busy rugs and garish pillows cluttered the village homes' floors. Their filthy, chaotic kitchens reeked of kerosene and cooking oil. Crude rope beds, cloaked in greasy blankets, occupied the corners. Blank-faced relatives stared down from canted wall photos. The floors were usually mud.

My father's cabin had a polished wooden floor. A headboard, carved from a single piece and as smooth to the touch as an old weaver's shuttle, stood framed against the pale back wall. A down-filled comforter contrasted its dark, waxy surface. The whitewashed walls were earthen like those in most Afghan homes, but they were accurately squared and tall. There were no trinket-filled nooks carved into them, no sooty candles. The little house had a sparse elegance about it. There was even a table and a set of chairs. It smelled of wax and old wood and clove oil.

I learned much about my father in the hours I spent in that little cabin. I learned that he was unpretentious, elegant, uncomplicated. He loved finely crafted things and natural textures. He was attentive to detail, perhaps even a little fastidious. Beauty fascinated him. It was no wonder that he abandoned his homeland for our stark mountains and my mother's captivating allure.

The cabin was a dangerous place for a woman to live alone, so when my father died, we moved in with Mother's family. It was a good arrangement. Unlike most families, we had our own house inside a small compound. It gave us privacy. I learned later that solitude is a sacred thing.

It was rare for a woman to own property, but my father's foresight, and perhaps his foreign sensibility, put my mother in a unique position within the family. It was not a large property, but it was hers, and Mother was proud of it.

Below the meadow was an apple orchard, also part of her land. The fruit from those trees was sweet and abundant. In the fall, when the air turned dry and cool, we spent weeks in the orchard. We cored and sliced the late-season apples and treated them with sulfur to keep them from browning. We spread the delicate fruit under gauzy nets to dry. Those dried apples were sweet and chewy and irresistible. My uncle took them in large cloth sacks to the markets in Kabul, where we could get a better price. The income Mother made from that orchard provided enough for us to live on throughout the year.

We never stayed the night in the cabin, but we spent long summer days there. Mother and I would trudge up from the village compound with our lunch in a shoulder bag, and we would squander the day lolling on the grassy slopes and napping in the cabin. The little cabin was perched on a small rise at the edge of a stand of pines. The slopes that rose behind it were steep and the land poor for farming, but the little meadow below was lovely. When the poppies and wildflowers were blooming, it was like a garden. Every spring my mother would remind me that poppies were the flower of love, but my aunt insisted they were the flower of the dead.

I once dreamed of butterflies as I napped alongside Mother in that gentle field. They brushed my face with wings as soft as breath, their vivid colors flashing bright. I have never heard a butterfly's sound, but in my dream the buffeting strokes of their wings made tender rumbles like distant thunder. I awoke to Mother's placid face. She was caressing my cheek with the soft petal of a poppy bloom. She had a face that glowed with kindness. In her deep doe-brown eyes, I saw bottomless pools of affection. I can recall only two moments in my life when I was angry with her, and though she had teased me from a restful sleep, I could not be cross with her on that sunny afternoon.

A person would have to make a deliberate effort to dislike someone like my mother. She had a soft, winsome face and full, expressive lips that often parted in a broad, open smile. She showed her pleasure effortlessly and her joy always made a way for her. She danced through life with a gracious ease that I did not understand until I was much older. As I roused from my slumber and my senses cleared, she mouthed silent words to me. I read her lips and I felt her tender breath on my cheek and I inhaled her sweet scent.

"I love you," she said.

Though I lived in a home that lacked the presence of a man, I understood love. I understood hope and desire. I understood the spontaneity of flirtation and careless companionship. I learned of those things from my mother and from the books that filled our days. I understood that the love I dreamed of was not the love the village women knew.

When the women gathered at the well or in the market, they told endless stories of shattered passion. One of my distant cousins married at sixteen to a fifty-three-year-old man. She was his third wife, and both the other wives were well past their prime. My cousin was attractive and the dowry exorbitant, which made the family happy, but her husband was fat and old and disgusting. She became his sole bedmate. She told me the nightly click of the lock on the bedroom door made her nauseous. She moved into his house in Kabul, and three months into her marriage, she was discovered dead in her room, an empty bottle of pills on the shelf at the head of her bed. Mother determined that I would never become one of those tragedies.

Mother and I both loved Persian poetry, and often I would catch her dabbing a silent tear from the corner of her eye as she read those ancient verses. I am certain there were times when loneliness was her only embrace, but she never pined for Father and she never complained. She had an extraordinary capacity to care for the women around her, though few of them deserved that courtesy. Her compassion was infectious and sometimes when we read I would weep for the women I knew around me. Few of them knew anything outside their village. Their lives were little more than endless suffering. They were petty and ignorant and malcontent.

In some ways, my life was like the lives of the young village girls I played with as a child. We had little in the way of possessions. Our days were simple. But in spite of the confines of our culture, I had enormous freedom. I knew of a world beyond my own. There were no boundaries to my dreams. The village girls were subject to the whims of their fathers, but I was subject to no one. I would choose my own destiny. I would marry the man I desired. I would pursue my own ambitions. I would not die by my own hand like my cousin, in some sad little room in Kabul.

When I heard of my cousin's suicide, I went to my field and sat under a pine as the sun set over the mountains on the opposite side of the valley. By the light of a full moon, I wrote a verse to her. And as the Milky Way emerged on that brilliant night, I buried it among the poppies.

Twilight Sowing

I mourn you, little sister
I grieve for what we lost
Your modest alabaster
Poured like milk
Before a ravenous dog

Chapter 2

Virgin—باكره

I suppose I was fortunate to find him so early in life. But fortune is a capricious thing. Fortune will taunt you in hope, then dash your heart on the stones of your ambition. It will tease you and rouse your dreams, then jeer your foolish longing. I suppose fortune must run its course before its true intent can be understood. Like unfamiliar seed sown with the winter wheat, it cannot be comprehended till root has taken hold. Then it is too late. You must make do with whatever harvest fortune has produced.

I saw him for the first time in my poppy field. I was barely sixteen and later learned he was twenty-two. He was watering his horse in the stream that meandered along the northern edge of the meadow. An early mist shrouded him. The horse was a dazzling stallion, well groomed and muscular. It pranced high-strung in the shallows of the stream, agitated over something and splashing his trousers with the icy water. He caught the beast's nodding head by its halter, pulled its face near to his, and spoke quietly. The horse calmed and lowered its head to drink deep from the pristine waters.

He had the self-control of a royal. I felt dizzy and steadied myself with my hand on the trunk of a nearby pine. He must have caught my movement out of the corner of his eye, as he turned in my direction. His motions had a strange confidence about them. He showed no panic, no startled shout—just calm attention to the stir he had sensed. He wore a gray *pakol*, the traditional Tajik woolen cap, placed on a jaunty cant. A sly, crinkled face and a sparkling gaze framed his coy little smirk. I was close enough to see his hands firmly gripping the sweat-darkened reins. His left hand, wrapped in a gauze bandage, wept thin, bloody serum through the soft knots that defined his knuckles. He wore fawn trousers and a shirt, handwoven in the old way. It billowed around him, clean and exotic. I could almost smell the fresh fabric. His chocolate-brown vest was crisp and trimmed with delicate gold thread in the Pakistani style. An antique silver cuff bracelet adorned his wrist; its dull carnelian stone emitted a warm, elegant glow. He kept his nails clean and carefully trimmed. I was most interested.

I stepped behind the tree but knew he had seen me. He made no sound, no movement toward me, no acknowledgment of my presence—nothing. He was unfazed by my spying, as if he were accustomed to young girls fawning over him.

I wanted to run, but was afraid. I wanted to call to him, but was ashamed. I wanted him to call to me, but prayed he would not. I felt a peculiar pounding in my breast, and my face warmed in a startled flush. I hid behind the tree, begging God to send him away and hoping God would not hear my prayer. And suddenly he stood before me, smiling, gazing intently. He kept a respectful distance and said in a gentle voice, "Hello, little one."

My face was uncovered, and I knew a crimson blush was visible on my throat. This man was not my relative, and it was scandalous for me to stand before him uncovered. I should at least have concealed the lower part of my face with my shawl. In 1962, few Afghan women in the villages wore the burka or the chador. The wealthy women in Kabul wore them, but it was more for status than for religion. In the countryside, a burka interfered too much to be practical. Nervous, I glanced around to see if anyone was watching us. He laughed—not in ridicule, but in an open, abandoned way that at once settled me, as if he'd cast some mystical charm over me. I smiled at him and felt a surge of desire. As surely as he had tamed the restless beauty he held by the reins, he had tamed my impatient heart.

"Perhaps we will meet again," he said with a faint smile, and in a moment, he was gone.

I watched his broad back as he disappeared down the trail that descended from the meadow. He paused just before the trail turned, half wheeling his horse to look back at me. He caught me staring, of course, but I held his gaze with a confident, bemused smile. I, too, knew a few secrets in the sorcery of love.

As I trance-walked along the dusty path back to the family compound, I remembered the visit of a wandering holy man who had appeared at the gate of our compound one evening. He stayed three nights.

The old mystic frightened me. He smelled of hashish. Fresh blood stained his rough tunic, and flagellation scars were visible on the back of his neck. His hair was unkempt, his fingernails long and black with dirt, his face weathered from wandering in the mountains. One night as he sat in our compound in meditation, he entered into a trance and murmured cryptic messages to some of the family members. Most of what he said made no sense to me, but he captivated the adults with his ramblings. He looked at my mother and after a long, unblinking gaze began to weep, saying nothing. His tears rolled strong, the large drops disappearing into his thick, disheveled beard, and though he wept, there was no expression of sadness in his hollow eyes, no quiver to his lips. He was serene. His passion seemed to make the men uncomfortable, but the women curious. Everyone shifted uneasily— everyone but Mother. Mother smiled and gazed into the night sky as if she were reliving a fond memory. I knew she was remembering the early days of her courtship with my father. The circle in the courtyard grew eerily quiet.

I sat on a mat next to my mother with my head resting against her shoulder and my hands entwined around her arm. The old mystic shifted his gaze from Mother to me and began to quote a poem written hundreds of years ago by Jalāl ad-Dīn Muhammad Rūmī, a famous medieval Persian Sufi. I recognized the passage. The mystic lilted in a soprano voice, as if he was singing the words.

The agony of lovers
They burn with passion's fire
They leave traces of their journey
The wailing of broken hearts
The doorway to God

After a long pause, he spoke to me. His voice dropped an octave, and his words flowed in a slow, almost caring cadence, as if he were a benevolent father. "Very soon you will discover your yearning," he said. "You will weep for joy, but your joy will become your mourning. And after a dark winter has passed, your mourning will become your solace."

It was the most coherent thing he said all evening, but it made no sense to me. My mother looked cautiously at me, concerned, and I heard some of the women begin to whisper to one another. The words unsettled me, but they also aroused my curiosity.

In my embryonic notions, I did not know that destiny and fortune could be altered. I thought that God had set my fate and chronicled the course of my life on the tapestry of his starry night. I believed in *inshallah*—what God has willed will be as God intended. I never dreamed that God could change his mind, or that forces beyond his influence might alter the course he had set for me. I assumed his providence would sweep me along in the tide of his altruistic love. I thought God's love and my husband's love were one. I believed God loved me as I loved him and I assumed he would send a man to me who would love me with the same loyal affections.

I thought I would journey into love in the way I journeyed from my village to the sanctuary of my field. I ascended to that field through meadows of wildflowers and scented herbs and graceful apple orchards. I climbed those gentle slopes on careful ancient paths, clinging to the cool, slender hand that guided me through my simple life.

That night I began my diary. It was not my diary, really, but my father's. It was a beautiful book, hand bound with soft, ancient calfskin. Graceful script filled the first twelve pages. I could not understand the French sentences, but

I did understand the title, *Mon Rêve Devenu Réalité*. I thought it was a fitting title for my diary.

My Surrender

You are my hope
And without regret
I bare my feet with you
And longing calls me
Rushing down
Like glacial streams
Swift and pure
And unashamed

Chapter 3

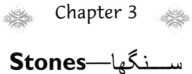

Stones—سنگھا

In early spring, the rain comes in torrents. The stream bordering my field swells and roars and gallops down the hillside, reckless and untamed. From the slope near the stream, you can hear rounded stones knocking together as the water hurtles past. The roar of the water muffles their banging, but the sound is unmistakable.

I have often thought of those stones. They did not begin their journey smooth and round. They began as jagged mountain rocks. As they moved season after season down our valley, their raw corners chipped away, and they became marvelously oval and, sometimes, perfect spheres. They were delightful to heft in the palm of your hand. Most were about the size of a man's fist, and they were smooth, substantive, and oddly reassuring.

The smaller ones made fearsome weapons in a sling, and in the early days of the resistance, one of the village boys killed a stout Russian with just such a stone. I had no interest in killing Russians or in gathering stones for house foundations or for lining wells. But I loved the sound of their violent journey. I loved that they started their descent as one thing and became another. I tried to imagine them rolling along the bottom of the stream, driven by a relentless force.

They were much like me, caught in an unbridled deluge. Like me, they were becoming something different. Like me, they were more beautiful in their aging than they were in their awakening. And that, I suppose, best describes what happened to me the day I met my husband—the beginning of a chipping away of the ragged edges of my heart.

I called him my husband before I knew his name, and I became so comfortable with the title that I preferred it. Maybe that was one of my mistakes. I do not know. Sometimes, it seems, all the weary efforts of reliving the past bring me to the same conclusion: that love is a relentless pounding of stone upon stone. But sometimes in that violent and weary journey, stones are broken. And sometimes they are crushed. And sometimes they languish in the bottom of deep and still and forgotten pools.

Some said my eyes were stones, but not the stones of the river. They are the turquoise stones from the mountains. Thanks to my French father, my eyes are a color I have never seen in any other pair of eyes in our valley. My mother said they were alluring. The ancient, illiterate village midwife said they were the eyes of a sorceress. My husband said they reminded him of the sea. He was the only one in our valley who had seen the sea. When he described its translucent depth, I felt proud of my heritage. He said he could contentedly drown in those deep-blue pools.

I lived for those brief moments of his devotion. Nothing made me more content, and nothing made me more fearful. I knew my bloom would one day fade, and I wondered what he would think of me then. I wondered if he would still desire me.

I was fascinated with my developing body, and I knew that as I matured I would be beautiful. After we were married, I would often catch him studying the curve of my hip as we lay together in our bed. It seemed he never tired of gazing along that soft flow. He said it reminded him of his favorite mare. I had laughed and playfully slapped him for comparing me to his horse. But deep inside I enjoyed his desire, and I longed for the caress of his hand as he traced that familiar curve. In the gentle days of our flirtation, I could only imagine those memories, but I knew someday they would be my possession.

It was a month before I saw him again. Spring was bursting, and the apple orchard below my field was a fine blanket of white-and-pink bloom. The poppies had not yet opened, but they were swollen with ripe potential. And the valley seemed full with the lust of new and fresh beginnings.

My young body was awakening, and sometimes at night I would ache with desire. I was moody, and for the first time I can remember, I raised my voice to my mother. Later I told her I was sorry, and I asked her forgiveness. She just smiled and said, "It's all right, my little lamb. Spring has come to your heart, and you are bursting with pent-up love. You do not yet understand, but in time you will. I will help you find your love."

He came up the muddy road to our home on the same magnificent animal I had seen him watering in the stream above my field. Red mud of the lower valley spattered the horse's lower flanks, but it pranced in vanity, if a horse can be vain. It was midmorning, and the air was clear and pungent with the aroma of the herb garden near our door. I was drawing water from the well when I saw him. Surprised, I dropped the bucket, and it clattered noisily down the well. The echoes of its descent sounded comical, in that hollow flutelike sound only a well can produce. I giggled and shyly covered my mouth with my shawl while he roared with laughter. It confused me that he had come to my very house.

Astride that silken horse, he towered over me—domineering, commanding, frightening. Though I laughed in feigned glee, my heart pounded in my chest. The brilliant clanging of the bucket in the well startled his horse and he snapped the reins tight, pulling the animal's mouth back toward its chest and arching its neck. The horse struggled against the bit, lolling its tongue. Its eyes, for a moment, gazed wild and unwilling. It pranced backward a few steps, dancing on spry, nervous legs, and reared. My husband never lost eye contact with me as he stilled the anxious beast. One of his sleeves billowed and I caught a glimpse of his powerful forearm. I saw corded bands of sinewy muscle ripple under his tanned skin. I imagined him sweeping me up and onto his saddle with that sun-darkened arm. I imagined him rushing off in wild, reckless abandon, my heart racing along with the pounding hooves of his thundering stallion. I thought that he would be a difficult man to manage.

"Is your mother home?" he asked.

"Yes, of course," I said. I waited, wondering what to do next, as he sat, smiling, holding my gaze. With great embarrassment, I realized that I should go and get my mother. I turned toward the door and was surprised to see her standing there, a broad smile spreading across her face.

"Make some tea, my lamb, and bring it to the courtyard."

It would have been shameful for them to meet alone, so Mother summoned my uncle, and when the men were seated, she poured the tea. They spoke for hours in low, muted tones, and it was clear they did not intend for me to hear their words. I was bewildered at first, but as their conversation continued into the second hour, I understood what was happening. He was interested in me.

I ran from our house in terror. My hands trembled uncontrollably, and my stomach knotted to the point of nausea. I ran to the only sanctuary I knew. I ran to my field of poppies. And there I dreamed impossible dreams of a pretty, young girl about to become a woman. And there I wept the last tears of my childhood and sowed them into the spring-softened ground. And there I noticed that the first of the poppies were blooming.

Song of the Stone

Stone upon stone
We tumble down
One upon another
And stone upon stone
We build our house
And fill it with dancing children

Chapter 4

Death—مرگ

From the vantage point of my meadow, I could see down the valley the green cultivated fields of three villages. In the growing season, barley and wheat and rye blanketed the terraced slopes in striated green hues. At harvest, workers filled the golden, dusty fields. From my distant little prairie, they looked like ants as they toiled through the day. I often wondered what their lives were like as they trudged through season after season. I wondered about their ambitions and their dreams.

I could see the markets filled with simple farmers and their families—most of them illiterate. The men argued endlessly over property or broken promises or politics or clans. Their conflict was endless. Sometimes they drew weapons, and sometimes they drew blood, and sometimes a woman returned home alone beating her breasts, her shrill trilling echoing down the valley. It all seemed so tedious.

Northeast from my meadow, I could see up the valley to the mountains. They are fearsome. Spicy pines forested the nearest. I once walked through one of those quiet sanctuaries with my mother on a journey to visit some of our relatives. We took a midafternoon nap on the pine-needle-carpeted forest floor. The wind whispered in the pines and lulled us into such a deep sleep that we did not awaken until dusk. We did not reach our destination until well into the night. It was terrifying to complete the journey in thick darkness, but I never slept so soundly as in that scented forest.

Beyond those steep slopes are rugged, barren peaks that in winter are blanketed in thick, brilliant snow. They are mysterious. Most of the men have journeyed through them, and some foreigners have scaled their peaks. My father was one of them. In the year I was born, he disappeared into those intimidating heights. My mother told me it was not the mountains, but the Hazaras who took him. I loathe those ancient peaks and the savagery they conceal. I loathe the violence and the anger and the destructive determination of men. I loathe their suicidal pride and their defense of honor and their stubborn will. I loathe everything about them. But in spite of my distaste, I am captivated by their self-willed vigor.

After we married and I saw my husband's body, I struggled with guilt over my perverse fascination with his scars. The knot on his shoulder marked the broken collarbone that he had suffered in a *Buzkashi* match; the scar at the corner of his eye branded the place where a man wearing a heavy stone ring split his face in a fistfight; the angry pucker on each side of his thigh noted a bullet's entry and exit.

My husband's hands are large and strong and wiry. The bold veins that snake up toward his powerful forearms fascinate me. He has a scar on his left hand from when he parried the slash of a knife with his bare fist. Gnarled white flesh runs across his knuckles, the remains of a crude suture. One of my cousins told me that he nearly killed a man in that fight. I am ashamed of this, but I have craved to touch that scar and run my slender finger along its length and revel in the strength of potential violence. Something in that gash charms me.

I thought of men, in those days of my simplicity, as toys. I thought that I could play with them as a child plays with her dolls. I thought I could tease them and lead them to the place of my choosing. But as a woman, I learned that men could be cruel beyond comprehension. They can crush a heart as easily as an egg and walk away without a backward glance. Men are not at all the playthings I imagined them to be.

My husband proved to be a reasonable man, willing to wait for me. I was ready, but Mother said I should not marry until I was seventeen. The wait frustrated me. I did not understand, in that tender season, the work of hope. Time was my enemy. I carefully marked the passage of days in my diary, ticking them off at first light. Before the day had begun, I had marked it off as completed. That should have been a beautiful year for me. I should have cherished my final season with Mother. But I did not cherish that priceless moment. I wished it along like an impatient child. That was a thoughtless season in my life—when nothing mattered but my dream. I did not know that love was selfless. I did not know how to serve love. I thought that love should serve me.

I saw my husband about once a month and always under the supervision of my mother and one of my uncles. Though it was awkward, I understood the wise restraints of our culture, and I did not mind. It gave me a chance to get to know him without the confusion of physical romance. But he would touch my hand when I handed him his cup of tea, and that soft brush was enough to give me palpitations. I often wondered how I would control myself when he truly touched me.

I had great doubting conflicts within myself over him. His eyes were so dark that they were nearly black, the pupils barely discernible. They were killer's eyes, my aunt had said. Like most of the women in our family, my aunt was superstitious. She wove dark predictions into even the most casual of conversations, reading the position of the stars or the patterns of milk in the tea or the double egg yolk. But even I saw something unsettling about his eyes. Sometimes they appeared as unsearchable dark pools and sometimes they sparkled with the light of boyish mirth. He would laugh and lean forward, cocking his head to one side, crinkling his eyes in sly mischief, and I would want to laugh along with him. Then, within the same hour, as the men drew him into some scheming tribal palaver, I would see his eyes darken to dull pits of violent ethnic prejudice.

He was always careful to be deferential to my male relatives. Sometimes he hardly spoke to me, preferring to focus his attention on the men. It was maddening, but I understood.

I was fair skinned and knew that at times I flushed. He was gracious enough to pretend not to notice. When we had first met, alone in the meadow and at the well, he had laughed at my awkward shyness. But with my mother in the background and the men present, he did not laugh once at me. I knew he would never embarrass me in public, but I also knew that when we were alone, he would be playful and teasing and fun. How I longed for that precious privacy.

My mother began to teach me about the intimacy a man and a woman share in marriage. Of course I knew about those things, but she taught me about the depth of sentiment that flows out of love. My cousins punctuated their talk of marriage with giggles and sly looks and pretension. My mother spoke of it as if it were a religious experience. She said, with reverence, that love was the closest thing to God we can experience in this life. She said her husband described the act of love as *la petite mort*, the little death. Mother said it was like climbing a mountain and leaping from its peak. The descent was brief and exhilarating, and for a moment, I would taste a sweet abandon as overwhelming as death itself. She said every act of love would demand that I die a little. Life, she said, was a series of little deaths, and the act of love was like a mournful song.

She spoke in hushed tones of the moving ecstasy of love, that love was not just physical, but emotional and even spiritual. She began to frighten me, and I asked her, "How can I know he will be pleased with me? If love is as deep and mystical as this, how can I know I can move his heart in the way he already moves mine?"

I began to weep uncontrollably. "Mother, I am terrified of this intimacy. How can I be all that he needs me to be?"

"The terror of love," she said. "Love is a wild and untamed beast that will frighten but fascinate you. It will tear you apart or make you strong. It will hold you captive or set you free. It is something to fear and something to embrace. It will destroy you or make you into something you never thought you could be. It is the greatest risk of life and the greatest reward. Yes, it is terrifying."

That night I threw up. I slept little, and when I did, I dreamed that I was a captive in an ancient tower, old and ugly and alone. And in the distance, my husband sat on his splendid horse at the top of a grassy hill, gazing up at me in displeasure.

I Am Afraid to Die

I want to die but am afraid
Afraid to disappoint you
Afraid that you will disapprove
Of me

If I do not satisfy you
There is no turning back
A forsaken grave remains
For me

Chapter 5

Respect—احـترام

Weddings in my valley are baffling riddles. They end just before dawn in a riot of barbaric rifle fire. The men shout and empty clip after clip into the night sky while the women cringe in the wedding tent. The children awaken from their slumber mats in terror. I have often wondered where those bullets land. I have wondered if they pepper the roofs of some distant village or fall harmlessly in an empty field or maybe strike by random some innocent child sleeping in the courtyard.

The ardent howl of bullets, the ring of spent casings ejected on the stones, and the violent metallic clank of the aging British Enfield's bolt action create absolute cacophony. It is such an insane irony, the maddening, irreconcilable worlds of men and women.

My mother was progressive, but change does not come easily in Afghanistan. For those few of us women who were educated, it made all the sense in the world to try to voice our desire for schools, health care, and social recognition. Some liberties came, but not without persistent resistance.

I spoke with my husband and uncle about the rifle fire during one of our tea visits and asked them if we could request that the men not shoot their guns after our ceremony. My husband almost laughed, then caught himself and with a smile said, "It's a tradition. We may as well ask them not to eat the mutton."

For the first time in our relationship, I became angry. "Weddings are a celebration of life and love and hope and family and all the things that we hold precious. Why must there be a display of violence?" I heard my mother clear her throat. I had violated protocol.

He spoke in gentle but firm tones. "Our traditions are important. In these days when foreigners threaten our lands and corrupt our blood, we must be careful to honor the age-old traditions, no matter how unnecessary you think they may be. We must have respect for the men who protect our way of life, protect our women, and provide for our little ones."

He cast a dark glance at my mother. I dared not look at her. Though he did not speak in anger to me, I resented that he spoke to me as if I were a child. I considered telling him just that, but halted when a striking revelation hit me. He would never allow me to question his leadership of our family, but more than that, he considered me the offspring of a foreigner. I would always be indebted to him. Hot tears welled up in my eyes, but I quickly regained my composure and lowered my gaze.

There was a long, awkward silence, and he placed his half-empty cup of tea on his saucer. "I must go," he said.

He was polite, but stiff. I feared that I had lost him forever. I knew it would be a mistake to speak and appear insolent. I kept quiet and I watched him leave. Uncle dismissed himself with a hostile stare at Mother, and when the door closed behind him, my mother and I had our first real argument.

"You must not question him," she declared.

"How dare he treat me like a child!" I answered.

"You are a child," she said, "and unless you respect him, he will treat you like a child. He has every right."

"How can he love me if he has no respect for me?" I said.

"And how can you say you love him if you do not honor him?" she snapped.

"Mother, he practically called me an outsider!"

"You are an outsider, and there is nothing that you or I can do about it." She began to cry.

I had never seen my mother cry. It shamed me, and I felt that I had failed her. But I was angry and hurt and in no mood to apologize. I stormed out of the house, slammed the door, and immediately stopped. Fat raindrops had begun to fall. They exploded on the thick layer of dust in the road in front of our compound like tiny meteorites, each of them leaving a soggy crater. I knew a deluge was coming, and embarrassed, I trudged back into the house.

My mother, cleaning up the remains of our little tea party, glanced up at me. "True love," she said with a wry smile.

"True love," I said with contempt.

And we began to laugh. And the rain pounded the roof, and I imagined my husband riding home in a miserable downpour. My mother threw a teacup into the fireplace and it shattered, spraying the room with fragments. I followed her lead and hurled a cup of my own, and we laughed until we could not stand. We laughed while the storm thundered down the valley. We laughed at men and guns and dim-witted girls and foreigners. We lay on our backs and held one another's hand and laughed at the ceiling. We laughed until she begged me to stop. And I never loved her more than in that moment.

The Ancient War

Last winter Grandmother died
And we bathed her paper body
And gently wrapped her in a cloth
And laid her down to rest

And after that my auntie birthed
An angry little girl
And as I rubbed her down with salt
She drifted soft to sleep

I marveled at her rage
Her screaming into life
How long, how hard would this one fight?
Before she wearied out

Chapter 6

اشـــتراک—Share

Some days I cursed the gift of literacy. Perhaps, if I had not known the magic of dreaming, I would not have been disappointed. Perhaps I would have lived a more realistic, more attainable, more modest life. Perhaps I would have lived a life like the women in my village. Perhaps my dreams were the greatest curse of all.

Sometimes my mother and I would visit my aunt who lived in a compound not far from our own. By the standards of our rural valley, both our families were privileged. I had been to Kabul many times and had seen the opulence some of my relatives enjoyed in that amazing city, but it seemed to me our life in the valley was far better by comparison. We did not have the luxury of electricity, and our roads were useless at times, but I preferred my uncomplicated life in the valley. I had the luxury of time to myself, and I could go about without the cumbersome burka women of status were expected to wear in the city. Most of all, I had the peaceful retreat of my poppy field.

When we women gathered at my aunt's, the house filled with high-pitched chatter. We would paint our toenails and tell bawdy jokes and make raucous fun of the absent men. Sometimes I would catch whispered conversations about the love affairs and secret liaisons of young women trapped in marriages to aging, petty husbands. Most often they were young village women forced to marry some austere middle-aged man who had no interest in romance. Abused by their volatile husbands for even the smallest of provocations, they were desperate for affection. Even as a child I understood their frustrations, but I also understood the harsh penalty for infidelity.

I had not yet possessed a lover and had no understanding of jealousy. I had not yet been consumed by passion's obsession. I had not yet owned love or been owned by love, but I was beginning to understand. I understood, as a child understands, that something that was mine should not be taken by another. And though my husband was not yet mine, in my tender heart I knew that I would never share my lover. I would rather die than share him, I thought. And though I resented the men's hypocrisy, I was beginning to understand the rage of betrayal. I understood that love could not be shared. I understood why a man could be driven to mindless violence when his honor was shamed by his wife's disloyalty. I understood the humiliation of shared love.

Men were bound to protect the family honor. They were obligated to execute any female relative who strayed. It did not matter if she was wife or mother or aunt or sister; if she was unfaithful, she paid the ultimate price. Husbands murdered their wives with their own hands. Fathers strangled their daughters, and brothers beat their sisters until they lay lifeless on their blood-stained mattresses. I detested the violence, but I also detested the women who so easily justified the betrayal of their promises. I suppose I should have been more patient with those superficial women. But I was young and without under-standing. I did not know how deep the wound of broken dreams could be.

My mother would never enter into the women's rowdy talk. She would smile and nod her head, but she was never one of them. I thought it odd. She was the only one in the group who lived without a husband, and yet she seemed the most content. I knew that it was because she had known love, and I knew the love she had known was sufficient for her. The magpies at my aunt's parties would never understand that mysterious contentment. Their bitterness seemed only magnified by my mother's quiet satisfaction.

About four months before the wedding, we visited my husband's home. He lived on the edge of a village about a half day's walk down our valley. He sent a wheezing Fiat for us, and we bounced down the crude, dusty road that ran along the river to his village. I was hot, cramped in the backseat with Mother and my aunt. Two of my uncles shared the front seat with the driver.

Summer was ending, and workers harvested wheat and barley in the fields. The sweet smell of curing hay filled the countryside. Even though the sun scorched me, I enjoyed the journey. It was my first time to ride in an automobile, and I did not want the trip to end. Some sections of the road were so bad that our speed was not much more than that of a horse, but there were long, smooth stretches where the driver used the vehicle's high gear. It was magical to cruise along to the rhythmic hum of the little Italian car and so much better than the cantankerous and over-crowded bus trips to Kabul.

As we approached his family compound, my heart sank. My husband was wealthy, and it frightened me. I do not know why. You would think his wealth would suit my dream to live in a palace, but somehow I always feared that I would never measure up to the expectations of my dreams. My simple life was about to be forever changed, and I was not sure that I was ready for life as a princess in the palace. I suppose that fear was the enemy of my dreams. I have always halted between hope and fear. As a child, hope was an elusive, airy thing, as difficult to clutch as water. But fear was a familiar companion. Fear was not difficult to grasp. Fear came without invitation.

The compound appeared to be about sixty meters by sixty meters square, and the walls towered at least four meters high. We screeched to a stop and unfolded ourselves from the tiny Fiat. My anxiety mounted as we entered the compound, and I glanced at my mother in panic. She smiled and held my hand by the tips of my fingers in a breezy, loose grip that spoke of self-confidence. She did nothing by accident, and I knew she was touching me to assure me, but doing it in a casual way to communicate an air of nonchalance to the other women.

The compound was overwhelming. My husband's father had three wives, and each of them had a separate home. Built with their backs to the compound wall, the houses made a complete square within the walls. A modest courtyard linked each home, providing a transition space between the dwellings.

In the middle of the compound was a large courtyard partially paved with flat fieldstones, but a good portion was grass, something I had never seen within a compound wall. It was luxurious. Green and soft, it must have cost a fortune to maintain. I saw some children's playthings scattered near a table with low benches, and I imagined that they must play there in the cool evenings. How I wished I could take off my shoes and run through that sumptuous living carpet.

An arched opening in the back wall of the compound led to another walled area, which I assumed were the stables. I knew my husband and his father were horsemen. They raised and trained the animals as a business. My uncle told me it brought in more income than their farming enterprise. We treasure horses in our communities, and the men talk endlessly about their value. They are worse than the women in the market who haggle over the price of a meter of cotton cloth.

My father-in-law's first wife met us. I was prepared to dislike her, but was pleasantly surprised. She embraced me and called me by my pet name with the same affection that her son used with me. Her dress was immaculate, and she smelled of fresh lilac soap. Her name was Huma. She was frightfully thin and her drawn face haggard, but she had an intelligent sparkle in her eyes and a sharp wit. She spoke in a musical, lilting voice and laughed easily. She had the vocabulary of an aristocrat and she supplemented her speech with poetic Persian phrases that she lifted from classic literature. I recognized some of the quotes and was amazed that she could weave them so easily into casual conversation. I relaxed. Mother dropped her loose grip of the ends of my fingers, and we settled in for a long, delightful afternoon of chatting, tea, and sweet biscuits.

Huma surprised me. I had a certain prejudice against women who shared their love. I knew that I was being unfair. I do not know why I was so mean-spirited. I suppose that fear drove me to unreason. I had heard all the reasons why men need more than one wife, but I had yet to meet an Afghan woman who was happy to share her love. Perhaps some of the first wives enjoyed help in the home or even relief from the never-ending sexual needs of their husbands. But I could not imagine that they were content to see the husband of their youth close the door to the private chamber of his second or third wife as they retired for the night. I could not imagine they felt comfortable when they heard the sounds of intimacy behind the door. I often talked to Mother about it.

"Love is not intended to be shared," she said. "Some women are willing to share their love, but it is only because they have not known love, or that they have no other choice."

I thought that my mother-in-law was such a woman. She was bright and gracious, and she never hinted at discontent. I came to know in the years following that she was as remarkable as my mother, but I also came to know that she was not happy. Her life was a compromise. Sometimes, I have discovered, we settle for whatever love we can find.

We talked mostly of the wedding. It was to be elaborate, of course, and a huge social event. Our families were only distantly related, something rare for a marrying couple in Afghanistan. The wedding would be huge, with relatives from two large extended families attending. The planning was endless. My mother seemed to like her. They chatted through the afternoon, detailing guest lists and food and music. I found myself drifting off in a daydream.

As the sun dropped below the mountains, the air cooled, and I caught a hint of moisture on the refreshing breeze. A pair of pigeons drifted down into the courtyard and cooed as they hunted in the grass for morsels. One was smaller, and they appeared to be a couple. Beautifully formed, they moved together in unison, as if some silent, unseen hand guided them. The sun glinted off their breasts, and brilliant iridescent colors sparkled on their necks in a rainbow of jewels. They are a good match for one another, I thought. My mother spotted them in the grass and without breaking her conversation nonchalantly tossed a biscuit piece toward them. I smiled when they both rushed for it. But at the last moment, one of the birds held back and allowed the other to devour the morsel. I caught my breath and felt a lump in my throat. And I wondered if my husband would care for me with such tenderness and such deference.

Covetous Sister

My love cannot be portioned
Like wedges from an orange
Or slices of a cake
Or a plate of dainty pastries

I cannot give love pieces
Or pour it out in cups
Or mete its modest secrets
To my eager friends

Turn away, my greedy sister
I will not share my love
I will not understand
Your craving

My jealousy will not quench
My rage will not still
If you dare to dip your hand
Into my cherished cup

Chapter 7

مان‌ی‌پ—Covenant

Winter 1963

My wedding day began at first light with a careful bath. I scrubbed until I was pink and washed my hair with Mother in the courtyard. I began to weep when she poured the water over my head. As I bowed my head for her to rinse my hair, I saw her bare feet on the same stool that I had stood on as a child. I felt as if I were looking back through the years at myself through her eyes. She understood and lowered the bucket, tears streaming down her face.

"I will miss you, my love," she said.

I could not answer her. I began to heave with great gushing sobs as she held me close, my soapy hair soaking her gown. We had never been separated, and I wondered how I could leave her here alone. I felt guilty and told her that I was ashamed for abandoning her. She smiled and held my face between her hands, gazing serenely into my reddened eyes.

"You cannot leave me, my love. I keep you in a place that cannot be abandoned. I keep you here."

She took my hand and placed it over her heart, and I felt its warm, persistent beat on my palm. It seemed as if life itself were calling me into something grand and eternal and mystifying—as if I were part of something beyond my control, as if love were an endless, flowing stream, clear and fresh and clean, and I were drawn helpless in its irreversible tide. And on that crisp, cold morning as the sun crested over the eastern mountain range, and my feet were scrubbed pink, and my uncorseted breasts pressed against my mother's warmth, I felt the curious, simultaneous mystery of overwhelming sadness and boundless joy. I had no words, but in that moment I felt pure and clean and holy.

Weddings in Afghanistan take place in winter and always at night. The night before my wedding was cold, but as the sun cleared the mountains, its radiance filled the courtyard. Mother and I took our time basking in the luxurious warmth. My aunt arrived as we were pouring our second cup of tea, and even though she interrupted the moment, she did not interrupt the magic that continued throughout the day. I would often catch my mother watching me with a contented smile. Though we were never alone again that day, there were times when it seemed we were the only two in the courtyard.

With the arrival of my aunt came other chattering female relatives, turning the rest of the day into an endless clamor of panic and veiled references to the wedding bed. I had to struggle to be patient and not be offended by their shallow teasing. They disgraced the enchanting purity of what I understood to be love. I was about to give a gift to my husband that I had been saving all my life. To have that gift cheapened insulted me, but I knew their simplicity and knew that I should be tolerant. They had once enjoyed a moment of hope. I prayed that I would not become like them.

We spent a splendid day together, lounging in the courtyard. I took a long nap that afternoon and surprised myself with sleep. I felt so pampered. When I awoke, my mother and aunt helped me into my dress. It was ornate to the point of gaudiness, and Mother and I had laughed over it in private. But Afghan weddings are traditional and I did not mind. I felt like a princess when the women began to arrange the heavy jewelry.

Around my neck I wore an ostentatious fortune of jewels, gifts from my husband's family. A thin filament of diamonds looped in a single strand around the top of my head and ended in a magnificent blue sapphire that lay flat against my forehead. I caught my breath when I looked in the mirror. It was exquisite. The blue in the stone flattered my eyes, and I could not take my gaze off the effect it created. I knew that I would be captivating to him and could not wait until the moment when I would remove the bridal veil.

At about six in the evening, a car arrived to collect me. Most of the women had already departed in a caravan of noisy buses. My husband had rented an antique Mercedes from Kabul to bring me to his village, and it arrived with a noisy clatter. I had never seen anything like it. Long and shiny and black, its brass and chrome fittings gleamed orange and red in the fiery light of the setting sun. It made an unusual tinkering sound as it chugged along the road.

My mother rode along with me in the leathered backseat, and my uncle sat in front with the driver. The two-hour ride was magical. Time stood still and flew all at once. I wanted the ride to last forever, and I wanted it to end. I savored the moment, but I longed for the destination. I did not want to ruin my makeup, and I wanted to let my tears flow. We arrived at the front gate of my husband's family compound at eight o'clock.

As I stepped down from the ancient car, I nearly fainted. The day I had dreamed of since I was a child was happening so quickly. I could not breathe, much less take it all in. The gauzy veil hindered my vision, but I could see my husband standing on a stage in the distance, framed against a background of strands of tiny, colored lights.

He wore a black Indian-style *Sherwani*. Intricately embroidered in fine gold thread, the long formal coat practically glowed in the soft light. His black wool Afghan hat added several inches to his height and the squared shoulders of the coat accented his broad frame. He stood erect and stately and still. I had never seen him in formal dress, and in the elegant setting of the pristine compound surrounded by the finely attired guests from Kabul, he was magnificent. I was never as proud of him as I was in that moment.

Hundreds of relatives and friends welcomed me at the gate. Their parallel lines formed a long greeting corridor, with the women on the left and the men on the right. The night was glorious, as if God himself had appointed the ceremony. A full moon crested over the distant mountains. It seemed close enough to touch. Well-stoked fires in temporary fire pits eased the chill around the compound. The effect was spectacular, creating an elegant, traditional atmosphere and adding magic to an evening under the stars. The moon was so bright we could have held the ceremony without lights. But the soft twinkle of the festival lights made it perfect.

My mother, aunts, and an entourage of female cousins followed behind me, and I felt as if I were welcomed as a queen. The musicians struck up the traditional Afghan wedding song and I walked slowly, as convention demanded. I found myself wanting to rush forward to hurry the ceremony along, but I knew that it would be a long night and that I should be patient.

My husband stood statuesque at the center of an elaborate stage in front of two high-backed chairs decorated like thrones. From there we presided over the evening and carried out most of the ceremony. The marriage contract was read and signed in private after the ceremony, but everything else took place on the stage in front of the wedding party.

My father-in-law passed the Quran over our heads for good luck, and we covered ourselves with a decorative shawl during a prayer read in Arabic. In ancient times, the bride and groom would cut their palms and mingle their blood as a sign of their covenant. I was grateful we no longer practiced that tradition. Instead, a precious dancing girl brought a silver tray with a small amount of henna, which was placed in the palm of my hand and on my husband's pinkie finger. My mother-in-law covered our hands with a silk fabric and whispered, "Good luck, little one."

My husband and I fed one another pieces of cake while the guests applauded then sat patiently as they were served with course after course. We spent the next three hours greeting guests, accepting congratulations, and posing for photographs. Then we endured hours of dancing, more congratulations, and more photographs, until finally, at two o'clock in the morning, we all danced the traditional *attan*. No one knows where this dance originated, but it dates back to before Islam came to Afghanistan. I was never happier to dance it. Drained, I hoped I had the stamina to please my husband.

The wedding had taken place in the spacious courtyard, a short walk across the compound from our newly prepared home. It was awkward, but he had the foresight to shroud the entire front of the home in a gauzy white cloth. It was very elegant, very tasteful, and very romantic. Freshly lit candles illuminated the interior of the home, and it was the perfect end to a perfect evening. I thought I was the most fortunate woman alive.

It felt strange to walk into our little home. It was small by his standards, but sprawling by mine. Three of my cousins accompanied me to our bedroom, where they helped me take off the elaborate wedding dress and put on a beautiful bridal gown. My husband waited outside with some of the men in his family until we were finished. I was exhausted when we entered the home, but as I changed and as the girls giggled, I felt my heart quicken and my senses come alive.

As they were leaving, one of them handed me a cotton handkerchief and a small vial of blood. Though my mother had explained to me what to do with it, I still blushed.

Proof of virginity is a life-and-death matter in my country. If the bride cannot give evidence of her purity, her husband's family has the right, and even the obligation, to take her life. Sometimes, my mother had explained, even though a woman may be pure, there may not be evidence to prove her innocence. The little vial of blood was just in case. By the time they left, my hands were trembling.

I waited alone in the bedroom, halting near the nightstand, feeling foolish. It seemed immodest to lie on the bed. As I fidgeted in the center of the room trying to decide what to do with my hands, he opened the door.

He smiled and stood transfixed in the doorway. I had kept the blue sapphire in my hair, and I could see in the mirror across the room that it sparkled in the candlelight. The gown was gauzy, and though it was long, the top was revealing. I felt self-conscious and lifted one hand to my chest, but at the same time, as I saw his eyes travel over my length, I reveled in the attention he was lavishing on me.

He stammered out that I looked beautiful, more beautiful than he had imagined, and when his voice cracked, I realized that he was nervous, too. Though my hands trembled with anticipation and my throat was dry, I felt a surge of confidence. I smiled at him and knew what to do.

My mother had told me that it would come naturally and that I should relax and enjoy the moment. If I was happy, she said, he would be happy. I walked straight to him and slipped my arms around his waist. He was trembling, too, and as I looked up at him, I thought he might faint. He mumbled something into my hair, and I felt his warmth and his firm body against mine. I could have stood there until dawn.

Though we had stood together during the wedding ceremony, held hands, and touched one another's faces as we fed each other cake, we had not yet embraced. My husband is tall, his chest deep, his shoulders powerfully built, his arms hard and well defined. I could not reach around him. His size startled me. Beneath the fading facade of cologne, and the more subtle hint of soap, I caught the carefully disguised fragrance of raw, warm masculinity. His faint musky odor intoxicated me. I realized, in that heady moment, that his scent would become my obsession and I surrendered myself like a hopeless addict, abandoned to a craving.

Our differences startled me. I had never felt a man's firm, unyielding flesh. I felt suddenly conscious of my soft femininity. I did not simply embrace him—I absorbed him. He sank into my compliant breasts and my yielding belly as easily as a hand vanishes into warm sheep's wool.

He fumbled, awkward and halting, his hands sliding up from my waist to my back. He stopped there and held me for a long while. I thought at first that he was lingering to savor the moment, but the quiver in his arms betrayed him. I raised my face to him and looked directly into his eyes. He held my gaze for a moment and then looked away. His face reddened and the vein in his neck pulsed as little sweat beads emerged in the furrows of his forehead. They appeared as if by magic, glistening in the candlelight, tiny shimmering testaments to the anxious thunder of his heart.

I touched his face with the tips of my fingers and cooed to him and calmed the trembling beast within his chest with wordless shushing.

I spoke the unknown graceful tongue—that mysterious, mystical language of the heart that I had learned in my mother's patient school of feminine enchantment. His breath stilled and as we lingered, my face upturned to his, I caught the faint and pleasant scent of the anise seed he had thoughtfully chewed in the courtyard while I had changed. The room stilled around me as the patient ticking of an ancient windup clock on his bedside table marked the passage of eternal moments.

It would be many years before I understood the tender vulnerability of that moment. I failed to grasp the significance of his tentative embrace. It was one of the few moments in our marriage when the window of his heart carelessly opened.

We stood together for a long moment, holding one another, until at last he tilted my chin up with his hand, and we kissed. My heart raced, and I dizzied with excitement. We walked trancelike to the bed, and before I knew it, I was slipping between the sheets with him. The press of our bodies together felt strange, and we giggled like schoolchildren.

I lay beside him on cool, crisp linen and felt a surge of terror sweep up from the core of my abdomen. I trembled under his roughened hand as he groped at the clasp on the front of my gown. My mother's careful tutoring had not prepared me for this awakening. Something within me roused from its mysterious slumber. A terrifying, mindless heat surged up to rumble through my heart. It trampled up into my head, roughshod and demanding. My cunning thoughts scattered, mindless and panicked and primitive. Once again I spoke the unknown tongue of the language of the heart—but this was not the tongue I was accustomed to speaking. It was not the gentle coddle of feminine affection. It was the urgent rush of unintelligible phrases that trampled upon one another in raw demand. It was the mindless tongue of Genghis Khan, who thundered down from the upper steppes and ravaged our gentle villages.

We fumbled through the night, both of us driven by a primal zeal we did not understand and could not bridle. We eventually consummated our marriage in an enthusiastic rush. I felt my body rise to meet his eager insistence, but somehow I could not master his demanding call. I felt something just beyond my grasp—some impossible peak that mocked my frantic quest.

Some months later, after I had become more skillful, I understood the startling thrill of fulfilled desire. I mastered the more primitive language that I did not understand on that night of my gifting. Though I tasted briefly of a man's powerful narcotic, I did not understand. What I understood that night was more innocent and more pure—the secret breaking of the vessel of my heart. I was an offering to my beloved. I poured my heart upon that intimate altar. On that night I did not take anything; I gave. I served love with no expectation of receiving. On that night I allowed myself to be a vessel, willingly broken. We lay together and my husband drifted off to sleep. As his breathing settled, regular and deep, I lay next to him warm and restful, and for a long while unable to sleep.

I somehow remembered to use the handkerchief to clean up. By the candlelight, I could see there would be no need for the supplemental vial. On the next day, I gave the cloth to my mother-in-law, as was our custom. I knew the women in the family would pass the cloth around for careful examination, and all of them would commend me for my virtue. It was barbaric and embarrassing, but I knew it must be done.

Covenant Love

Last night I cut my covenant
I sealed it with my blood
My love affliction
My wound
My offering

Cherish it, my love
I give it only once
My wound will heal
My heart will not
If you despise my gift

Chapter 8

Man—مرد

Living in my husband's family compound was more challenging than I expected. From my earliest memory, I had slept in the same room as my mother. It was unsettling to share the bed with a man, and I felt self-conscious. My husband rustled through the night, turning, sometimes snoring. His scent, so captivating in our intimate moments, grew more pungent through the night. By morning, I could not escape its overpowering presence. I longed for the familiar feminine aroma of fragrant oils and soap.

I eventually slept our first night together, but the second night I lay on my back after he had gone to sleep and wept quietly. I missed my mother and wanted to share my joy with her. I was happy, but at the same time, I yearned for her. It was cold that winter, the nights long and dark and weary. Sometimes, when I could no longer bear the lonely chill, I would snuggle near to my husband's back but it seemed to annoy him. When our bodies warmed he would move away from me and toss the covers aside.

As a child, I could not leave our family compound without my mother's permission. I never went out alone, unless it was to my poppy field. That privilege was a rare thing in our culture, and solitude was not something most women enjoyed. My mother had stood firm in the fiery arguments with my uncle about my freedom. He would send one of my young male cousins to follow me when I went to my field. I seldom did much more than sit on the porch of the old cabin, reading. They would tire of watching me and disappear to fly their kites.

As a married woman, I could not go out alone. If I wanted to visit my family, I needed my husband's approval. Even my mother had to ask his permission to visit. My life was completely subject to him. I was fortunate that he was reasonable, but custom and family demanded that I honor the traditions and respect him without question. If I disrespected the family or brought shame to them, I would face immediate wrath.

Spring came early that year, its rains pleasant, frequent, and warm. During a three-day drizzle, we spent most of our time indoors. As my husband and I shared tea early one morning, my father-in-law's second wife erupted in shouts from her adjacent house. One of her daughters had apparently overturned a bottle of fresh milk, just delivered from the village. The distinct slap of an open hand on chubby flesh echoed across the space between us, followed by the child's piercing wail. I waited patiently for the fracas to settle. By the time it was quiet again, my tea was cold.

A rose-ringed parakeet landed on the top of the wall in our courtyard. It was unusual to see them this close to the village. It preened for a few moments—its bright red beak combing through emerald feathers—then startled when a new round of screaming began next door.

"Where do you go when you need to think?" I asked my husband.

He looked perplexed, drank the remnants of his tea, and said, "I don't really have much to think about. What horse to sell, what horse to buy, what mare to breed, what field to collect on. These things don't require much thinking, they just happen as I go along."

"Don't you ever want time alone?" I asked. "A time when you can dream?"

He smiled and looked toward his empty teacup. I anticipated his want and dutifully poured his second cup. "I know that you are accustomed to solitude," he said. "Your mother even talked to me about it during our betrothal. I understand that need. Someday we will have a place of our own. Someday I will build us a compound like you never dreamed you would have."

He launched into an animated description of a stately complex that would stretch across the field adjoining his father's compound. He spoke of a large central house with guest cottages and barns and spacious courtyards. He described the fountains and tiled walls and slate walkways and play areas for the children.

I did not imagine the grand compound in the same way that he imagined it. He saw majestic buildings filled with furniture and artifacts and guests. I saw the need for servants, and the chatter of socializing, and the constant demand of expanding enterprises.

"I don't want much," I said.

"I will give you all you've ever dreamed," he boasted.

He means well, I thought.

I came to appreciate his mother, Huma. She was a second cousin of my husband's father, Jahangir, and came from an influential family in Kabul. Her family had been reluctant to allow her to leave the city, but Jahangir's father was persuasive and generous with his dowry offer. Jahangir's family land was in the richest area of the Panjshir Valley. He held vast fields and had built a successful farming and horse-raising enterprise. What Jahangir lacked in sophistication, he made up for in entrepreneurial zeal and business smarts.

Huma had married at eighteen, and by the time she was twenty-five, she had birthed four children. My husband was her firstborn, and she was proud of him. She spoke passable English and often listened to shortwave radio broadcasts at night. I came to enjoy visiting with her in the evenings and listening to the international news.

Her Kabul education had opened her eyes to a world beyond—the Western world. She loved politics. She would squabble with the radio then grow increasingly passionate as she gave me her opinion on how the world should be. She was so unlike my mother. Mother loved quiet evenings with books and long, reflective solitude. Huma loved to argue.

I had never met anyone so world aware. She introduced me to American and British pop music on the shortwave. Elvis Presley was her favorite, and we would listen with the volume turned down low, huddled near the speaker, giggling like schoolgirls. I memorized "Love Me Tender." She taught me the meaning of the English words, and even though I was singing in a language I had little knowledge of, the song moved me every time I heard it.

Huma developed female problems after her fourth child and lost a considerable amount of weight. She would not talk much about it and she never recovered. At the time of my wedding, she was in her midforties and very thin. Jahangir had chosen to take a second, and later a third, wife.

His second wife, one of his first cousins, was a voluptuous village girl. Though she was pretty, she was dim-witted and difficult. She had three children, all girls, and all with the same cantankerous attitude as their mother. Childbearing and the sedentary life had taken a toll on her, making her fat and lazy and an insatiable gossip. I disliked her.

Jahangir's third wife was twenty years old. He had married her when she was seventeen. She had not given him any children, and he spent most of his nights in her little two-room house. She was sweet but similar in many ways to his second wife, illiterate with a village mind-set. She had never been more than twenty kilometers from her home and had no idea of life in Kabul, much less the rest of the world. Her life was limited to the family compound, nearby relatives, and occasional visits to the village market.

I found the tedious bickering of the two younger wives insufferable at times, but Huma never criticized them. It baffled me, and I asked her how it was possible for her to bear the indignity of sharing her husband with two shallow, petty women.

She looked at me for a long while without saying anything. I thought I had offended her, and I was about to apologize when she began to speak in a soft, thoughtful voice. "Life has a way of wearing a person down," she said. "When we first married, I was determined that I would never tolerate another woman in my home, but my life has not been what I expected it would be."

I tried to keep my composure. She was, after all, my mother-in-law, but I could not keep the tears from spilling down my cheeks. I turned away from her in embarrassment while she continued. "I know that my son loves you," she said. "But there are other influences in his life that I cannot control." Her voice trailed off in a resigned sigh, and I felt a great sadness.

I watched her until silence demanded that I speak and finally said quietly, "Thank you, Huma."

We sat for a moment in silence. I never dreamed that I would find another woman as open as my mother, and I never dreamed that such a woman would be my mother-in-law. I was grateful for whatever coercion of fate had brought us together. I felt such a strange kindred spirit with her, as if we were part of some clandestine sect of sisters who knew deep, inscrutable secrets about life and love and one another. No woman would ever replace my mother, but Huma became part of our confidential league.

Jahangir, to his credit, took time each day with his wives and their children. He would visit one wife in the morning for breakfast before he made the rounds of his fields. Tenant farmers leased most of his land, so there was little he had to do with them other than collect his portion at harvest. He would work with his horses through the morning and have lunch with another wife. In the evening, he ate late with his third wife.

Though I loathed him for taking three wives, I developed an unanticipated respect for him. Almost all the men I knew ruled their families like intolerable sovereigns. Some were violent, and some browbeat, but all of them subjugated their wives with an unbending, unreasonable devotion to tradition. Jahangir enjoyed each of his wives and he treated them with deference. But the more my esteem grew for him, the more I worried that the irresistible erosion of a subjugated life was wearing me down. It disturbed me that I could respect a man who was doing the very thing I despised and who had a greater influence on my husband than any other person.

Even though Jahangir was in his late fifties, his body was as hard as stone. He interacted with his horses in the same way my husband, with patient mastery. He was kind to them, and spoke to them in affectionate murmurs, as a benevolent father would speak to adoring children. The horses seemed to respect him. They would sense his presence and turn docile faces toward him, watching with rapt curiosity, their ears sharp and swiveled in his direction. They would drop their heads when he approached them, bowing in subtle, graceful submission. He would not overly coddle them but neither was he cruel. He was courteous, almost deferential, but always in control.

But sometimes a horse can be obstinate. He bought one scruffy stallion from west Afghanistan that he intended to breed. The horse was small, but strong and self-willed and wild. Its former owner had seen its potential, but had been unable to tame the little animal. It was unclear if the scars on the horse were from the man or from scraps with other stallions.

Jahangir worked with the little stallion for three days, trying to win its trust. It did not go well. On the fourth day, I watched him rope the horse and run him around the compound with a whip. He fashioned a halter and noose that he could tighten around the animal's neck to control its breath. The stallion ran wild-eyed in circles and stirred up such a cloud of dust that I could hardly see either of them.

Jahangir never raised his voice. He ran the horse until it lathered. He ran it more, tightening the noose, and as the horse's tongue began to hang from its mouth, the animal wobbled pitifully and stumbled. Jahangir lowered his shoulder, ran forward, and knocked the stallion down. The hit was ferocious, unexpected, and violent. He stunned the animal, and before it could scramble to its feet, he hobbled it with a loop of the rope then sat on it, keeping it pinned to the ground. Whenever the horse struggled to rise, Jahangir shifted his weight, tightened the hobble and the noose, and controlled the animal with his legs. The little stallion struggled mightily, angrily trying to nip at him, but he knew just how to avoid the bites. Finally, the horse tired and wallowed. Its lather mingled with the arid dust forming clumps of thick mud on its neck and shoulders.

As the horse stilled, Jahangir tightened his hold even further; then, leaning into the horse's ear, he spoke in a hushed voice. "I am your master," he said. "I will not tolerate your insubordination. You will obey me, you will respect me, and you will serve me." It was bizarre, but the horse quieted, and I saw a defeated submission in its whitened eyes. I knew in that moment that the little stallion was broken.

I once watched a little boy catch quail near my village. He set simple traps made from woven cane baskets at the edge of a millet field and lay in the standing grain, waiting for the birds to discover the seed under his traps. He lay there for hours until a fat quail entered one of his traps. When he pulled the fine kite string he had tied to a stick, the trap was sprung. The captured quail flapped violently in the overturned basket, but the boy remained prone in the field. Finally, the bird tired and lay panting in the hot soil. The boy rose, walked quietly to the trap, and carefully lifted its edge. The bird was exhausted and had no struggle remaining. The boy reached in, caught the bird, pinched off its head, and slipped it into a small sack tied to his waist. There was a covey of birds nearby, but the boy's crafty movements did not disturb them. By the end of the day, his sack was full of quail.

I suppose that none of those little birds realized they were trapped until it was too late. Their panic was short-lived and vain. I remembered that young boy while I watched Jahangir crush the last hope in the heart of that little horse. I remembered the boy's wise, patient cunning. And I wondered if there was some mysterious skill passed down from father to son in an ancient ritual hidden from the eyes of women.

My Lovely Prison

My beautiful, violent man
Rules with iron and stubborn will
And plaits with cunning patience
My halter

Some days I submit
And some days I resist
Some days I do not care
And some days I abandon to tears

And in the deafening boredom
At times I want to scream
But I still my restless heart
And pour another cup of tea

Chapter 9

Isolate—شـده یـمـنزو

I suppose that my romantic fantasies were unreasonable, but my husband, at least in those early days, met every one of them. I could not imagine a more caring man. He was a head and shoulder taller than me and strapping. I had lived in a woman's world and never felt the strength of a man. I found it frightening, but exhilarating. He could lift me by the waist, and he loved holding me up and watching my feet flail in the air. He would laugh and call me his little puppy and then pull me to him, my feet well off the floor, and kiss me with such tenderness that my heart would melt.

His contrast of strength and gentleness never ceased to overwhelm me. Sometimes I felt as if I were in control of a powerful stallion and that

I could move him by the slightest touch of my hand on the reins. I could meet his gaze from across the room and know that with a smile and a pat on the mat, he would come to me like a docile child. He would lay his heavy head in my lap, and I would stroke his broad forehead, and within minutes he would be sleeping soundly. I enjoyed the intoxication of knowing that like a sorceress, I could charm him at will.

In the evenings, I would prepare his tea and bring it to his mat in the courtyard, where he sat contentedly smoking his water pipe. He would lean back against the courtyard wall with his eyes half-closed, and when I bent near him with the tea tray, I would catch him looking down my blouse. I was always careful to position myself where he could see me and always pretended not to notice. I could feel his eyes watching me as I returned to the kitchen, and I would walk as gracefully as I could.

If the weather was pleasant, we would have our meal together on the same mat, sharing food from one plate and feeding each other choice portions of lamb or candied almonds. As a little girl, I had watched my uncle eat lamb with great relish, licking his fat, greasy fingers and belching loudly. It repulsed me. But my husband ate with dignity, as if we were at a social event and I was the guest of honor. He was just as I had imagined the Persian royalty in my childhood books: respectful and courteous and attentive.

In our bedroom, he was a considerate, tender lover and patient with me as I learned the skills of pleasing him. Though I enjoyed him, he was more fascinated with our lovemaking than I was, and sometimes I pretended to be satisfied. I did not mind. It gave me a deep contentment to know that he was pleased with me. We often talked in the quiet afterglow about his dreams for us and our family. I imagined that we would enjoy idyllic days, have happy children, and grow old together.

My husband seldom told me that he loved me unless I said it first.

"I love you," I would say when we had finished our lovemaking.

"I love you, too," he would answer.

"I love you, Husband," I would say when he left our home in the mornings.

"I love you, too," he would answer.

Sometimes he would compliment me on the evening meal. I worked hard on every meal: fretting over each dish, worrying that none became repetitious, sometimes throwing away the dishes that did not turn out as I'd expected.

"This is delicious," he would say.

"I love you, dear," I would answer.

"I love you, too," he would say without looking up from his plate. He would continue eating with serious focus until the last morsel had disappeared.

The candle that I always placed between us in the evenings would illuminate his strong, dark face and I would smile, basking in its warm, golden glow. I loved the way he looked in the candlelight: his black, inscrutable eyes; his rough evening beard; the light sun-fashioned crinkles at the corners of his face; his rugged, angular jaw.

But late one evening when I was engrossed in a Persian translation of *The Old Man and the Sea*, he said, "I love you."

I jolted out of my reverie and stared across the tiny, dimly lit sitting room. He sat across from me on a cushion in the corner smoking a cigarette, its long ash about to drop on my new Iranian rug. I disliked his smoking, but I was, at last, getting accustomed to the nicotine scent that clung to him.

"I love you, too," I said.

"I love the way you crinkle your forehead when you're reading. You're so focused, so intent, so cute," he said.

I did not want to gush, so I kept quiet and smiled broadly, my heart warming in my chest, my affection pouring across the floor like the spreading pool from an overturned vessel.

He caught the dangling ash in his hand just as it dropped and took another long drag on his cigarette. The ember's glow illuminated his face in its tiny blaze. He exhaled a long stream of smoke directly at my face. He knew how I hated that.

I flung my book at his chest and he laughed, flipping his half-finished cigarette out the open window and into the small courtyard that was the centerpiece of our little home. I was sitting with my legs extended toward him and he snatched my ankle and dragged me toward him. I felt the carpet burn my hip. I struggled in his strong grip, pretending to resist. And as the evening chilled, and the crickets sang, and a brilliant moon illuminated the silent courtyard, we made love on my new Iranian rug.

I was content in those days and thought often of my husband's vision to build our compound. Our children would live around us. I would teach them about love and fidelity, and they would live as couples are supposed to live—not in quarreling and jealousy, and not with multiple wives, but as couples who respected and honored one another. They would know love, and I would watch over them like a benevolent queen. I was happy beyond my dreams.

But I grew restless.

Huma employed a few village girls to help with chores around the compound, but none of the other women had help. They complained, of course, but I could not imagine why. There was little to do. I spent my days preparing meals for my husband, but he was easy to please. He ate breakfast with his father whenever Jahangir ate at his mother's house, which was about every other day. Sometimes he would take his midday meal in the fields or in the village, but he was always home for our evening meal together. He allowed me to have my books, and I was surprised to find that Huma had a good library of her own.

I had time alone nearly every day, but I missed my poppy field. I missed the open views and the quiet solitude. In the compound, there was the continuous sound of four families living together in a common area and the steady comings and goings of the farm and horse business. Men constantly came to the gate looking for my husband or his father, and the chatter of the women and children was never ending. For a full year, I lived in relative contentment, but finally I could bear it no longer and asked my husband if I could visit my mother.

"Of course, my love," he said. "I'll take you there the day after tomorrow."

"I would like to go alone, and I would like to spend the night," I said.

"Absolutely out of the question!" he responded with a sharp, angry look. "Why would you want to spend the night, and why would you want to go alone?" His voice rose to a level he had never used with me. His piercing stare unnerved me.

I stammered something about missing my poppy field. I tried to explain how important it was to have some time to myself in an enchanting place where I wrote in my diary and thought about my future and looked into the distance. I watched his face flush to crimson as he struggled to throttle his rage.

"You have your time alone here every day. There are no children to care for. You have your books. What exactly do you need that I have not provided?" His voice began to shake and his fists clenched.

For the first time in our life together, I felt threatened. I began trembling and burst into tears. I tried to speak, but could only stammer. He stood, and after a long, hard look at me, he turned his back and walked out of the house. He left his lunch untouched in the courtyard. He slammed the heavy wooden door so hard that it cracked near the top, and the boom resonated inside our home like thunder.

I spent the rest of the day fretting about the cottage, cleaning, and recleaning. I had his supper ready an hour early and waited until past nine o'clock for him to come home. When at last he did return, he told me he had eaten something in the village, and we went to bed. With his back to me, he was soon snoring. I lay through most of the night, vacillating between rage and fear, replaying our conversation in my thoughts. The next morning I apologized to him and asked his forgiveness.

"I forgive you," he said, his voice flat and harsh. His cold stare disturbed me. I understood in that moment that my feminine magic had its limits.

His anger lasted for days, and I wondered if we would ever be the same. I tried to talk to Huma about it, but she, too, was angry with me for wanting to leave. She seemed suspicious and began to ask probing questions that at first seemed almost laughable until I realized that she was serious. I could not believe she was questioning my loyalty to my husband, but as she persisted, I realized there were limits to her kindness. I would always be something of an outsider in this family.

My husband and I took a long walk one evening about a week after our argument. It was a new path for me, southwest of the village and down the valley into a large wheat field that lay in the fertile flats near the river. He laid his coat along the irregular stones of an abandoned dry well and motioned for me to sit as the sun shimmered down into the dusty horizon.

"This is one of my most productive fields," he said. "It has been in my family for a hundred and fifty years. My great-grandfather bought it during the time of the British. The Afghans slaughtered the English soldiers as they retreated from Kabul to Jalalabad. My great-grandfather killed an officer in a field like this one with a breech-loaded Jezail. He fired from behind a low wall and dropped the man with a single shot, dead center to his chest, from three hundred meters."

I gazed across the breeze-swept swells of ripening grain and tried to imagine a grizzled Afghan warrior peering along the heavy octagonal barrel of a handmade antique weapon. I tried to imagine a British officer in his smartly tailored uniform, three hundred meters away. The heavy bullet from the Jezail would have lifted him from his feet and laid him prone in the soft, fertile silt. He would have died quickly, on his back, the thunder of the ancient weapon rolling past him, the grain waving gently over him, his rich, dark blood gurgling into the thirsty ground. He would have thought of his loved ones in their hearth-warmed cottage on his distant, misty isle.

"Have you ever killed a man?" I asked.

He gazed at me for a moment, his dark and inscrutable eyes searching my face. "I have done what was needed," he said.

I laid my palm on the top of his broad, warm hand and said, "I am sorry I offended you."

"And I am sorry I was angry with you," he said.

He met my gaze and held it for a long moment, his thoughtful face softening in the dusk. He spoke quietly to me in the voice he used with his horses—the voice of patient reason, the voice of firm, respectful care, the voice of the law.

I learned from that soft, deep voice the rules of my behavior: how and when I could leave the compound, how I would dress, whom I could see and not see, how I would behave when men were present.

The law came down as if from God himself, firm and commanding and benevolent. It was all for my best interest, for my protection, because he loved me, he said.

I thought often of my father during that season of my loneliness, and I began to study French. I had picked up some vocabulary from my mother, mostly out of curiosity, but my curiosity became an obsession. With laborious effort, I translated most of the lines he had written in his diary. One of his poems moved me in a way that was difficult to describe. I suppose, for the first time, I understood the life of a foreigner in an unyielding land.

Alone

I lay upon a ridge
In the heart of Hindu Kush
And watched a single eagle
Glide silent over me

And on the restless draft
I joined my hermit brother
And drifted gently down
The lonely valley

Chapter 10

Debt—ی بـده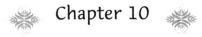
Summer 1964

The following week I missed my period. I thought at first it might be due to stress, but when I became nauseous after breakfast in the second week, I knew I was pregnant. I waited another week and told my husband that I believed we would be having a child.

The news could not have come at a better time. His sullen suspicion turned to childlike glee, and he began babbling about what we should name the boy. I wanted to wait until we were sure before telling his family, but that night we went to his mother's home, where he breathlessly spilled the news. Later in the evening, he told me that he wanted to send for my mother and that she should stay a few days with us. Nothing could have made me happier. It was as if our fight had never happened. I prayed that it would be a boy.

My mother's visit was like a fresh breeze over a spring field. I had seen her only twice in the year since I left home, and both of those visits had been brief. We spent three luxurious days together and talked endlessly about my new life, but mostly we talked about the baby. I decided not to tell her about the fight with my husband and later wondered why. I suppose I had hoped that our brief unhappiness was behind us. I ignored the nagging fear and turned my thoughts inward to the little one forming in my womb.

How peculiar it is to know a love growing within you. I could feel the strength of my own life flowing into the little child. I wanted to make my husband happy and give him a gift that only I could give him. That would seal our future. I spent many sumptuous afternoons lounging on the mat in the courtyard of our little house.

It was a dreamy, peaceful season in my life. My husband smothered me in his affection, and sometimes I wished he would leave me to myself. I enjoyed the attention, but he doted over me like a mother hen, while the house filled with kites and wooden horses and marbles. I prayed to God every day that the child would be a boy.

One evening, while I was lying quietly on the bed, I felt an odd sensation in my belly. The child had moved for the first time. The movement was so slight that I thought I had imagined it, but I felt it again a few moments later. I did not say anything to my husband. As the weeks progressed, the movements became much stronger. I found myself spending long, pensive moments staring off into the distance, with my hand resting on my drum-tight abdomen. I would wait for the slightest motion, place my palm over the place where I felt life, and imagine myself caressing that vulnerable little one.

On a night when the baby was active, I put my husband's hand on my swollen belly. The evening was warm, and I was wearing a light cotton nightshirt. I could feel the heat of his huge hand as he spread his palm gently over my tummy. The child made a strong, sudden kick, and it startled him so much that he cried out and pulled his hand abruptly back. The revelation was instantaneous, and he roared with laughter. He laid his face against my stomach for nearly an hour, waiting for the slightest movement. And he wept. I did not want to embarrass him, so I lay still as his tears dampened my gown. I had never seen him display such emotion. It disturbed and excited me. I never mentioned it to him, and he never brought it up, but in that moment, I experienced such a deep tenderness for him and for life itself that I had no words.

"What was your father like when you were a little boy?" I asked.

"He was as a father should be," he said. "He was strong. He taught me the ways of horses. From the time I was weaned, I went everywhere with him."

"Did he ever tell you that he loved you?" I asked.

He looked at me curiously, thoughtfully. He had that way, a sort of cunning patience whenever anyone asked him a serious question. He broke eye contact and stared blankly at the candlelight that trembled on the bedroom wall. I waited, enjoying this rare reflective moment.

"I know you think my father is a hard man," he said. "And in many ways, he is. But there is a part of him that you have not seen. He taught me how to put a horse down when it was suffering, and he taught me how to deliver a foal. He taught me how to slaughter a lamb, and he taught me how to care for an injured ewe. He taught me how to handle a weapon, and how to be kind to the poor."

He was quiet for a moment as we listened to the ever-present ticking of the antique Turkish clock at our bedside, dutifully marking the passage of time, making me aware of the valuable heirlooms surrounding me and reminding me of my lack of ancestry.

As if reading my thoughts, he said, "I suppose you may think that you missed something by not having a father. In some ways you probably have. But your mother did well with you. There does not seem to be anything lacking."

He laid his heavy, dark hand over mine. "My father told me many times that he was proud of me. And yes," he said with that boyish smile of his, "my father once told me that he loved me. But don't you dare tell him I told you!"

We laughed together and the metronome of the Turkish clock faded into the background.

I cannot express what I felt in that gentle evening. It was beyond tears, beyond joy, beyond any passion. I felt a mysterious calm, as if I were floating on Aladdin's carpet on a magical journey across a vast, cloudy expanse.

I heard the deep, inexplicable call of eternity. I was a part of an ongoing itinerary and this little one was my contribution to a miraculous process. I had heard the teachings of the imams. I had read the poems of the Persian mystics. But something about a child growing within and the wonderful hope of that little life was moving beyond words. None of the mystics had captured what I felt in that enigmatic summer evening. Though I did not have the breathtaking solitude of my poppy field, I felt my language of expression returning, and I filled my diary with my buoyant dreams.

My Love Debt

I cast myself onto love's tide
And drifted aimless in that current
Like dandelion spore
In pleasant early summer

I abandoned to its benevolent whim
With unquestioning loyalty
And I did not care of destination
Or purpose or design

I only cared
That I give offering
To something greater
Than myself

Chapter 11

Sorrow— غم
Winter 1975

In the season of my disillusionment, I gave birth to three boys. They were born two years apart, and they grew up in a man's world of horses and weapons. While they were young, they were mine. I introduced them to music, and all three were reading by the time they were six. The school in our village was nowhere near the standards of the schools in Kabul, but it was a start. I supplemented their education with a disciplined home environment. But as my first son neared puberty, I noticed a not-so-subtle pulling away.

My husband had them on horses by the time they were walking. By ten my oldest son was a warrior on his little stallion. His rash abandon terrified me. My husband worked with him every day, shouting instructions to him as he wheeled and cut in the tight confines of the training area in the back of our compound. He built a beautiful complex that joined the west side of his father's compound, and he enlarged the stables.

His horses had always been in great demand for the *Buzkashi* matches, but he began making real fortunes when he imported an Arabian stallion from Iran and bred him with his most agile Afghan mares. He developed a Thoroughbred pony perfect for polo and trained them to sell to the foreigners and wealthy businessmen in Kabul.

Though some foreign women had seen *Buzkashi* matches, no Afghan women I knew had seen them. But I knew enough to know it was dangerous and bloody. I had seen the casualties: men with broken teeth, broken limbs, and crushed skulls.

Buzkashi is a brutal sport, brought to Afghanistan by Mongol invaders centuries ago. The rules, if there are any, are simple. Two teams of men on horses fight over a headless goat carcass and try to drag it to a circle at one end of the field. It is barbaric and gory. Men are often maimed and even killed in the competition.

When I saw my oldest son at eleven snatch a sack of sand off the ground from a full gallop, I felt queasy. It was a breathtaking feat. He ran the horse hard in the opposite direction of the sandbag, and as he approached the compound wall, he threw his weight back on the haunches of his sleek little stallion. The horse slid on stiff forelegs; its hindquarters squatted back, as if braced for a collision with the wall. Just a meter from the wall, the horse wheeled back toward the sandbag and rising on its rear legs drove toward the bag in relentless fury. From across the compound, I could see the intent, wild-eyed focus on my son's face matched in the eyes of the little horse. They were, it seemed, a hell-driven machine intent on self-destruction. My son lay prone over the stallion's back, his left hand low and flat on its front flank. As he approached the bag, he leaned impossibly low, his high-heeled boots locked in the stirrups, and slid his hand down alongside the horse's furiously churning foreleg. When he caught the bag, it nearly jerked him from his saddle, and for a moment he faltered, but as the bag swung behind him, he used the momentum of its weight to swing himself upright. I could see the white flash of his teeth in contrast to his sundarkened face as he beamed proudly.

I knew it was just a matter of time before he would ask his father if he could compete in the *Buzkashi*. I knew his father would be proud of him when he did. He had named him Zemar, which means "lion," and from the time Zemar could walk, he had challenged him to be fearless. I learned that it was pointless to argue with my husband when it involved the boys. He captivated their imaginations with knives and horses and guns and kites.

Every Afghan man owns at least one weapon. They are seldom without them. My husband maintained an arsenal in a large, overly elaborate upright case covering an entire wall in our bedroom. A local carpenter built the case from dark walnut. Although the doors were fitted with locks, my husband did not use them. I despised the case. Grandiose and sinister, it dominated the room. It reeked of oil and aged steel. In it he kept three ancient Jezails: heavy, ornately decorated muskets with curious stocks that curved downward at awkward angles to the weapon's muzzle. I could not begin to imagine how one would hold such a monstrosity, much less fire it with any accuracy.

He also kept copies of British Lee-Enfield bolt-action rifles—exact replicas of the famous

World War I weapon—fashioned by Afghan and Pakistani craftsmen in their grimy shops on the border straddling the Khyber Pass. He had an array of Afghan knives, some of them as long as my arm, along with Russian assault rifles and dark, menacing pistols. But he kept his most prized weapon—a Norwegian sniper rifle with a large scope—carefully wrapped in a clean felt cloth. He babied that rifle. Not a scratch marred its surface and its barrel gleamed from his careful polishing. He said he could hit a cantaloupe from five hundred meters with that weapon. No one was allowed to touch it.

He began taking the boys down to one of his fields near the river in the afternoons to teach them to shoot. He started them with a small-caliber rifle and from the first day, they were picking off little pottery jars that he lined across the top of the low stone wall of a sheep pen. They returned at dark, full of bluster, boasting to one another of their prowess.

"I wish we could wait a little longer before we teach them the ways of war," I said.

"It is not the way of war," he said. "It is the way of self-reliance, the defense of honor, and the protection of our land."

I did not want to fight. I was outnumbered anyway. He stood still in the doorway as his minion soldiers rushed past and crowed to me of their budding manhood. I smiled and kissed their grimy cheeks and told them to wash for dinner.

I never understood the fanatical fascination my boys had for their kites. It started when Zemar was eight years old and his father took him to his first competition. My son made the kites himself, fragile, colorful contraptions he would loft in the slightest breeze and work deftly into the sky. His fingers would fly over the wooden spool as he pulled and released, wound and unwound with a skill that seemed almost innate. My husband showed him how to treat his kite string with a mixture of paste and ground glass, making the string abrasive. He learned to maneuver his kite around and cut the string of other kites in the competition by sawing his line against theirs. Then it was a mad rush to catch the opponent's falling kite and claim it as his own.

I was dismayed when, at nine years old, Zemar came home with a blackened eye and another boy's kite. Apparently, a fistfight started when both boys reached the tumbling kite at the same time. His father could not hide his pride as Zemar recounted the tale of the kite battle, the race to capture his prize, and the savage boxing of a neighboring boy his age at the spot where the kite touched earth.

My husband and I walked to the village soccer field one late winter afternoon to watch the boys fly their kites. Zemar flew the kite and his brother Padsha helped him. The two boys worked together, with Zemar guiding the kite and Padsha feeding the string from a wooden spool. I marveled at their dexterity. I had never realized that my boys could be so graceful and quick or cooperate with such fluid precision. At home they fought constantly, but with a kite in the air, they worked together with hardly a spoken word. They seemed to anticipate one another's actions, and often ran forward or backward at the same instant with no visible communication.

There were at least twenty kites in the air and sixty boys on the field. The unexpected beauty of so many kites flying together mesmerized me. Their bright colors dazzled in the vivid, cloudless sky, and they swooped with a speed and grace that mimicked agile birds in flight. Sometimes the boys would dive the kites low, and I could hear the crisp rustle of their paper coverings and the sing of the taut string in the wind. As the boys released meter after meter of line, the kites resembled small, colorful, distant swallows.

I noticed Zemar's bright teal-and-orange kite flying in tandem with a brilliant copper-and-green kite flown by a boy who stood near my husband and me. The two kites moved almost in unison, like a brace of pigeons racing over a field. I never dreamed flying kites could be so beautiful or so entertaining. I watched in silent appreciation, my hand shielding my face from the afternoon sun and my eyes tracking the quick, sudden dives of the kites. I heard Zemar shout something to his brother and glanced at the two boys about twenty meters away. Padsha furiously wound his spool, desperate to recover the string that lay strewn on the ground. From what I could gather from the shouting, Zemar wanted to run forward, but could not for fear of tangling the string. Padsha eventually spooled up the line, and both boys ran forward and to their left, releasing a few meters of string as they ran. They stopped abruptly, and Zemar jerked the kite string back, barking instructions to his younger brother. I looked up and saw the reason for all the excitement. The two kite strings had somehow intertwined, and both boys were working their strings furiously, sawing back and forth in an attempt to cut their opponent's line.

My husband cursed. His intent eyes focused skyward and his right hand jerked unconsciously at his side, as if he could guide the kite by the sheer force of his will. Zemar's kite fluttered off in the wind, and his limp kite string dropped hushed to earth. I saw him backhand his little brother on the cheek. In an instant, my husband was between the two boys, pulling them apart.

They argued all the way home about whose fault it was they had lost the kite. My husband intervened and gave them both a solid cuff to the backs of their heads. As we walked home in silence, I could not stop thinking of how something so beautiful and artistic had so quickly become violent in the hands of my sons. I wanted to speak, but knew better. As surely as that taut string had slipped through the agile fingers of my oldest son, my influence in their lives slipped through my hands.

That night I crept into my sons' bedroom. None of them had bathed, and they smelled of sweat and earth and anger. I sat for nearly an hour on the edge of their bed and watched them sleep. How I wished I could keep them in the world that I knew and loved. How I wished I could hold them as I did when they were toddlers and rest my cheek against their curls and breathe in their childlike sweetness. I longed for those tender moments when I nursed them by candlelight in the quiet solitude of a dark and early morning. But they were being rapidly drawn into a world of coarse violence.

I will never forget the sorrowful image of a beautifully crafted teal-and-orange kite wafting slowly to earth from its lofty flight. I will never forget that beautiful, heartsick day.

My Little Man

Little boy, my little man
How tragic is your journey
From heaven's sweet and innocent soft
To bitter fields of earth and hell

Chapter 12

Driven—طلب جاه
Summer 1976

The year of my thirtieth birthday was a heady time in Afghanistan. The Russians, the British, the Americans, and even the Iranians competed to gain a strategic advantage. Clever Afghan politicians worked all four against one another. Foreign money flowed into the country like water, and some of my husband's friends grew rich. Polo became a popular sport with the foreigners. Wealthy Afghans, who already had a deep love for horses, joined in the weekend matches, but good polo horses were hard to find.

My husband's bold move to import an Arabian stud proved to be brilliant. Afghan horses are small, but strong and courageous. No horse is better suited for the mountains, and they are lords of the *Buzkashi*. My husband always said that in the *Buzkashi*, it was better to have a good horse and a poor rider than to have a good rider and a bad horse. But in the game of polo, which requires finesse, the long-legged and long-winded Thoroughbreds were superior. And they were splendid animals.

Thoroughbreds are temperamental creatures, frisky and eager in the mornings and sometimes cranky and prone to nipping or kicking one another in the hot, dry afternoons. One of the mares, tall, sleek, and black, carried herself with a regal, inspiring attitude. I admired her self-confidence. When my husband allowed the horses to run in the early mornings, she would trot eagerly across the open field with her head up and alert, her neck arched, her forelegs snapping high, and her tail erect and flowing behind her.

The connection I felt with her was eerie, almost mystical. She reminded me somehow of my mother. The mare's thick, black mane and her stately manner took me back to those innocent, dreamy days. Sometimes I would tell her my secrets.

My husband would have his breakfast before sunrise, and after I had prepared his meal, I would steal through the soft ground fog of dawn to the stables with an apple hidden in my palm. The mare would nicker softly the moment she heard me enter the stable. While she devoured the apple, its sweet juice running out the bottom of her mouth, I would stare into the deep pools of her huge, lustrous eyes. I would see my reflection in their glassy surface and tell her everything. She would gaze deep into my soul and unhinge my heart. I would rest my forehead against hers and breathe of her rich animal scent and hear the thunder of imperial hooves in a prehistoric desert valley.

I wondered whether the mare felt the same appreciation for me as I felt for her. I wondered what she thought of me. Was I beautiful? Did I fascinate my lover? Was I worthy of his devotion? And I wondered if, in all her noble bearing, she sometimes doubted herself, as I doubted myself.

Mother would have scoffed at my insecurity over turning thirty. She would have told me that I was beautiful, and now wise as well as attractive. She would have scolded me when I worried over the little lines forming at the corners of my eyes and on my forehead. But Mother never grew old with her husband. He was preserved in her memory, young and strong and faithful. And she was preserved along with him in that memory, lithe and beautiful. She never competed for his affections with younger, more vigorous women with shining hair and glowing, eager faces.

Though she reminded me of Mother, the mare was more like me. I had watched her jostle the other brood mares as they romped in the field. I had seen how she carefully positioned herself between those mares and the stallion who watched over them all with ardent interest. The mare understood the competition with the young and the strong, yet she carried herself with supreme confidence.

And sometimes, when I had poured out my secret fears to her, the mare would speak to me with the voice of an ancient Persian queen. She would gaze, serene and unblinking, into my reddened eyes and nicker, deep and rumbling and patient. She would tell me to be strong.

The Russians built a new road into our valley, and my husband bought his first car, a beautiful powder-blue Peugeot. He bought many new things: Russian rifles for the boys, a pistol he always carried, silk and jewelry for his mother and me. It was too much too fast, and it was changing him.

I tried to talk to him about it one evening when he was relaxing in his favorite spot in the courtyard, pulling slowly on his water pipe. He had tiled the courtyard and installed a little pool in the center. Soft lantern light made it a tranquil haven, and he spent most of his evenings relaxing there. He had lavished a small fortune on the construction—a copy of a courtyard he had seen in a French embassy official's home. I had to admit, on clear starlit nights, when the courtyard filled with the music of his pipe's soft gurgle, it was my favorite place, too.

On one of those balmy nights I told him that I worried about all the money he spent on the endless favors for the endless needs of his endless line of relatives. I told him that I felt we were in danger of losing our priorities, that I was concerned about the new money and the new foreign friends. I told him we would be caught in a political crossfire if we continued to associate with the foreigners.

He looked at me thoughtfully, took a long draw on his pipe, and exhaled slowly, watching the dense smoke flow up toward the night sky. "You worry too much," was all he said.

I knew him well enough to let it go at that. He did not like discussing money and bringing up the subject had been risky.

When he took an interest in the polo horses, he began to study English. He surprised me with how quickly he learned. I practiced with him, and although my grammar was good, I could not match his vocabulary. He had more opportunities to speak than I did, and showed a quick intelligence. I was proud of him. He had a strong accent, and he often got his word order backward, but his personality and enthusiasm more than made up for his limitations. Foreigners seemed to like him.

His interaction with the foreigners changed him in ways that worried me. He began making weekend trips into Kabul. After two years of regular visits, he shocked me when he invited me to join him. He astonished me even more when he bought me a Western dress and asked me to wear it to a Sunday brunch at the Kabul InterContinental Hotel. It was a modest dress, with long sleeves and a high neck, but it did show my calves, which made me self-conscious. He had promised to take me to the Kabul museum afterward, and for that I would have worn a sleeveless dress.

The brunch was much more fun than I had expected. I tasted my first Iranian caviar. We ate it with thick, heavy cream on a delicate cracker. The briny, sensual flavor burst in my mouth with such intensity that I giggled. I had to refrain myself from taking more than would have been appropriate.

My husband's customers were charming. Most of them were British or American, but there were also French, Germans, Italians, and, of course, Russians. They were educated, gracious, and fun. Many of them spoke Persian, the language of choice among the Kabul elite, as well as English, and conversations flowed in both languages. It was a delightful, stimulating afternoon. I clung to my husband's arm while we wandered through the crowd. He seemed to know all of them.

Near the bar a short, overweight Russian approached us, his drink sloshing with his tipsy gait. His leering focus on my chest embarrassed me. My husband eased himself between the man and me, gently positioning me away from the other man's gaze. The ruddy little man did not take the hint and continued to stare at me while he spoke to my husband in heavily accented Pashto. Through the babble of voices around us, I heard him mention the museum.

My husband said something I could not quite hear and moved away from the man. He moved too quickly and as I stumbled, I clung to his arm for support. I was not accustomed to the Western heels I wore. I hoped that no one had noticed my clumsiness.

"How does he know we are going to the museum?" I asked.

"He arranged for someone to give us a tour," my husband answered.

"Is he one of your customers?"

"He works for one of my customers," he said. "He is not important."

The little Russian seemed out of place. He was not refined like the other foreigners at the brunch. While my husband had been comfortable with everyone we spoke with, he seemed nervous and unsure of himself in that brief encounter. Something I could not quite grasp troubled me about the man, but I dismissed it as we continued the dizzying, champagne-fueled tour of smiling foreign faces.

Several men told him I was beautiful, and I blushed at their straightforwardness. To my surprise, my husband seemed to enjoy their compliments. Afghan men are notoriously jealous over their women, and my husband was no exception, but the freewheeling lifestyle of the foreigners seemed to influence him.

I found the experience of these two dramatically different worlds uncanny. That morning I had a simple breakfast of tea and a boiled egg in a primitive village and by midday, I had indulged with the Kabul elite. I enjoyed the afternoon, but a nagging fear continued to haunt me. I knew how quickly fortunes could turn, and I knew that outside Kabul, powerful clan leaders resented the change that foreigners were bringing to our nation.

In spite of my fears, I was proud of who my husband had become. He worked hard, he loved his boys, and though he could be maddeningly stubborn, he treated me respectfully. At thirty-six, he was strong and handsome and full of unshakable confidence. He prospered in everything he did, and a cunning intelligence had emerged in him. I loved him more than ever, but to that love, I added a growing esteem.

Though he was wealthy, he had never hinted at taking another wife. Age added to his strong masculine appeal, and among the foreigners at the brunch, I had seen women notice him. Some even approached him, engaging in flirtatious conversations. He held their gaze with charming, confident wit.

I was unaccustomed to women toying with men and I could not judge the seriousness of their interest. They stood with a cigarette or drink in one hand, while the other hand punctuated their conversations with gestures and sometimes a casual touch to my husband's arm. They tilted their hips provocatively and leaned forward when he spoke, gushing over anything remotely interesting.

He seemed unfazed by the attention, but their interest still troubled me. I worried that in a moment of weakness, he could be seduced. They were attractive enough to draw any man's interest. They roamed the room like hummingbirds visiting flowers, quick and curious and fetching, equally interested in every conversation. They were dizzying to watch. I could not tell if their behavior was cultural or wanton.

In Afghan culture, a woman would never behave in public with such forwardness. We flirted, of course, but it was subtle. We flirted with our eyes, but the Western women flirted with their bodies. In spite of my hatred for the stifling social limits of our way of life, in some ways I preferred the restrictions I lived under to the unrestrained morals of the West. It unsettled me to imagine a life in the emotionally competitive social circles of the foreigners. I had heard that affairs were common among them, and I wondered how they endured the shame and trauma of betrayal and broken dreams. Their gaiety, I thought, was a thin facade covering shallow, meaningless lives.

Around three in the afternoon, we left the brunch for the museum. I rested my head against the doorjamb of the Peugeot and with the window down enjoyed the warm breeze. Kabul had become a magnificent city with tree-lined boulevards and paved streets. I glanced at my husband and smiled at his concentrated focus. He still drove the car uneasily, and his furrowed brow and clenched hands betrayed his anxiety.

We came to an intersection, and he seemed confused over which way to turn. I thought the museum was to the left, but I said nothing. He seemed to start in that direction, but chose at the last moment to go straight. Fifteen minutes later, after circling through several confusing backstreets, we arrived back at the same intersection. This time he turned in the direction I first felt we should go. I said nothing and dreamily watched the passing of walnut trees that lined the street. It seemed to me that in many ways we were headed in different directions. Our differences in the early years of our marriage were insignificant, but the longer we lived together, the more noticeable those differences became. The more we continued on our paths, the further apart they grew. It was not our intention; it just happened.

I wondered, as we whisked along that empty street, whether my love could evolve with him. I wondered whether I could become a different person for the sake of love. I wondered if I was not happy with my new persona, whether my love would prevail. And I wondered if I changed with him, whether he would still love the person I was becoming. I could not decipher who he wanted me to be. I thought to ask him, but I knew he would not understand. Love, it seemed, had its own selfish agenda. It captivated my heart; then without informing me, it changed the rules. I fretted and sputtered and objected that it was not fair. But love continued on its relentless course, and I had no choice but to blindly follow.

I understood, in that tranquil intersection, that we had drifted apart. I had watched him become someone else, someone who was not at all the person I first loved. Without breaking from my reverie I asked him if he knew where we were going. I was thinking of where we were going in our marriage.

"Of course I know where we are going," he snapped.

I felt foolish when I realized that I had spoken aloud a thought that I had intended to keep to myself.

"You seem lost to me," I said with a little more force than I meant, my voice rising, shrill and angry.

He started to speak, then stopped. His fingers tightened around the Peugeot's steering wheel and his face flushed. The prominent vein that pulsed in his neck when he was angry began its persistent beat. I watched him struggle to regain his composure. He took several deep, slow breaths and the vein retreated into his brown, leathery flesh. After a few moments of clenching his jaw, he spoke in calm, measured words.

"Do you want to go to the museum, or not?"

"Yes, of course," I said, suddenly meek and submissive.

But something troubled me. It was not like him to manage his anger. I seldom won an argument with him. He would usually berate me, or intimidate me, or simply overpower me with irate shouts. I could not remember a time when he had so effectively corralled his unpredictable temper. He had given up too easily. Something that I could not quite define nagged me through the remainder of our drive to the museum. Something was dreadfully wrong.

My mind wandered as we drove down that dreamy, tree-lined avenue. Perhaps the city had unsettled me. Perhaps the rich food and the gaiety and the champagne had addled me. Perhaps my fears were imaginary. I closed my eyes and envisioned the simple serenity of our unsullied village.

There are two paths to the market from our compound. One is hardly a fifteen-minute walk along a dusty road. In the dry season, passing trucks kick up a fine, chalky dust that covers everything and makes breathing difficult. In the rainy season, it is a muddy quagmire. The other path meanders along the river bordering the wheat fields behind the village. It goes by an abandoned prehistoric threshing floor, of massive flat stones darkened by hundreds of years of weather. An ancient wall lining part of the path, with stones neatly stacked along both sides, has remained unchanged for centuries. I imagine those walls were built before the time of Genghis Khan, who invaded us eight hundred years ago.

The land along the path is terraced on the upslope side, and the wall is about my height. The musty smell of decaying moss and the rich aroma of the fertile fields combine with the sudden silence of the high-walled passageway to make it a magical place. In many ways, it is the sensory opposite of my poppy field. Instead of wide and open and fragrant, it is narrow and confining and pungent. But the effect is the same. It is a place of solitude. Shielded by the wall, I always slow my pace when I walk that path, enjoying a brief moment of quiet.

The river path is at least thirty minutes longer, and in spite of the stern warnings from my husband and mother-in-law, I nearly always took it. I suspect that if my husband were inclined to go to the market, he would take the direct route.

My Lover's Journey

My lover is determined
Ambitious in his course
He charges blindly down
A dark and fearful mountain

And I meander in the hills
And daydream in the pastures
Admiring the driven man
My wayward lover

I call to him from distant heights
And my heart tumbles down
An avalanche upon the slopes
The rubble of my dreams

Chapter 13

Beast—جانور

The Kabul museum in 1976 was one of the finest in the world and the pride of the nation. Located in the crossroads of Asia, my country has been inhabited at one time or another by Buddhists, Sikhs, Hindus, Greeks, Muslims, and even Jews. The city is more than three thousand years old and some of the museum exhibits display treasures predating Islam by more than a thousand years, including Hellenistic gold coins, Buddhist statues, and ancient pagan gods and goddesses. From the time I was a child I had longed to visit the museum, and now, to have only a few hours to browse through its cavernous rooms frustrated me. But I was grateful for what I was given.

We entered through a long arched hallway and my husband guided me toward a marbled staircase. He appeared to know where he was going. I was overwhelmed. He glanced at his watch and scanned the vast foyer. He seemed oddly determined, and without the slightest hesitation, he led me upstairs to the Greco-Bactrian Buddha statues. Carved in the third and fourth centuries, the limestone figures were bizarre in the context of our Islamic culture. I found it hard to believe that Buddhism had once influenced our country. I had never seen anything like them.

I walked with a light hand on his arm as he guided me up the marble staircase. My sudden intake of breath as we entered the exhibit hall seemed to please him. The next hour went by so quickly that I almost panicked. I did not want to rush through this afternoon.

As a child, I had spent hours leafing through the glossy pages of my mother's large book of the museum exhibits. Printed in Pakistan, the book was a black-market copy of a British publication. Someone had carefully translated the English text into Urdu. It was of excellent quality, filled with large color pictures, and one of the most interesting books she owned. I surprised even myself when I began to explain some of the exhibits to him. I awakened in the glow of his interest.

I felt proud as we drifted from one exhibit to the next and I answered his probing, sometimes insightful questions. He seemed to look at me in a new light, as if he were discovering a new intriguing facet of my personality. I could not have been more content that afternoon in that absorbing conversation. We discussed ancient history, but I experienced rekindled love.

We rounded a corner in the exhibit hall and nearly bumped into a tall, very beautiful foreign woman. She was directing three men as they struggled to mount a heavy bronze statue on a waist-high pedestal. Apparently, she had overheard our conversation about the Bactrian era and asked in lightly accented Persian, "Would you like to know about the Bactrian gold?"

"Yes, of course," I stammered, having no idea what she was talking about.

"Hi, I'm Ivana."

She extended a slender hand to me and smiled pleasantly. Her nails were clean and carefully polished. She wore an elegant gold bracelet with onyx stones that tinkled daintily as we shook hands. Nearly as tall as my husband, she towered over me. I felt intimidated. Her immaculate suit clung gracefully to her impressive feminine form. She wore a modest skirt, just below her knees, but the skirt could not hide the beguiling beauty of her willowy legs. She is no archaeologist, I thought.

"I'm Czechoslovakian," she said, "and I'm here from the National Museum in Prague to help categorize the Kushan gold."

"I have never heard of it," I said.

I stole a glance at my husband. His face was a befuddled, expressionless mask, as if someone had cast a strange enchantment over him. Ivana's long, curly blonde hair tumbled over her shoulders in an elegant, scented profusion. She had eyes even bluer than my own and a flawless pale complexion. She smiled confidently at my husband, showing perfect white teeth. To my surprise, he did not respond. Bewildered, he searched for words. After an awkward moment, he stammered in a dry voice, "Please, tell us more."

"We've found ancient treasure," she responded. "We're working together with the Kabul museum staff to excavate near Sheberghan. We think the find will rival Tutankhamen's tomb in Egypt and we've uncovered some pieces that look very promising."

She then described, with sincere enthusiasm, first-century Afghanistan and the unparalleled riches that traveled through our nation along the famed Silk Road. Her clean V-neck blouse emphasized her broad shoulders and ended just low enough to reveal a hint of cleavage. At the base of the V, a simple gold cross hung on a slender gold chain. My husband took interest in that cross.

Christian! I thought with contempt.

At last, he discovered his voice and engaged Ivana in a discussion of the area they were excavating. He knew the region and location where they were digging, though he had no idea of the riches hidden there. He seemed amused that poor melon farmers had been scratching out a miserable existence on a site where untold wealth lay buried.

The museum was closing, but with a charming smile Ivana said, "Don't worry, workers will be here for three more hours setting up a new exhibit and I don't have any obligations this evening. Would you like to see more?"

"Of course!" my husband replied with a little too much enthusiasm. We followed her along the broad marbled hall to another exhibit, her heels echoing in the empty corridor. I noticed him studying her round bottom as we trailed behind her and realized that I had not said a word for the past twenty minutes.

I tried to enter the conversation, without appearing competitive. Ivana graciously deferred to me when I spoke, never contradicted me, and added only occasional comments to things I left out. She even complimented me on my knowledge of the exhibits. But in spite of her deference, her presence dominated our time together. A casual toss of her hair and a delicate waft of perfume would drift over us, intoxicating my witless husband. The constant click of her heels and the swing of her lithe arms mesmerized him. Her long, slender fingers gestured toward this object or that and her musical voice echoed softly in the cavernous rooms, accompanied by the faint jaunty tinkle of her bracelet. My husband followed her through room after room like a hungry puppy eagerly waiting for the next morsel to drop to the floor.

For the first time in my life, I hated a woman. I wanted to snatch that obscene cross from her neck and hammer her face with the spiked heels of her flawless pumps. She was a jinn from hell itself and turned the next two hours into a torturous eternity. Desperate, I tried to match wits with her, but in the end, she conquered me as easily as she had charmed my clueless husband.

On the long, dark drive home he rambled on and on, inspired by his newfound enthusiasm for ancient Afghan history and undiscovered treasures. Patient, I listened to him with a sweet smile, but in my heart a tiny rip had begun

I have never understood how a person could abandon the passion of first love. That a person could be persuaded by a seducing devilment to throw away the fragile, tender sweetness of their first kiss as casually as changing into a fresh garment was incomprehensible to me.

I rested my head against the doorjamb and let the warm breeze flow over my face as we sped through the dark night. Love, I thought, is so all-consuming, so terrifying, and yet so destructive. I was so deeply disappointed. The day had begun in a magical adventure and ended in foreboding dread. My tears dried quickly in the turbulent wind, but their burning salty residue remained on my raw cheeks like a crusty, irritating abrasive.

That night we made love and my husband seemed unusually eager. He finished quickly and I hardly had time to respond. Although he was with me, I knew his imagination had carried him somewhere else. And I could not compete with golden locks and full painted lips and scented foreign lingerie.

My husband had a magnificent Arabian stallion. That horse frightened me. When freshly groomed, his coat gleamed black and glossy, and his muscles rippled under his skin in flowing rivers of corded strength. I saw him nearly kill one of my husband's men with a single kick that splintered the man's ribs, punctured a lung, and split his breastbone. I have seen him stand watch over his brood of mares, his nostrils flaring, his ears swiveling to the slightest sound, and his hooves pawing the ground in fearless intimidation. I have watched him nuzzle and flirt with one of those mares before mounting her, and then do the same to another mare within that very hour. I have seen a mare deliberately position herself upwind of the stallion and whisk her tail and entice him with her scent and completely captivate him.

My husband's stallion may be controlled by bit and bridle, but it is a delicate and dangerous and precarious task.

The Beast

The beast devours one by one
Weak defenseless lambs
They bleat and shuffle stupidly
To the slaughter of their hearts

Chapter 14

حمق‌ا—Fool
Fall 1977

I had mixed feelings about moving to Kabul, but I was happy that the boys could attend a real school. Zemar, my oldest, was thirteen and though I could keep up with him in literature, he was beginning to ask math questions that were above me. The rote-style teachers in the village school were useless, but the Kabul schools would challenge him.

Mohammed Daoud, Afghanistan's prime minister, had introduced sweeping changes into the country. Playing Russia and America against one another, he brought massive injections of foreign capital into our nation and transformed Kabul. The city was clean and bustled, with all the major streets paved. But the greatest changes were cultural.

Men and women wore Western clothing. It was common to see a woman walking alone on the streets, unaccompanied by her husband or a male relative, wearing a Western blouse with her skirt above her knees. Women still wore the burka, but they were becoming more of a rarity. Occasionally, a fundamentalist attacked a woman, throwing acid on her face for not being properly covered, but the city government worked hard to rein in the mullahs and the radicals. There were movies and restaurants and theaters. Foreigners hosted endless parties.

The private schools we visited were outrageously expensive, but they met Western standards. My husband said that I should not worry about the cost. I was grateful that my children would have the best schooling possible, but I found the changes in the city troubling. The Russians had invested heavily in the Afghan military, offering training, weapons, and Russian Army advisory officers. The Afghan Communist Party was gaining power. It seemed to me that it was just a matter of time before the Russians made some sort of military move. Nothing could stop them from occupying us, just as they had taken Tajikistan, Uzbekistan, and Turkmenistan, our northern neighbors. I worried about it constantly.

Moving to Kabul took us one more step away from my mother. As it was, I saw her maybe twice a year. Now, from the city, it would be an even greater challenge. My husband had a driver and told me I could take the car any time I wanted to visit her. That would mean an overnight trip. I could not believe the same man who would not let me leave our home when we were first married now encouraged me to travel alone with a male driver and stay with my relatives unsupervised overnight.

He changed in many other ways. He turned the day-to-day activities of the horse and farming business over to his brother. From our village, he had taken weekly trips into Kabul that started as weekends and became weeklong. By the time we moved, he spent only weekends at home. Sometimes I would not see him for two weeks. He began selling more Thoroughbreds, but I couldn't see how the increased business accounted for the unusual amount of money he was making.

He bought a beautiful villa in one of the most affluent areas of Kabul. There had been a huge influx of Afghans, as well as foreigners, moving into the city. Soviet-built apartments sprang up everywhere. The Afghans loved them and boasted to their village relatives about indoor plumbing and electricity and telephones. But those buildings were ugly concrete towers with families stacked on one another like pigeons in a coop.

At least my husband had the good taste to find us a real house. It was small, much smaller than our compound in the village, but I loved it. A high wall surrounded it and between the wall and the home were lush, well-established gardens. I had a full-time gardener and a maid. But it was too much, too fast.

I scarcely saw my husband. He began sleeping late and would have a quick breakfast around eight in the morning, which was the time I was busy getting the boys off to school. By the time I settled down at the table for a cup of tea, he was engrossed in the daily paper and hardly looked up at me. Most nights I had no idea when he came to bed. Our lovemaking dwindled to once in a fortnight at best.

I began to enjoy afternoon movies at the theater. Indian Hindi films and even foreign films had become popular in Kabul and there was something new to see every week. I spent long afternoons in the library, and in the evenings I helped the boys with their homework. I wanted desperately to go to the Kabul museum again, but I could not bear the thought of seeing Ivana.

One afternoon I was browsing in a bookstore not far from the Kabul InterContinental Hotel. I glanced up through the large storefront window and happened to see my husband's car flash by outside. He was sitting in the backseat talking animatedly with a foreigner. Curious, I stepped out of the bookstore and watched the car cruise down the street and turn into the InterContinental.

I considered walking down to the hotel, but could not conjure up the nerve. What would I say if he saw me, and why was I so intrigued? I tried to put it out of my mind, but all afternoon I wondered what it was he did with so many foreigners, staying out late at night, about town without so much as an office. Where exactly did he go each day?

Several weeks passed and I obsessed over his secret life. One afternoon as I watched a large woman in a burka amble down the street, I realized that no one on the street gave her so much as a glance. Not many wore a burka in Kabul anymore, but it was still common enough to blend into the scenery. That afternoon I bought an indigo burka and hid it under my bed.

It took me several days to get up the nerve to wear it. I tried it on several times in my room and remembered why I hated the garment. The heavy crochet screen trapped my breath inside the headdress. The stale air made me claustrophobic. I felt nauseous at the very thought of putting it over my head. Visibility through the tiny face grille was limited. I could not see my feet and had to anticipate by several meters where I was walking. I could not see to either side without turning my entire body, which was tedious. It took some practice to get used to wearing it, but at least it was November and it would not be so hot.

I took a taxi to the InterContinental the next afternoon and planted myself on the sofa in the lobby. I was fretful, but after a moment I settled down and began to enjoy the experience. In the burka I could watch in complete obscurity. A couple sat on the couch near me and engaged in a conversation without acknowledging my presence. I noticed that mine was the only burka in the lobby and the doorman had been watching me. He finally walked over to me and asked politely, "May I help you with anything, sister?"

"I'm fine, thank you," I said. "I'm just waiting for my husband. I'm sure he will be along soon." He seemed satisfied with my answer and went back to his duties at the entrance. The hotel lobby was busy with a constant stream of foreigners and Afghan businessmen. Smartly dressed men in suits and an occasional woman filed in and out of the revolving door on their way to meetings or engagements.

In spite of the limitations of the burka, I watched in fascination as the cream of Kabul filed past my anonymous vigil. But by five in the afternoon, I began to grow weary. The boys would be home by now, and though I did not need to prepare supper for them since I had house help, I liked to be there for them and find out about their day. Besides, I thought, I might sit here for days before my husband comes through that gleaming brass door.

I was about to rise when he walked in. He looked attractive in his pin-striped business suit. His heavy beard had begun to show an afternoon shadow, but otherwise he looked crisp. I saw him every morning in his suits. Meticulously tailored in the same shop that most of the diplomats used, they were dark and creased and molded to his form. He fussed over them, spacing them evenly in his closet, each one in a zippered plastic suit bag. Though I saw him dressed for business every morning, I had never seen him in the prim setting of the Westerners. Our home bore the vestiges of our medieval village life—handcrafted utensils, frayed rugs, floor mats and cushions— but the hotel lobby was furnished with polished Western-style couches and Iranian rugs and elaborate Islamic artifacts. At home he seemed awkward and out of place in his foreign clothes, but here he walked with the alert confidence of an ambassador. He had even grown a little plump in the city, like the group of Russian men who lounged at the bar.

He scanned the lobby and apparently did not see who he was looking for. I watched him go to the front desk and speak briefly with the clerk, then turn and walk directly toward me. My heart leaped into my throat as I watched through the thick gauze of the burka's grille. I kept my hands folded in my lap for fear he would see them shaking, but I had no reason to be anxious. He sat across from me, and without a glance in my direction, nonchalantly lit a cigarette as he picked up a newspaper from the coffee table between us.

It was bizarre to watch him like this. I felt like a scientist studying an interesting specimen. But unlike a scientist, my emotions were deeply invested in the subject of my study and my yearning heart went out to him in deep, anguished longing. How I wished to hold him as we had held one another in our early days. How I wished I was still the awestruck young girl and he was still the confident young man on his spirited horse.

I began to feel guilty for what I was doing and had decided to leave when the Czech woman walked in through the front door. She wore a simple black dress with a single strand of pearls, black heels, and a three-quarter-length cashmere coat. Her white, unblemished bare legs gleamed in the sunlit lobby. I thought it was not quite cool enough for the coat, but I had to admit, she was stunning. Every man in the room turned in her direction.

She smiled broadly and walked toward my husband. He had his back to her and did not see her, but I knew he had been waiting for her. I felt nauseous and feared I was about to be sick. I panicked and bolted up from the couch, brushing by her as I lurched across the lobby. I was dizzy and could hardly see through the burka's veil. I stumbled when my shoe caught in the long hem of the garment, and, not knowing what to do, I walked straight across the lobby to the elevators.

I needed something to steady myself against and the wall by the elevators was the nearest spot where people were not congregated. When I reached the elevators, I placed a palm on the wall beside the door and leaned against the wall for support. I pushed the elevator button, thinking I would get inside and ride it up to the top floor, then back down to the lobby. That would give me time to compose myself. The elevator took an eternity to descend and as I stood there, I sensed someone standing behind me.

The doors opened and a smartly dressed, elderly foreign man stepped out. I had to move back to make room for him, but once he was clear, I rushed into the elevator and grasped the rail along its back wall. I turned and to my horror, Ivana and my husband were entering through the closing doors. The room seemed to be tipping and I felt as if I were in a Dalí painting. I could not breathe. I thought I would faint. The palpitations in my temples were so loud I feared the two of them might hear my pounding heart. Ivana pressed the button for the sixth floor, then, smiling, looked at me as if to ask which floor I wanted. I shrugged and nodded, hoping she would think I wanted the same floor. I prayed she would not speak to me.

The elevator creaked and began to grind slowly upward. For an eternity we crawled up, and up, and up. My husband and Ivana stood in front of me, their eyes on the floor indicator above their heads, occasionally glancing at one another and smiling. When the doors finally opened, they stepped out holding hands and began to walk briskly down the hall. I waited for a moment, and then hesitantly, as if in a trance, stepped out of the elevator and began walking slowly after them.

They stopped at the door of a room and my husband fumbled with the key. As I approached them, he pushed the door open and they stepped inside, closing the door as I passed. I could go no farther. My legs quivered and I would have fallen had I not braced against the wall. A step past their door I stopped, leaned my back against the wall, and waited for the shaking to stop. My breath was rasping inside the burka and I nearly threw it off to get some fresh air. The last thing I wanted to do was linger outside their door, but my body would not move.

I heard Ivana's musical laugh, just on the other side of the wall, and a high-pitched squeal. There was some bumping against the door, more laughter. They were fondling one another less than a meter from where I stood. I crumpled to the floor and for a moment I must have passed out. When I came to, I was on my hands and knees propped against the wall with a relentless pounding in my ears. In a mindless panic, I somehow got to my feet and ran back to the elevators.

I do not remember the trip down, or racing blindly through the lobby, or even the taxi ride home. I only remember walking through the front door of my house and seeing my sons at the kitchen table doing their homework. Quizzical, they raised their heads. I realized I was still wearing the burka.

Fool

Love made a fool of me
And stole my heart away
And though I heard the whispers
I still would not believe

And I became a king of clowns
And ruled my petty kingdom
And wondered how and wondered why
Love made a fool of me

Chapter 15

Curse—گفتـــن ناسـزا

S omehow, I got the boys to bed without breaking down. When I tucked in Babur, my youngest, I nearly lost my composure. He was nine, with big, sensitive eyes and a persistent cowlick. I unconsciously wet my finger on my tongue and tried to smooth it down, as if by fixing that little imperfection I could fix everything else that had gone wrong. It annoyed him, as it always did when I tried to groom him, and he said sternly, "Stop it, Mommy!"

"I'm sorry, dear," I said. "I'm so sorry." A huge, single tear forced itself against my will from one eye. It dropped with a heavy, sodden thud on his crisp bedsheet. He noticed it and looked at me, perplexed.

"Mommy, it's all right," he said. I could hear the worry in his voice.

I wanted to climb in the bed with him and hold his warm, chubby body against me. I wanted to sleep there with him and cling to him through the night, as if by clutching to my youngest child I could somehow hold on to the fading memories of a time forgotten. I could not bear the thought of going alone to my bedroom and waiting in persistent dread for my husband to come home. But I did not want to alarm Babur, so I kissed him softly on the forehead and said, "Go to sleep, dear. I love you."

He seemed satisfied and turned his back to me, adjusting his pillow as he turned. I stood at his door watching him sleep, postponing the grief that I knew would arrest me the moment I was alone. I poured a hot bath and my tears flowed into those soap-clouded waters until they were cold. They flowed until my cries were nothing but dry heaves and desperate gulps for air. I could not breathe. I suppose it was not that I could not breathe, but that I did not want to breathe.

I lay on my back in the bed and shivered from the persistent chill that gripped me. My heart was a heavy, aching stone within my chest. I wanted to die.

Death, I discovered, is not a moment, but an inevitable digression to an inevitable end. Like love, death has its own persistent agenda and its own stubborn, selfish will. And though I feared to die, and though I despised all it represented, for the first time in my life I wanted to embrace that cold and heartless conclusion.

I heard my husband open the front gate and drive his car into our compound at about eleven thirty that night. I turned over on my side and waited. It was a long while before he came to bed. I heard him in the kitchen eating, then the soft splash of his bath. When he slipped into the bed and I caught the faint scent of his soap, I realized how long he had carefully concealed his affair.

I lay comatose through the night. I wanted desperately to sleep, to have some brief respite from the determined ache in my chest. But sleep tiptoed just beyond my grasp and sunrise brought a dull, throbbing headache. By the time the children were awake, I had drunk three cups of tea. I somehow managed to have a polite conversation with my husband over breakfast, but I have no recollection of anything I said.

I only remember being surprised that I was not angry with him. I felt a deep and longing sadness and oddly, regret. I regretted that I had not done things differently. I regretted that I had not been a better wife and mother. I regretted that I had not fulfilled his needs. I regretted that somehow I had failed him and failed my children and failed my mother and failed love.

For the next three days, I shuffled about in a state of piteous numbness. But on the fourth day, after getting my children off to school and my husband off to the city, I gave the maid and the gardener a day off. It was cold that day and I took a blanket and a thermos of tea and sat outside in my favorite garden chair. Out of my numb and bitter heartache, a seething anger began to surface from deep within until finally, rage overwhelmed me.

In the backside of my garden, I paced back and forth near a pond where placid goldfish swam and I muttered out loud like a woman gone mad. I cursed my husband and I cursed Ivana and I ground my teeth in my rage and cursed God. I cursed my mother for planting the lie of hope for true love in my stripling heart. I cursed my father for all his foolish talk of *la petite mort* and loyalty. He knew nothing of life or love. He knew nothing of betrayal or abandonment or loneliness or vulnerability or failure. I cursed him for his witless naïveté. I cursed the day I was born. I fell to my knees on the rough, cold stones that encircled the goldfish pond, and my rage became a spate of filthy words that I had heard, but never spoken. As if driven by a hellish jinn, my phrases degenerated to unintelligible mutterings. My tears poured upon the stones in great salty pools. I swore upon those stones that I would never again write in my diary, that I would never again gaze on fields of poppies, that I would never again dream of love.

Chapter 16

 Trap—افتـــاده بـــدام

Winter 1979

When the Russians invaded, my country and I began a long and sorrowful funeral march. I never understood why we could not resolve our internal conflicts. The tribal divisions made us vulnerable through the centuries to outside invaders. I did understand why external forces continually razed Afghanistan and fought one another to control her borders. Located at the crossroads between the West, central Asia, and India, Afghanistan has been conquered, ruled, destroyed, and rebuilt by world empires for nearly three thousand years. Cyrus the Great, Alexander the Great, Seleucus, Sultan Mahmud the Great, Genghis Khan, Babur, and the

British all pillaged Afghan cities and ravished her people. The Russians were just another of a long line of empires that have come to dash themselves on the inscrutable, resilient rock that is Afghanistan.

The Soviets began with good intentions and through the seventies, they made astonishing improvements in our educational and medical systems. They paved our roads, invested in housing projects, and opened highways through the mountain passes. As Prime Minister Daoud continued to walk a tightrope between the United States and Russia, the Soviets tired of his cunning politics and developed the Afghan Communist Party.

An indigenous communist party had operated in the country since 1965 and it was their support that helped Mohammed Daoud Khan overthrow his cousin, Mohammed Zahir Shah. In 1978, with help from the Afghan Army, they assassinated Daoud and his entire family in an attack on the presidential palace. They formed the Democratic Republic of Afghanistan that year. Their party legislated land and social reforms that inflamed most of the countryside and infuriated my husband.

The Democratic Republic's socialist agenda was radical and wide reaching. Men were required to cut their beards, the burka was banned, and people were prohibited from going into the mosques. Land-reform laws released tenant farmers from debt and land usury was abolished. The traditional practices of the bride price and forced marriage were banned and the minimum age for marriage was raised. I welcomed many of their reforms, but I did not trust the socialists. It was clear there was going to be trouble. It was a very complicated time and once again, we became a pawn in the struggle between world empires.

When the United States engineered a peace agreement between Israel and Egypt in March of 1979, the Soviets saw it as a threat to their influence in the Middle East. With their strategic position threatened, the Russians began to strengthen their presence in central Asia. In late December of 1979, the Russians lost patience with the infighting that had gripped my country and KGB units airlifted into Kabul. They killed Hafizullah Amin, whom they had set up as their puppet ruler earlier in the year, and the next day Russian Army troops poured across the border from Uzbekistan.

I had seen the conflict coming for years, but my husband had been too preoccupied with his business and his mistress to engage in a conversation with me about politics. Though he had become liberal in his social life, he was still very conservative regarding my role in the family. As far as he was concerned, I was a woman with little comprehension of the grand scheme of politics and business.

His hypocrisy enraged me. I had long since given up making love to him. I could not bear the thought of him touching me, knowing that he had touched another woman just as intimately. I struggled constantly with the images in my mind of him and Ivana embracing. The memory of their laughter haunted me. For him to abandon the purity of our love was heartbreaking, but I made the decision to ignore his indiscretion for the sake of my children.

I remember a night, not long after I discovered his affair, when I could not sleep. There were many sleepless nights in those days. My husband was snoring and it irritated me that he could rest soundly while I lived in restless, agonizing torment. I went into the kitchen and made tea. I fidgeted at the table until finally, with my steaming cup in my hand I wandered aimlessly through the house. I watched the boys sleep for a while and ended up at the door of our bedroom, gazing mournfully at my former lover.

I found myself vacillating between love and hatred toward him. Those conflicting compulsions had been warring in me ever since I discovered his adultery. I would remember the happy seasons and think that I should move past the aching hurt. Then I would remember that day in the InterContinental and a rage would seethe inside of me and provoke irrational thoughts.

He kept a loaded revolver in the drawer by his bed and I thought of tiptoeing to his bedside, carefully removing that heavy pistol, and finishing him there as he slept. But I knew that I would never be able to gather the courage to pull the trigger. My hands were shaking at just the thought. I knew that I would not be able to bear my shame when my sons scrambled out of their sleep at the sound of the shot and came running in terror into our bedroom. I thought of turning the gun on myself, which was a more intriguing notion, but I could not bear disappointing my boys.

I thought of going to a mullah, but I knew he would somehow find a way to blame me for my husband's infidelity. To meet with a mullah, I would be required to bring my husband, which meant I would have to confront him first, or surprise him in front of the leader with what I had done. That would make me vulnerable to accusations of deception for hiding behind the burka. It was all so complicated. Every scenario I played in my head led me into an inescapable trap.

When an Afghan woman commits adultery, if her husband or relatives do not murder her, she is publicly stoned. If a man commits adultery, he, too, is supposed to be stoned, but I have never heard of that happening, unless the woman he is caught with was also married. In that case they would both be stoned. If the man were married and the woman unmarried, the man would be required to take the woman as his second wife. The fact that my husband was involved with a foreigner complicated things and I knew the mullah would side with my husband against me. It was pointless. I leaned against the doorjamb in the dark until my tea was cold. I was cold, too, and shivering, but I could not bear the thought of crawling back into bed with the traitor who was living with me.

A few days earlier, I had discovered the rotting carcass of a rodent behind a linen trunk in the hallway. As I lingered in the entrance to our bedroom, I could still detect the faint scent of death. The odor hung soft and pervasive in the background, reminding me of all the rare moments of my past when I had caught the waft of decaying flesh.

Death is one of those smells you never forget—an odor that loiters in the chamber of your throat and haunts your hollow soul. It is a pungent, insidious thing that rouses your deepest fear. Once you know the stirring horror of that reek, you are forever changed. There is no turning back from that awakening.

I had always been a trusting person and had looked for the best in people. My mother had taught me that. But my mother had never been betrayed by her lover. She had never experienced the assassination of her dreams. She had never known the silent, powerless fury. She had never shared her love. I was becoming a person who trusted no one, who believed in nothing, and who cared for nothing. The only thing I cared for were my boys. That night I slept on a mat in the front room of our home. I slept in restless fits and dreamed of rotting mice.

I was startled out of a deep sleep at about five in the morning by a rough hand shaking my shoulder. "What do you think you are doing?" my husband said in an irritated voice. He was standing over me in his nightshirt, his breath stale, his face rough and unshaven.

"I could not sleep," I stammered.

"You're sleeping now!" he bellowed.

He grasped me by my upper arm and jerked me up off the mat, setting me forcefully on my feet in front of him. I felt a strong and over-whelming panic as I rose from that groggy, prone place on the floor, but the moment my feet touched, an obstinate calm settled over me. He had never been physical with me and I had never defied him, but I determined in that moment of supreme anger that he would not conquer me. I determined to stand my ground. If I am to die, I thought, let it be by the hand of my lover.

I suppose it was a strange revenge, but it was a thought so lucid that it made maddening sense. I would die at his hand and he would bear his guilt. And that would be my retribution. And for the rest of his life he would know that he could not break me or subjugate me or make a fool of me.

I stood defiant, my hands at my side, my chin thrust boldly forward, and my unblinking eyes locked on his. I glared up at him and my seething rage became a stubborn, driving determination. I was ready to die. I wanted to die. And I would defy him to the end.

He gave me a ferocious slap and the force of the blow spun me around. For a moment my cheek stung and a curtain of darkness descended over my eyes. I shook my head, regained my balance, and took a step closer to him. He slapped me again, this time much harder. My ear rang and I knew that my eardrum had probably ruptured from the blow. But I would not be crushed.

I stood again and rage took control. I refused to cry. I refused to ask for mercy. I refused to back down. I refused to strike back. I would take his strength and turn it into my own. I would crush him in my defiance.

I heard a whimper from the doorway and watched through a fog as he turned toward the sound. It was a distant, forlorn cry, like an echo from some lonely canyon. It sounded like the bleating of a sheep. I turned to see my youngest son standing in the doorway, his pillow in his hand, and his mouth open. At eleven, he was too old to cry and too young to protest. His attempt to speak came out strained and garbled and crude.

My husband seemed confused. He looked back at me in bewilderment and I held his gaze, staring unblinking at him through a haze of pain, in tenacious insubordination. I knew in that moment that I had won. He stormed out of the room, brushing past Babur, and I crumbled to the floor. Still the tears did not flow. They would not flow again for many years.

Anger insulated me from pain. I retreated into an anesthetized, defensive shell. I could not and would not be moved. Something inside me died that day. For many years it lay in a quiet, forgotten grave.

Chapter 17

Unworthy—ستهیناشـــا
Summer 1982

Afghanistan became a magnet for Islamic jihadists. They journeyed from all over the Muslim world to fight against the godless Russians. The mujahideen resistance was born and from the very beginning, the determination of radical Islam surprised the Soviets. Kabul's tight security made the capital safe, but the countryside was a baffling death trap for the Soviet Army. Mujahideen forces could strike from seemingly nowhere and disappear into the mountains without a trace. Supplied with weapons from the United States and funding through Saudi Arabia, all channeled through Pakistan, they became a chaotic and divided, but stubborn resistance force.

Though the Soviets controlled the cities, the mujahideen controlled 80 percent of the countryside. The Panjshir Valley was the most tenacious region of defiance. Ahmad Shah Massoud led a highly organized opposition out of our valley that was never defeated by the Soviets. From the very beginning Massoud, the lion of the Panjshir, was like a ghost in the mountains of the northeast. The Soviet tanks were easy targets for Massoud's fighters, who would attack from the high ridges with rocket-propelled grenades and shoulder-fired missiles. He eventually commanded more than fifteen thousand Afghan fighters, but even in the early days, with small, efficient units of men, he held the Russians at bay.

For several years the fighting in my valley was limited to hit-and-run guerrilla missions. The mujahideen were clever and they would allow Russian patrols to penetrate their defenses. The tight mountain passes gave them a strategic advantage. Once a patrol had driven deep into a mujahideen-controlled area, they would close in behind them, isolate the patrol, and attack with focused vengeance. They did not take prisoners and the morale of the Soviets spiraled downward. The Afghan conscripts who were fighting with the Russians abandoned by the thousands and joined the resistance, taking their AK-47s with them.

The CIA set up camps in Pakistan near Peshawar and began to supply modern assault rifles, ammunition, and training. Over the next four years, Massoud consolidated the divided factions in the Panjshir Valley and with the help of the Americans, just across the Pakistani border, he became a legendary freedom fighter. The more he entrenched in the mountains, the more the Russians were forced to increase their commitment of resources to my valley. They resorted to indiscriminately bombing the Panjshir. My village was one of the first hit with high-altitude bombing runs.

My mother was one of the first casualties.

We heard about the bombing on the radio, but it was three days before word came from our relatives that my mother had been killed. A Russian fighter-bomber dropped a five-hundred-kilo firebomb directly on my uncle's compound. Mother died instantly, along with all three of my uncle's wives and five of their children. The attack happened midmorning and none of the men were in the compound.

Mother was buried by the time we received word.

It had been five years since I had discovered my husband's infidelity. I knew he was still seeing Ivana. Our relationship had evolved into a courteous coexistence. He must have known I suspected something, but he never broached the subject of his secret life and I never asked. I continued to sleep on a mat in the front room. I would rise early in the morning, before the boys were awake. They had no idea their father and I led separate lives.

I told my husband that I wanted to visit my mother's grave. He looked at me thoughtfully and chewed on the corner of his mouth, a queer habit he had when he was about to argue. He thought better of what he was about to say and nodded his head in agreement.

"You may take the car and the driver, and you may stay as long as you wish," he said. "You know it is dangerous, and you know the risks. There will be long delays when you pass through the checkpoints. You will need to spend the night."

I nodded, said nothing, and packed a bag for an early-morning departure. The Russians had entrenched themselves in Kabul and made it difficult to move in and out of the city. Armed forces guarded every exit road and long queues formed at the checkpoints. Because the fighting in the Panjshir had been so heavy, security tightened on the northeast highway that ascended into the valley. The driver and I left before dawn and by midday we had not yet reached the narrow valley entrance.

At every checkpoint I showed my particulars and the letter from my family telling of my mother's death. Each time we had to step out of the Peugeot while the soldiers searched it, and I would answer the same series of questions. What was my mother's name? How did she die? What village are you visiting? How long will you stay? Are you aware of the dangers? Are you helping the mujahideen?

I answered the questions in a flat, bored tone, which seemed to irritate the Afghan conscripts working the checkpoints under Russian supervision. One of them had difficulty believing me because of my lack of grief.

"You do not seem to be a woman who has lost her mother," he said. "Were you not close?"

I stared at him, cool and arrogant, through narrowed eyes. I could see that it confused him to speak with a woman who seemed to have no emotion and who appeared to be challenging him. As I stared him down, I thought of what a puzzling person I had become—demanding and defiant and confrontational. I did not understand my sentiment. I lived in a perpetual state of smoldering rage.

"Why don't you shoot me, little brother?" I asked. "Are you afraid of a woman?"

My insult infuriated him and he raised his weapon, pointing the muzzle at my forehead. I smiled at him and said, "Do it, my brother."

I knew as I held that soldier's gaze, I would not care if his finger squeezed the trigger against the only resistance that separated me from my suffering. It would be a long-awaited relief.

A bored Russian commanding officer sauntered over to me and gazed curiously as I stood my ground before the Afghani. I looked at him with the same defiance. He took a long drag on the cigarette dangling from his mouth, exhaled softly, and smiled. With an eerie familiarity, I understood him. He knew that he was consigned to die and did not care. His smile faded and we held one another's gaze in sad resignation. I felt sorry for him. He was already dead.

The drive up into the valley overwhelmed me. On the distant mountain slopes, I saw blackened rifts in the forests where Russian bombs had ignited fires. I could not recognize the villages amid so many bomb-flattened homes. In one place an entire village was gone. I could not be sure where we were. I saw nothing along that decimated roadside but ruins.

When we reached my village, I was surprised to see there was not really a great deal of damage. My relatives' compound was the only one hit. It looked as if a Soviet pilot, having finished his bombing run farther up the valley, had dropped a leftover firebomb on my mother's home. Nothing remained of the compound but mud-brick rubble and charred debris.

Men sifted through the wreckage, picking up odds and ends—kitchen utensils, pieces of my mother's books, partially burned roof timbers. They looked pitiful. Their tattered, filthy shirts hung from their bony shoulders and their hands and faces were blackened from the soot that drifted up whenever they pulled something from the dusty ruins.

My uncle walked with me to the cemetery and waited respectfully at a distance while I trudged to her grave. I stood near the fresh-turned earth and stared at the large round stone that marked her resting place. I thought I should say something, or shed a tear.

The sun was setting as I reached the cemetery. Though the summer air began to cool, the baked earth gave off a persistent radiated heat. I was sweating under the dark traditional garment I wore. As I stood there, I remembered when Mother and I had watched a village boy, for no reason, kill a beautifully colored cuckoo with his slingshot.

"Why did he do that?" I had asked.

"He does not understand how precious life is," she said. "And he does not understand the pain someone has gone through to bring a new life into this world. To him, life is cheap. But life is not at all cheap. It is very precious.

"Women understand that cost," she continued. "They understand how fragile life is. And they understand the privilege of our purpose."

"Was it painful when I was born?" I asked.

"I suppose it was," she said. "Some women scream when they give birth. I may have done the same. I do not remember. I only remember that my sister caught you as you emerged and cleaned you and laid you on my chest. I remember how you clutched the end of my little finger in your tiny fist. I remember that you were pink and wet and dainty. I remember counting your fingers and toes and thinking that you were the most breathtaking little thing I had ever seen. I remember thinking how fortunate I was to have you."

She had smiled and caressed the side of my face with the backs of her fingers. As a child, I had not understood that sweet moment, but when my first son was born, I understood.

Mother had a gentle way about her, a way that did not impress you at first, but that, as time passed, would gouge deep chasms into your heart. She was taller than I was and more slender. I had resented her sinuous beauty. I was curvier, which my husband liked very much, but I wished I could have inherited her graceful limbs. By her stature alone, she transcended our petty village life. She lived above it all, noble and elegant and proud, while the rest of us wallowed in our earthy ambitions.

I could not judge my father's stature from the mantel photograph. Mother had told me he was lean and strong but not heavily muscled like my husband. "He was supple," she said, "and he had a more inquisitive gaze."

I had always read between the lines of anything my mother said. She had that way, too. A way of saying more than what she said. I decided that my father had been a more engaging man than my husband, perhaps more reasonable. I imagined him listening to me with an open expression, lifting one eyebrow in rapt curiosity as he leaned forward to study my face. My husband listened with a furrowed brow and calculating eyes, always two steps ahead of me in our disagreements.

As I stood over that hot, sunbaked grave, and as dusk settled on my war-torn valley, I felt very sorry for what I had allowed myself to become. I felt ashamed that I had drifted from my moorings. I had forgotten who I was. Some mischievous regressive gene, some throwback to my tribal ancestry, had reared its dreadful head in my midlife passage. Hot, pent-up tears flowed down my cheeks. Deep springs of grief gushed from the bottomless caverns of my heart.

"I am so sorry, Mother," I said. "I am sorry that I cursed you in my grief. I am sorry that I forgot the lessons you taught me. I am sorry that I have been bitter and angry and hurt. I am sorry that I shamed your memory. I am sorry for who I have become."

I felt unworthy to stand on the sacred ground that was her resting place. I lifted my eyes and gazed up toward the slopes where my poppy field lay. It was quite a long distance from the cemetery, but I could see that secluded hill in the soft twilight. And I longed to go there to rest and remember. I was very tired.

I heard my uncle clear his throat behind me and knew that I must go. He mumbled something about the danger of being out on this unprotected field and I began the long, sorrowful walk back to the dark, grubby village house where we were to sleep that night.

Chapter 18

Revenge—انتقـــــام
Winter 1983

The war became unbearable. Spared much of the fighting, Kabul remained peaceful, but the countryside fell into chaos. The Russians continued to carpet bomb our valley from high-altitude aircraft, determined to break Massoud's persistent rebellion. I had not been back to my village since my mother's death, but the news coming out of our valley was grim. We heard reports that entire villages were leveled and that once-fertile fields were seeded with land mines and unexploded munitions.

Refugees from the countryside poured into Kabul and the population in the city doubled. With security concerns and checkpoints throughout the city, traffic crawled. My boys continued their schooling, but by Zemar's final year of secondary school, the Afghan communists recruited him for the military. When the war began, the communists pressured boys to join the army and fight alongside the Russians against their own countrymen. As the war progressed, young men were not given a choice. By the end of the war, militants forcefully picked up boys as young as fourteen off the streets, gave them weapons, and threw them into the chaos of the front lines. Most of them were wrapped in burial shrouds within weeks.

My husband encouraged Zemar to play along with them, but delay his enlistment. The boys were the only common bond I shared with my husband. The times we discussed their future gave us a brief respite to our tacit coexistence. Though I worried constantly about Zemar, I enjoyed when we talked about them. My husband had not struck me since the day I stood up to him. Somehow, we reached an unspoken compromise that morning, but outside of our conversations about our children, he lived in a constant state of agitation. His daily routine remained the same as it had been since we moved to Kabul.

It disappointed me that he never initiated any intimacy. I may not have responded to him, but it hurt that he had shown no interest. I sometimes thought that I could learn to share his love. I thought he might respond to me if I made the first move, but I could not bring myself to do it. So as war raged around us, I pitifully clung to those brief moments of familiarity.

Zemar did not take my mother's death well. He had been her favorite. He had her strong traits and there seemed to be an unspoken bond of appreciation between the two of them. In many ways it was self-admiration. Zemar had inherited her soft brown eyes and gentle cheeks. Though both of them were long boned, their faces were placid, rounded, almost out of place on their athletic bodies. When he was younger, he had been insatiable in his quest for knowledge. He would lift one eyebrow and tilt his face in amused curiosity and probe my limited knowledge of his little-boy fascinations. I would catch a glimpse of my mother's penetrating gaze, peering into my heart from long-forgotten decades, asking questions I could not answer.

After I returned from the graveside visit, I sat with the boys on a mat in the front room. We shared a quiet tea together and I told them about the village and my mother's compound and the things I had seen on the way into the Panjshir Valley. The two younger boys remained sober as I spoke and asked a few simple questions when I finished. Zemar brooded through the entire telling, looking steadily at the floor. When the younger two rose from the mat to return to their studies, he stayed behind.

"I will make them pay for what they did to Grandmother," he said.

His hands trembled as he spoke and a vein on the side of his neck protruded. I could see the throb of his heartbeat in that vivid purple bulge. It was uncanny how much he was like his father. At nineteen, he had matured into a sturdy young man. He spoke with a strong and resonant voice. He had large hands. Although he was developing a heavy beard, he had my fair complexion and his pale skin made him appear vulnerable. His voice had cracked when he mentioned his grandmother and I thought he would cry. I even hoped he would. That would have been better, but he choked back the tears and regained his composure.

I told him that people seek retribution when something they love is taken away from them. I did not tell him of my own battle with the need for vengeance, but I thought, as I spoke, of my private war. Revenge, it seemed to me, was motivated by either love or desire. Someone he loved very much had been stolen from him and it was natural for him to want justice. While I spoke, my thoughts ran ahead of my words and I considered my own desires.

True love had been my yearning. For my entire life I had pursued my ethereal dream of pure love. When it was stolen from me, I wanted a settling of scores. I wanted someone to pay for the theft. I am ashamed to admit it, but I wanted my husband to suffer for his sins.

I thought often of how sweet that revenge would be and I daydreamed of elaborate plans to trap the woman who had taken my husband. I never took action. I knew that my revenge would not restore what I had lost. It would only ensure that someone else did not have what I wanted. I knew that if he was not happy with me, it would not matter if the other woman was gone. Her absence would not make him love me. Though I was obsessed with the notion of getting even, I knew it was an empty pursuit.

As I tried to explain revenge to Zemar, nothing came out right. I tried to help him see that a force that could not be satisfied would consume him—that his obsession would be his ruin, but he would not accept my reasoning and he would not be consoled.

"Someday," he said again, "I will make them pay."

From that moment, I knew that I would lose him to the war. He began speaking of joining Massoud up in the Panjshir. He was as tall as his father and though he did not have the same thickness in his chest, he was strong, clever, and fearless. Massoud would want him, I thought.

About a month before his twentieth birthday, Zemar left for school and did not return that afternoon. I found a note addressed to me in his bedroom. He had written it in the terse objective style of his father, straight to the point and heartbreaking.

That evening, my husband and I decided to send Padsha and Babur to Pakistan. We had discussed it before, but I had refused to consider the option. One of our relatives lived in Rawalpindi, where he and his extended family of sixteen subsisted in a tiny, unfinished two-room apartment. Within a week, my sons left with a cousin on a rickety, overloaded truck that took them through the Khyber Pass to Peshawar, where they boarded a bus to Rawalpindi. They joined tens of thousands of Afghan refugees who had already fled. It was a miserable existence, but they were safe. At least they did not live in the squalid refugee camps on the outskirts of Islamabad or Rawalpindi.

About a year later, one of my uncles came to visit. As we sat together on a mat, he told me of Zemar's heroism. He was filled with pride as he described what my son had done, but his story only increased my dread.

The resistance leaders had been interested in Zemar. Massoud was a brilliant man who spoke five languages, including French. He loved literature and poetry and as my uncle breathlessly told of Zemar's personal friendship with Massoud, I regretted that I had poured a love for reading into my young son. My insistence on his education would contribute to his eventual death. I was certain that his intelligence had attracted Massoud. I had seen what the Russians were capable of and knew it was just a matter of time.

The Russians came up into the Panjshir Valley in their low-profile T-62 tanks, but the terrain of the Panjshir favored the resistance army. Narrow passages through the mountains were deadly traps for the Russians. The CIA in Pakistan had been supplying the resistance with shoulder-fired rocket-propelled grenades. When the Russians traveled through those confined passes, the mujahideen would assault a line of tanks with a team of four men, all armed with grenade launchers. By concentrating their fire on the first and last tank in the convoy, they could halt the entire line of tanks and attack the trapped vehicles in the middle.

Zemar and another young man were assigned to attack the rear of a column. Zemar placed a strategic strike on the vulnerable turret and crippled a tank. He ignored the danger and abandoned his position behind the rocks to stand in the middle of the road, directly behind the line of tanks, but his recklessness saved his life. The Soviet grenade launchers used by the rebels leave an exhaust trail that identifies the position of the man carrying the weapon. The Russian counter-fire came immediately, directed at the beginning point of the vapor trail. The return fire killed the young man who had been with Zemar.

My son fired another grenade that incapacitated the second-from-last tank and then he ran into an open field where he could draw a line on the third tank. With tracer bullets arcing toward his vulnerable position, he fired a third round that hit the rear of the tank at the same time as the leading team fired from the front. Every Russian in the tank was killed. They destroyed five tanks that day and Massoud himself recognized Zemar's bravery.

It was snowing the day my uncle told me that story and I knew that Zemar was hiding in some remote cave in the stark heights of the Panjshir. There was not a night that passed that I did not lie for long hours in the hostile dark thinking of him. It was difficult to imagine the tender child I had birthed shivering in the humid cold of some dismal cave. I knew food was scarce up in the valley and that he had lost weight. I knew, in spite of the accolades of his superiors, that he was not satisfied. He would never slake his thirst for vengeance and it would drive him to greater risks. I knew deep in my weary heart that like so many other idealistic boys, he would come home, still and silent in a filthy shroud.

Chapter 19

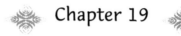

Jealousy—حسـادت
Winter 1989

I n early February, I received a surprise visitor. As I read in the front room, a steady, cold rain fell on the city. The miserable day suited my mood. It had been raining for three days. A sober, fateful resignation gripped the city, as if we finally understood the dreadful destiny that had fallen upon us.

I heard a persistent knock at the front door followed by a muffled conversation. In a few moments, my houseboy stood, hesitant, at the entrance to my front room. I had snapped at him earlier in the morning and he was skittish. With his eyes cast down at the floor he said in a timid voice, "Madame, an urgent message has come." He held a sealed envelope in his hand.

"Well, bring it to me," I said impatiently.

The envelope was addressed to me in a feminine, looping handwriting. I opened it slowly and began reading the Persian script.

You may not remember me, but we met some years ago in the Kabul museum. I must see you immediately. My driver is waiting outside and he will bring you to the museum. Please come to where we first met and please do not tell anyone where you are going. I know it may seem strange, but this is urgent. —Ivana

I stared dumbfounded at the elegant script and noticed my trembling hands. I did not know what to think. Why would she want to see me? I was afraid, but at the same time interested. I had no desire to see Ivana, but my prurient curiosity aroused me in a mysterious, inexplicable way.

When I was a little girl, I saw a large snake at the edge of my poppy field. I spotted it lying on a sun-warmed stone in the late afternoon, dark and menacing and fat. I had been sitting nearby for nearly an hour and had not noticed it. Apparently, the snake had crawled onto the rock with such deft cunning that I never perceived the movement. It just appeared. It unsettled me, but something about that serpent had captivated me. I watched it with careful interest, fighting the impulse to run, and surprised myself with my fascination with something so dangerous and frightful.

I suppose Ivana intrigued me in a similar way. She mesmerized me and repulsed me in the same moment. I decided to see her.

"Tell the driver I will be out in thirty minutes," I told the houseboy.

I spent a great deal of time getting ready. I wondered, as I applied my makeup, why I felt so energized and so alive. I had no idea what I would do or say when I faced her, but the thought of that meeting awakened a long-forgotten will to fight for what was mine. Surprised by primitive, violent thoughts, I imagined myself slapping her with the back of my hand. The vision made me smile, but my enthusiasm waned when the car turned in to the museum, a grand and intimidating building. I felt a sudden and overwhelming dread. I almost demanded to be taken back to my home, but curiosity won. So, with small, tentative steps, I entered the cavernous museum. I steadied myself with the handrail as I climbed the stairs to the second floor. The echo of my footsteps in the deserted foyer spooked me. I felt very uneasy.

She was seated in a small chair in a corner near the Bactrian exhibit, reading a document from a thick folder. She stood as I entered the room and walked toward me, unsmiling. Her appearance shocked me. She looked tired. She had lost weight and seemed to have aged twenty years since that day I saw her in the elevator of the InterContinental Hotel. Deep lines had formed at the corners of her eyes and her face was drawn and weary. She still had an abundance of golden hair, but it had lost its youthful sheen.

I'm forty-three and I've borne three children, I thought smugly. She is five years younger than me, but she looks five years older.

She extended her hand to me with a weak smile and said softly, "Thank you for coming."

Without another word, she turned and walked slowly down a long corridor toward the rear of the building. I followed her for a few steps, then increased my pace to walk alongside her. I would not follow her lead like some frightened child.

My confidence mounted as we walked side by side down that empty hallway. I felt my heart steady and my stride lengthen with each bold step. I was comparing myself to her and I felt a sober satisfaction as we walked along. She no longer intimidated me. She was still pretty, but something had sucked the life out of her. I hoped guilt had stolen her sheen. She turned into a small alcove and motioned for me to sit beside her on a narrow couch.

"You are in great danger," she said softly in Persian.

"Whatever are you talking about?" I said with amusement. "We are all in danger these days."

"Yours is urgent," she responded.

I turned toward her on the small couch and startled when our knees touched. I blanched in revulsion and slid back to put some distance between us. I moved a little too quickly. She seemed to take notice, but did not say anything.

"Your husband is involved in some very dangerous business and I am afraid that you may be hurt if you do not leave the city immediately," she said.

"How would you know anything about my husband's business?" I replied.

I watched her through narrowing eyes. She could not hold my gaze and averted her eyes to stare stone-faced out the window. Though it was uncomfortable, I let the silence hang and watched smugly as she fidgeted with her hands. Her discomfort gave me enormous satisfaction.

After a long pause and an audible sigh, she said matter-of-factly, "I work for the KGB."

I think my mouth fell open. She continued, "Your husband has been supplying horses to the mujahideen and he is cooperating with the Americans to supply weapons into the Panjshir. He does not move the weapons, but he is part of the intelligence chain. He is directing the flow of supplies through his relatives in the valley."

She might as well have slapped me. She spoke rapidly in a low voice, and I noticed that she kept watching the hallway. My mind raced as I digested the quiet, dumbfounding words that poured out of her.

"He has been working with a corrupt Soviet Army lieutenant to supply large quantities of raw opium. He is taking money from both sides. The Americans know what he is doing and they know we are aware of the drug trafficking. They will not warn him or protect him. Their Kabul operatives are not inclined to take an active role and they do not care what happens to him. He has outlived his usefulness to them."

"Why should you care what happens to him?" I spat.

She looked at me thoughtfully and after a long pause said, "I am weary of seeing innocent people hurt. You and your family will die with him."

"Aren't you in danger by telling me these things?" I asked.

"I am already dead," she replied. She stared out the window, ignoring the hallway, and spoke barely audible words in a language I did not understand. I guessed she was repeating the phrase in her native tongue.

"I know about you and him," I said slowly.

Now it was her turn to be stunned. She lowered her head and lost every pretense of confidence. I felt no compassion for her, but curiously, I felt no hatred. I simply did not care if she lived or died. I wondered whether she felt guilty for what she had done. She sat motionless in the deafening quiet of the cavernous room, her eyes focused on the floor near her shoes.

"He was my true love," I said simply. And I choked on my words. Despite my efforts at control, I could not speak of love without a deep, heart-wrenching throb between my breasts. The old and familiar ache welled up from deep inside me and with frantic persistence tried to escape my throat in an agonizing, primal cry. But like always, the cry lodged in my gullet, paralyzed my breath, and crippled my thoughts.

"I do not know true love," she said. "But I thought I loved him."

"You know nothing of love," I said.

"You are right," she answered. "But I am beginning to understand."

I felt a white-hot anger flush my face. My hands shook in rage. I leaned close toward her, thrusting my chin within inches of her face, and in a low growl said, "I will never forgive you for what you have done to me."

"I am truly sorry," she said simply.

She looked directly into my eyes. I could see the vivid red veins stress had etched in the whites of her eyes. I knew she was genuine and for a brief moment, I felt sympathy for her. I held her gaze until I felt embarrassed and turned away to stare unseeing through the window.

A long silence followed as I digested her words. In a strange way, I felt sorry for her, but I could not get past my own bitter heartache. I could see her sincerity, but I wanted her to pay some price for what she had done. She had stolen my only dream. She deserved to suffer.

"I will never forgive you," I repeated. I spat the words through clenched teeth in determined resentment. I hated her in that moment with a vile and bitter gall that I never dreamed capable of having. I felt as if I were possessed with the same demon of murderous rage that had haunted my heartbroken country and driven it into a relentless orgy of bloodlust.

I shifted forward to stand, but something obliged me to stay. I suppose it was my curiosity, or perhaps, in spite of my anger, my empathy for her. I did not know, but I could not rise from the edge of that couch.

With her eyes locked on the rug at our feet, she spoke in a slow, thoughtful cadence. "The Russians recruited me in Czechoslovakia when I was finishing the last year of my studies. At first I was not interested, but the opportunity was difficult to ignore. They were persistent. I was young and inexperienced.

"This country was my first assignment," she continued. "I was afraid, of course, but I was drawn into the adventure and I appreciated the benefits. I had privileges here that I would never have enjoyed in Prague. By the time I met you and Amir that day in the museum, the Russians had been watching him for months. They staged that visit to the museum. Amir knew he would be meeting someone, but he did not know it would be me. They asked me to try to get close. To my surprise, I enjoyed being with him."

I snapped my head up and stared intently at her. It shocked me to hear her say his name, Amir. To hear that name on her lips was profane. I rarely uttered his name in public, preferring to call him Husband. It was my way of honoring him. He seemed to appreciate that respectful token. Even in our casual life, I called him Husband. I do not know why. I suppose I developed that habit from when we first met. Before I loved him, I loved the idea of him. I loved the idea of marriage. I loved the idea of Husband. It was later, when we visited together under the watchful eye of my uncle, that I loved Amir.

Only when we were finally in bed together, naked and shameless and innocent, when he whispered into my hair, *I love you*—only then did I call him Amir. And sometimes, in the avalanche of passion, I lost the discipline of my tongue and called him Amir. And sometimes, as I basked in our gentle afterglow, when he was incoherent with sleep, in those moments I whispered his name to the soft embrace of the dark—Amir. It grieved me to know that she had whispered his name in their private moments, that she had whispered her love for him and that, perhaps, he had whispered to her and called her Ivana.

She seemed not to notice my vexation and continued her story with her eyes locked in a distant stare. "Amir is clever and he would not talk to me much about his business. But through what little information I gleaned and because I knew his schedule, we were able to piece together the details of his enterprises."

"Please do not say his name," I said. My voice quavered and I struggled to keep my heart within myself. I was more sad than angry. I choked on deep and bitter grief and glanced away from her. She seemed to understand and moved as if to grasp my hand, then thought better of it and fidgeted.

"Why are you telling me this?" I asked.

She seemed moved by my asking her not to say his name and paused before continuing. "We have all the information that we need from him.

I do not know when, but I know he will be picked up for interrogation soon. Once that happens, you will never see him again.

"I have thought carefully about what to do," she said. "I am to meet with your husband today. For what it is worth, it will be in a public place. I plan to tell him everything. I will beg him to flee the city. If he listens to my advice, you must go with him. If he does not, you must persuade him somehow to leave. I will not tell him that I met with you."

"Do you still love him?" I asked.

She ignored me and continued speaking. "When I was an infant, my mother separated from my father. He was a violent drunk and I do not remember him. She left me with my grandmother and disappeared. I do not remember her either. My grandmother is a Christian and she—"

I interrupted her in sudden, uncontrollable resentment. "I curse your Christian god," I said as anger displaced my grief. "How dare you speak to me about God? You know nothing of God."

"You are right," she said. "But I do know something about shame."

"You will burn in hell," I hissed.

"Perhaps," she said. After a long, thoughtful pause, she continued. "My grandmother sent me a letter last week. It's very strange. It seems to be something from her Christian book. There was no explanation. I have translated it for you and I want you to have it."

She thrust an envelope toward me, but I pushed it away. I stood abruptly and walked away from her, but she caught me by the elbow and spun me back around.

"Please take it." Her eyes pleaded with me, making her insistence difficult to ignore. Someone entered the hallway, walking deliberately toward us. On impulse, I snatched the letter and, without a word, spun on my heel and strode down the corridor. I pushed past her driver, who was waiting for me outside the museum, and caught a taxi on the street. As we wound our way through the city, I opened the envelope and began to read the graceful script.

Love is patient

Love is kind

It does not envy

It does not boast

It is not proud

It does not dishonor others

It is not self-seeking

It is not easily angered

It keeps no record of wrongs

Love does not delight in evil

But rejoices with the truth

It always protects

Always trusts

Always hopes

Always perseveres

Love never fails

1 Corinthians 13:4-8 NIV

Chapter 20

Truth—یی راست

That afternoon, the sun broke through the tedious mist that had enshrouded the city for the past three days. I sat for more than an hour in my garden among the dripping leaves of the still rain-soaked trees. Emerging from three days of somber quiet, the birds gushed in cheerful song. But I felt no joy that day and I fretted over my husband's return.

He came home much earlier than usual. I was giving instructions to my servant boy about what to prepare for the evening meal when I heard his car enter the gate. I had decided on one of his favorite dishes, qabili pilau.

Though my mood was still foul, I felt a stirring of hope that I could rekindle my love for him.

With Ivana no longer a part of his life, maybe, in time, I could love him.

When I was eleven years old, I lied to my mother. It was the only time I ever lied to her. During a visit to my auntie's house, I stole one of her rings. She had a box full of beautiful jewelry and I took a simple ring, thinking she would not miss it. For two weeks she did not, but when she discovered it had disappeared, she flew into a frightening rage. She decided her house girl had stolen it and beat her all morning. Everyone in the compound could hear the poor girl's screams as she insisted that she had not taken the ring.

I was terrified and overwhelmed with guilt. An innocent young girl, just a few years older than me, suffered because of something I had done and I cowered on my sleeping mat, wishing the day would end. My aunt wearied of beating the girl and banished her from the compound. The young teen sat trembling at the front gate throughout the rest of the day. As the sun set, it occurred to me that she would spend the night outside the compound wall. I could not bear my shame.

My mother sensed something was wrong and asked, "Do you know anything about that missing ring?"

"No," I replied, a little too quickly.

She watched me thoughtfully for a few moments and then asked me to come to her, motioning for me to climb onto her lap. At eleven, I was too long legged to sit in her lap, and it was awkward. We had not cuddled in that way for years. I sat facing away from her and she pulled my resisting head gently back to rest against her shoulder. She encircled me with her arms and we sat in silence for a long while. After what seemed an hour, she spoke softly, her mouth only a few inches from my ear.

"True love is only found in truthfulness," she said. I did not understand what she meant, but I knew enough to know that she was disappointed that I was hiding something from her.

"When you love someone," she continued, "you are not afraid to tell the truth. If you are afraid, you do not truly love them. There can be no fear in love and there can be no secrets."

I thought deeply about what she was saying. I suspected that she knew I was hiding something, but by now I was so ashamed of what I had done that I could do nothing but snivel.

"Shame," she continued as if she were reading my mind, "is a good thing. It helps us know when we are doing something wrong. But shame can be a bad thing. It can drive a wedge between you and the person who loves you most. When you are ashamed, you are alone. Most people settle for an incomplete love. Most people live their entire lives bearing their shame. They never take the risk to discover love. They never take the risk of truthfulness."

By now, my tears were flowing freely. Mother spoke with earnest tenderness. The kinder she was, the more guilt I felt. I wanted to die, or at the very least go to bed without my supper.

After a long silence she said, "I think I know what happened to the ring. I think you can help me understand. I could question you until you tell me the truth, but that would not be love. You must love me enough to speak honestly with me and you must take the risk that my love for you is also true. You must believe that I will do what is best for you."

My confession spilled out of me in great gulping sobs. I wept so hard that I thought I would be sick and I told her everything. She let me babble until I could say no more, then held me tight to her until I settled. And time stood still. As my anguish abated, I began to feel weary. I sank back against her soft breasts and felt such a stillness that I do not recall if we rested there for moments or hours. It could have been days and I would not have cared.

"Bring me the ring," she said simply.

Timid, I bought the ring to her and, holding it gingerly, I dropped it into her outstretched hand. She looked at it thoughtfully and gazing into my eyes said, "I love you with all my heart, my little lamb."

I felt so unworthy of her love that I burst into another round of sobbing. She held me until I stilled and said, "Wait here."

She left our little house and within a few moments, I heard the distant shouts of my still furious aunt. I could not understand what she was saying, but she was beyond soothing. I heard long pauses of silence between the tirades and I realized that my mother was reasoning with her in the same soft kindness that she had used with me. When she returned, Mother said simply, "Do not worry any more, my love. The matter is settled."

As my husband entered the front door of our beautiful little Kabul home, the home I knew I would soon be leaving, I longed that he would be truthful. I longed for him to sit across from me and look deep into my eyes and tell me everything. I longed to hold his massive head against my breast until his tears wet my blouse and his repentant sobs abated. But I knew that love was beyond his grasp. And I knew that in his pride and his fear and his shame, he would lie.

He called to me as he entered the house. I stepped timidly out of the kitchen to greet him. He looked exhausted, but I felt nothing for him. My bone-weary sadness shrouded me in a dark, heavy complacency, numbing every emotion.

"We need to talk," he said.

I followed him into the front room and as he settled on the mat near the window, he sighed heavily. He looked out the window and for a moment I thought he would open his heart to me. Instead, he took a deep breath and said, "The Russians are about to withdraw."

"That's wonderful news," I answered.

"Maybe not," he said. "The al-Qaeda has gained strength. Foreign Arabs are pouring into the country. They are determined to form a pure Islamic nation here. They will want to control

Kabul. The Russians are gambling that their puppet, Mohammad Najibullah, will maintain control of the city, but those Afghan Army troops will never stand up to the mujahideen. Everyone is fighting the Russians now, but when the Russians leave, they will all fight one another. This city is the key to the country. I believe these factions will destroy one another for control of the city. They will destroy Kabul in the process and we will be caught in the crossfire."

"How do you know all this?" I asked.

He paused for a moment and, breaking eye contact with me, said softly, "I have been working with the Americans to supply weapons and information to the mujahideen in the Panjshir. The work I have been doing is very important for our people and it has been dangerous. But it has also had its rewards. This house and even our compound in the valley are some of those benefits—the private schools, the car, our house help, our driver, everything."

I said nothing, hoping against hope he would tell me all.

"I did not tell you any of this because I wanted to protect you and I did not want you to worry," he continued. "But we must leave immediately."

"You mean now?" I asked incredulously.

"Tonight," he said evenly.

"Why not wait until the Russians leave?" I asked. "Wouldn't it be safer to move to the valley then?"

"No one knows," he answered. "Perhaps, perhaps not. I have arranged to get us out of the city, but we must leave tonight. After tonight, there will be no help. We will be on our own."

I began to weep. I imagine that he thought I was upset about leaving our home, and about the danger we would face, but I had no care of danger. I did not care if I lived or died. Though I would miss our home in the city, I was not weeping over my loss. I was weeping because I now understood how skilled he was in deception. If he could tell a partial truth, he could lie easily and without remorse.

Since that day I lied to my mother, I had not deceived anyone that I loved. To me, love and truth were one. But I understood now that my husband had not been instructed in the ways of love. He had learned the skills of deceit. He knew better than to tell a complete lie. If he could tell enough truth to give the appearance of honesty, he could deceive someone completely, just as he thought he was misleading me. I debated whether I should tell him that I knew everything, but I decided against it. I suppose I held on to the remote hope that someday he might open his heart to me.

Weary, I looked out the window and watched the sun descend over the western hills. The rain had cleansed the air and the few lingering clouds reflected a brilliant orange and red spectacle. I thought sadly of my life with him. I wondered about every conversation and every shared moment. And I wept because I could not tell what was real and what was counterfeit. I wept because I did not know what part of his love was true. And I grieved, not only for my loss of love, but also for my loss of trust. And I knew, in that regretful moment, that like the fading sunset that bathed my front room in soft pastels, my life with him had been a beautiful, tragic mirage.

Chapter 21

Home—خانه

The city was under a curfew and I wondered how my husband planned to leave. He was resourceful, but moving at night would be risky. He told me that we would leave one hour after dark and would spend the night with a relative in a little town just past the last Kabul checkpoint. We would travel on into the Panjshir the next day.

We left most of our belongings in the house. Both of us packed a small bag and he told me that he would have someone bring the rest of our things later. At about eight o'clock, a Russian jeep with two Afghan soldiers groaned to a stop in front of our home. We had been sitting in the Peugeot since sunset. Without a word to them, my husband eased the little sedan behind the battered jeep and we began our timid journey through the empty city. I surprised myself with my own trembling. I sensed his anxiety as his hands gripped the steering wheel and his eyes locked on the rear of the jeep.

When we reached the first checkpoint, he left me in the Peugeot and walked to the guard with a thick envelope in his hand. He returned without the envelope and drove grimly through the checkpoint, telling me to keep my eyes straight ahead. The same scenario unfolded at the second and third checkpoints. Before one hour had passed, we were on an open road and headed to the Panjshir. My husband visibly relaxed. By ten o'clock we reached Charikar, a little town near the entrance to the valley, where we spent the night with a relative. Though it was not late, the trip out of Kabul exhausted us, and we fell asleep in our clothes on a single mat.

The next morning, as we were eating boiled eggs and chapattis with our relative's family, my husband surprised me by telling their boys a story about following orders. He was in a remarkable mood considering our circumstances. Despite the wasteland he knew that we would see as we entered the valley, his engaging wit had the boys rolling on their mats in laughter.

"Did I ever tell you about how your cousin Atash lost his sheep?" he began.

"No," they said together as he pulled them into his yarn.

"Your cousin brought a herd of a thousand fine Arabi sheep down from their summer pasture. He was high in the mountains and had to cross a suspension bridge stretched across a ravine more than a hundred meters deep.

"The lead ram panicked halfway across and jumped from the bridge. The entire herd followed. Over a thousand sheep died in less than two minutes. Every one of those stupid animals followed their leader off that bridge. I told him that he should never have bred those Iranian sheep to his Afghans."

At that, he and the boys roared in laughter. I could not understand why they laughed and said, "That is absurd."

"They were Iranian," the oldest one howled. "Afghans would never blindly follow their leader."

As the boys strangled on their tea, my husband said proudly, "A true Afghan has no master."

I marveled at their stupidity. Proud and careless men, driven by their arrogant egos, were ripping our nation apart. And it was not just the Afghani. The foreigners were no better. And while we rested between a city about to be leveled and a demolished valley, this impossible man told foolish jokes and reveled in pride and self-assurance, when just a few hours ago his hands had trembled as he lit a cigarette. We bantered over tea and chapattis just miles from our valley, where I knew that unimaginable suffering was taking place. It seemed irreverent to be joking in the face of such dread.

I found myself watching my husband with a strange detachment, as if I were no part of him or the bright-eyed boys who fawned for his attention. I knew how young boys starved for strong male companionship. They lapped greedily of his words as he lavished them with his crude, raw masculinity.

I knew his magical spell—his charm. The dizzying turbulence of his bright-eyed wit had once carried me away. I knew the longing. I knew the deep and anxious desire to somehow matter to

him, to be worthy of his affection and his friendship and his devotion. For a moment, back in
Kabul, I had been optimistic that we could begin
again. Perhaps, as the devouring lust of jealous
warring tribes leveled our city, we could hide
away in our forgotten medieval valley. Perhaps
we could return to the simplicity we once knew.
For a moment, I had hoped. But it was a distant
fancy that wafted away like the faint illusive scent
of morning glories. And as I watched that foolish
man, I knew that my hope had been equally foolish. It was a troubling beginning to a troubling
day.

My husband helped me into the Peugeot and
returned to his cousin's house. He spent a long
while inside and I could hear the soft murmur
of their subdued voices. I had no idea what they
were discussing. I guessed it had something to
do with the family business in the Panjshir. I
thought of Zemar. He was somewhere in the
valley we were about to enter. Perhaps by some
miracle I might see him.

The derelict house was in a small compound on
the outskirts of the town, part of an ancient little
village. When we had arrived the night before,
there was little I could discern of the village. By

the morning light, I could see the waste of the long war with the Russians. A little boy with a stump of an arm toiled to draw water from a well nearby. Part of the stone wall around the well had collapsed and the boy stumbled in the rubble. I thought he would fall into the well and I cried out involuntarily, but he righted himself and continued in his tragic struggle.

From where our little Peugeot was parked on a small knoll, I could see other dilapidated homes along the twisting lane that led up the little hill. Most of the houses were scarred with bullet wounds. Kalashnikov rifle rounds had shattered against the thick mud walls and knocked out huge pockets in the cement-hard earthen bricks. Some of the homes had holes blown through them, no doubt the result of a grenade or a tank round. Through one of those shattered walls, I could see a family squatting around a small fire. A thin woman carefully lifted a steaming kettle from the fire and poured milk tea into a little girl's outstretched cup.

Today I will be home, I thought. But I realized with a heavy sigh that the home of my dreams was not my husband's lavish complex. It was the earth-scented, two-room hovel I had shared with Mother in my uncle's modest place. I could close my eyes and see the ancient, worn timbers that supported the flat, earth roof. The roof had been constructed in layers of timbers, thick mats of straw, and finally a layer of hard-packed earth. From my sleeping loft I could see the blond straw stems through the cracks of the roof between the massive timbers. The layer of straw kept the packed earth from falling into the home. But fine particles of dust would filter through the straw and cover everything in golden talc. When the roof heated up in the summer sun, my loft smelled of sweet, cured hay. But sometimes, during a heavy rain, the roof would leak and soil my bed, and I would spend the next day scrubbing the stains out of the cotton cloth. I could still smell the pungent mildew that filled the house during those rains.

In the hot season, Mother and I would go up on the roof at night and enjoy the cooling breezes. Most of the men slept in the open on the rooftops at night. They dragged their wooden frame and rope beds up to the roof when the spring rains finished and would not take them down until the weather cooled. Forbidden to sleep in the open, the women lingered well into the evening, lounging on their mats, and watching for shooting stars. Sometimes I would fall asleep, my head resting in Mother's lap, my heart soothed by her soft, delicate hand stroking my cheekbone.

As my legs sweat against the plastic-covered seat of the little Peugeot and my forearm stuck to the shiny vinyl door rest, my heart broke with longing for that unrefined life. I stared out the window at the dusty war-torn village and murmured to myself, "I so want to go home."

But there was no home for me. Mother was no more, and the Russians had leveled our little house. There would be no nostalgic return to a warm stove where fresh chapatti baked and filled the room with rich aroma. I was an exile—doomed to wander through a war-ravished world in search of an illusion.

I could not identify what it was that I wanted. Somehow, my memories had filtered out all the heartaches and disappointments of my childhood. What remained was the recollection of an impossible, frivolous world. I knew that I could never recapture those untarnished days, but how I hungered for them. How I wished I could be naive and simple again.

Perhaps if I had a daughter, I thought, everything would be different. I would tell her of the world that used to be and we would share my wistful melancholy. And she would lay her head on my shoulder and our bereavement would pour from us in a single feminine tear. And as the world crumbled around us, we would crawl into a sacred cocoon. And we would have no need for words because we would understand one another's hearts.

My husband startled me from my reverie by snapping open the door of the Peugeot. He seemed annoyed. Without a word, he fired up the car and eased down the twisting lane. The narrow passageway was designed more for donkey traffic than vehicles and the rubble strewn along the way forced him to pick his line carefully.

He had to gather speed as we neared the highway to give him enough momentum to make it up a slippery mud embankment. We skidded sideways onto the main road, spewing dark, sticky mud behind us. The Peugeot whined and rocked and I screamed as a Russian Army truck nearly struck us as it thundered past. A soldier in the back of the truck lifted his weapon as if he intended to fire at us and the driver shook a hostile fist out his window.

In the distance, a pillar of dark black smoke rose ominously. At least a dozen vehicles followed behind the speeding truck. They roared past as if hitched to one another with hardly a space between them. A monstrous vehicle in the middle of their caravan forced us off the road. Dark diesel exhaust belched out of its side pipe, blowing hot, noxious fumes into our open windows. My husband struggled to keep the Peugeot from slipping into the deep ditch along our side of the road. Ahead I could see another line of trucks approaching in the same hell-bent fury. I cowered as they rumbled past while he cursed angrily. Haggard, grim-faced Russians filled the truck cabs.

I understood their seething fury. I understood their disguised fear. I understood their bone-weary and fateful resignation. I knew the heart-throbbing startle of their night terrors. Like me, they skirmished with an insidious, heartless enemy they could not see and could not understand. They were betrayed by day and ambushed by night. They would never comprehend their enemy's language or reasoning or motivations. And like me, they were a long, long way from home.

Chapter 22

Corpse—نعــش

As we entered the valley, I entered through the dusky raw veil of a young woman's wasted heart. I was unprepared for the flood of emotion that washed over me. That lonely, broken young girl emerged from deep within me in a violent, fearful vengeance. She would not be consoled.

Angry tears streamed steadily down my cheeks. Their rivulets collected along the sharp line of my jaw and mingled with the mucus pouring from my nose. A slimy drool hung from my chin and I made no attempt to wipe it.

We had to drive around a shattered Russian truck overturned in the highway. I saw a lump of bloody rags strewn beside the rear of the truck and I realized without pity that it was the headless, bomb-riddled torso of a Russian soldier. Both legs were severed from the man's body and one of them lay in our path. My husband hesitated, then drove over the leg, his face ashen and his hands trembling. I felt the Peugeot bump over the soft limb, but I felt nothing for the Russian.

We wove our way through a minefield of war-molested corpses and limbs strewn haphazardly across the cratered road. One corpse stared back at me with expressionless blue eyes. The face was unmarred and young and beardless.

My husband drove grimly on through five hundred meters of fresh battlefield. Oddly, I heard no sound and I wondered whether my senses were failing me. A vulture landed heavily near a fallen Afghan and my husband's shouting broke the eerie silence. He blew the Peugeot's horn and hammered the side of the car with his open hand. The vulture stared at him, unblinking and defiant. It tore at the man's face and my husband cursed the bird in a violent, filthy stream.

I glared at him as he shouted. "What right do you have to curse?" I spat. "You are the cause of this—you, and your pride and your greed and your medieval ways."

I cursed him with the same vengeful rage he had aimed at the vulture. I cursed his violent land and his bloodguilt. I screamed virile obscenities at his astonished face. He lifted his hand as if to backhand me and I preempted his strike with a blow of my own, smacking him soundly in the face with my open palm. I cursed the Russians and I cursed his foreign white whore. I watched his jaw fall open in astonishment when I spat her filthy name.

"Do you think I am a fool?" I shrieked. "Do you think I do not know what you have done?"

And as he negotiated the little car through the remains of broken men, I dismantled him limb by limb. I told him what I had done that afternoon at the InterContinental. How I had disguised myself in a burka and ridden with him in the elevator and followed him to his room. I told him of my meeting with Ivana and of how the Russians and the Americans had used him like an adolescent schoolboy.

As rockets thundered in the distance, I rained my own grenades down on his shell-shocked soul. I dismantled him piece by piece until nothing remained of him but a bloodied torso and sightless staring eyes.

When I was nine years old, I watched my uncle butcher a young sheep at the edge of a field of lentils behind our compound. He turned the animal toward Mecca, soothed it by laying his meaty palm over its eyes, and prayed to Allah. His knife was so sharp and quick that the lamb had not whimpered or stirred when its throat was opened. Blood had pumped from its gaping jugular and spread in a wide pool at the edge of the field.

While one of his men poured boiling water over the hide, my uncle scraped the wool off in large, dirty clumps. In minutes the carcass was hairless, its skin white and smooth and flawless. They rubbed saffron into the flesh until it was a deep yellowish orange and gutted the sheep with a single quick rift in the animal's belly. While the liver roasted in small, seasoned pieces on a bed of coals, they quartered the lamb. I had filled myself on the delicious spiced liver while they cooked the rice and mutton, and by the time my relatives were feasting, I had fallen asleep.

I had a troubled dream. In my dream, I gorged on roasted flesh while sitting among the dismembered limbs of a fat sheep. The severed head lay on the ground nearby, bleating pitifully, its tongue hanging grotesquely from the corner of its mouth. In my dream, I licked my greasy fingers and smacked obscenely and belched.

While my husband soldiered on in grim shock, I reveled in the gore of his dismantled self-assurance. And when he stopped to retch violently out the window from the stench of battle, I sat still and smug and strong. And when I wiped the dried remains of my tears, an insane calm covered me like a prophet's mantle. Although I feared the madness, I embraced its calm and rested my head against the door pillar of the car. I muttered crude obscenities while my husband stared at me, stupefied. I smelled his fear and smiled coyly at the spreading wet of urine between his thighs.

Chapter 23

Madness—جنــون

My insanity lasted about a week. The
madness comforted me, but looking
back, I was not mad at all; I was overwhelmed. The long siege of love had starved my
soul as efficiently as Sultan Mehmed had taken
Constantinople from the Christians. And in my
famished state, the raw horror of the battlefield
had broken all my resolve. I suppose madness
saved me from destroying myself.

I remember only scraps of that week. I do
remember that we lost the Peugeot, not long after
we entered the Panjshir. The road had become
impassable and the car useless. We stopped at a
narrow gap between two huge rocks that had been
rolled down onto the road from the craggy cliffs
above. A Russian truck had stalled between the

rocks, and its crew worked frantically under the hood. A pair of soldiers saw us and fired rounds into the grille of our car. We abandoned the car in the middle of the road and fled into a narrow ravine, hiding behind several large boulders.

As gunfire cracked below us, I heard the roar of a Russian tank. The tank passed in front of us and simply crushed the Peugeot under its treads. I could see soldiers crowded on the turret of the tank with their weapons shouldered and pointing in every direction. Though they did not see us, several of them fired rounds in our direction as the tank passed the opening to the ravine. Bullets whined over my head and I remember laughing at their odd musical resonance. As they ricocheted off the rocks, they sang in long, mournful shrieks that slowly died as they echoed up the ravine. They were the cries of the Russians, I thought. They were the cries of men abandoned to fear. I had no empathy for them and no regret for their suffering. Those Russians were paying the price for their sins and their bullets' mournful song was a fitting ballad to their careless retreat.

It took us a week to reach my husband's compound. We abandoned the road that ran along the valley floor and climbed along the ridge, traveling mostly at night. We had no food and little water. We found small platoons of Massoud's men and slept with them in filthy caves near the top of the ridge. The haggard men were battle scarred, but jubilant. The Russians abandoned the valley en masse, discarding weapons, munitions, and vehicles along the way. The Afghan Communist Army assumed control of the strategic outposts, but Massoud's men knew the Soviets' pawns would be no match for them.

The men talked excitedly of the great victories that Allah had given them and of the final defeat of the infidels. I remember one glorious night, we built a bold fire in one of the caves and roasted a bony sheep one of the men had packed in on his back. Someone gave me a piece of the leg and I gnawed it clean of every succulent morsel of flesh. I cracked the bone on a rock from the cave floor and hungrily sucked the soft marrow. It was not enough, but it nourished me. I remember sleeping peacefully that night, huddled from the cold on a greasy blanket near the fire.

I have often thought of that mysterious, mindless week. Oddly, I have no regret, but it frightens me that I cannot remember what I did or said as we toiled along that jagged mountain ridge. I do remember early one morning, shivering in the cold on the top of the ridge and watching a lone Russian jeep bounce along the cratered road in the valley below. I could see by the way it lurched that the engine was straining and I knew the Russians were vulnerable. Massoud's men knew it, too, and a small group of them positioned themselves ahead of the jeep. They took it out with a quick volley when it reached their position. They had not even tried to hide, but boldly stood in the open and fired on the Russians. From my position, they looked like hungry roaches as they scurried down from the rocks and fell on the injured men in the jeep. Although I could not see it, I knew they were savagely ripping the men's throats with their knives.

I was in a deep and dreamless sleep near a fading fire the morning my madness lifted. Daylight had not yet broken and the air was misty cold. I heard a familiar voice and opened my eyes to see two men crouching by the fire, talking softly. One was my husband and the other was my oldest son. I thought at first I was dreaming, or that I was having a vision. I felt awake, but this did not seem real.

I do not know why I did not rush to him. I suppose I did not have confidence in what I saw. The past week had been a disjointed dream and I found it difficult to tell what was real from what was not. I could not trust my senses or my thoughts. But I heard Zemar call me Mother.

The sound of that word ripped open my soul and laid me bare on those numbing rocks. In that single moment, I heard all the tiny voices of his childhood. I remembered when he first called me Mother. I remembered when he fell from the wall in our compound and fractured his wrist. A wail had escaped his lips and he'd cried out for me. He quickly recovered, embarrassed that he had betrayed his independence. That moment had been precious to me and I still cherished the memory. I still desired to be needed. Though I could not rush to him and comfort him as I did when he was a child, I wanted him to need me. Reluctantly, I had to admit that though I still despised the man who squatted next to him, I wanted him to need me, too. With startling clarity, I realized that my insanity made me vulnerable and needy and a burden. I realized that I still wanted to be loved. I realized that if I were to be desired, I must be strong.

As the sun broke robust over the distant ridge, burning off the morning mist, the cloud of madness lifted from my ravaged soul. I lay for a long while, listening to the comforting mummer of Zemar's voice. He was lean and bony and squatted easily by the fire. His shoulders were still broad and strong, but their sharp edges protruded. His left arm appeared to have been broken and not set properly. I noticed that he favored it when he moved. I saw an obvious knot halfway between his shoulder and his elbow.

His beard made him look forty, not twenty-five. I rose from the greasy blanket and moved to sit across from him at the fire. He met my gaze and smiled cautiously. My husband watched warily, concerned over what I might blurt out. I understood his reluctance. I ignored him and smiled warmly at my son.

"It's good to see you again, Zemar," I said. "I have missed you, my little lion."

He smiled again, but said nothing. He had a vivid purple scar along his cheek. The skin around the scar puckered, as if it had been burned. The lower part of his ear on that side was missing, giving him an uneven face. As he stirred the coals and added a piece of wood, I gazed at his hands.

He still had gentle hands. They were not the hands of a warrior, but of a scholar. He could have been a doctor, I thought, or a philosopher or a teacher or a musician. He had always been intelligent and he still had a bright sparkle to his eyes. But I knew those gentle hands had taken the lives of men. I knew that with his quick intelligence, he had devised cunning attacks on hapless Russians. I suspected that he had satiated his lust for vengeance and had slit the throats of wounded infidels. And though I despised what he had done, my love poured out across that lonely fire and my soul stirred strange and warm within me. And in a moment of great clarity I realized that I could forgive him for all the things I hated about him. I could forgive him and I could love him. And I wondered why I could not do the same for his father.

Chapter 24

Butterfly—پروانـــه

For the next three days, Zemar traveled with us as we trekked along the high mountain routes to my husband's compound. Chaos had scarred our valley. The Russians had never been able to control Massoud's powerful forces in the Panjshir region. The Soviets occupied most of the central valley and maintained fortified outposts, but the mujahideen controlled the side valleys that ran up into the mountains. In about four months, the Russians had systematically transferred power to the Afghan Communist Army across much of the country. My husband and Zemar were confident they could overwhelm them in the strategic main valley positions. I overheard them discussing Massoud's plan to crush the communists and from his Panjshir stronghold, eventually take Kabul. Though he was young, Zemar was rising as a leader and my husband was proud of him.

Even my husband was shaken by the approach to the compound. The area had been controlled by Massoud for the entire war, but it had not escaped the high-altitude Russian bombers. He had not been to the valley since the early days of the war. I had seen the destruction when I visited my mother's grave seven years earlier. There had since been dozens more bombing campaigns in the valley and the ruin was difficult to comprehend. We walked for a week along high trails well above the valley floor—routes once shaded by graceful pines and filled with songbirds. I did not hear a single bird the entire week and saw only a few scraggly pines.

To walk for days without color or song or beauty disturbed me as much as the gore of the battlefield. The brief, bloody day of our flight from Kabul traumatized me. But to walk for a week across bleak, endless ridges of barren rock left me weary beyond words. I had never in my life been more tired. I contracted body lice from one of the filthy blankets I had slept on in the caves and I scratched even in my sleep.

About midday, we stopped on a windswept ridge about a kilometer from where my husband's compound had been. Neither my husband nor Zemar had spoken all morning. We had not eaten since early the day before and I assumed they were fatigued. When we stopped, my husband pointed in silence to the valley floor. I realized in horror that he was pointing to what was once his boyhood home. He sat heavily on the rocky ground and shook. I watched in amazement as he sobbed uncontrollably. Zemar, who had lived in the conflict, seemed unable to comprehend the mourning that racked my husband. He stared into distance and would not look at his father.

I could not take my eyes off him. I had seldom seen him lose his composure. He had always been a rock of strength. I had seen him weep twice in our entire relationship, but I had never seen him completely lose control. It was exhilarating.

Land, to Afghan men, is spiritual. They call it *khawk* and it is much more than property. It is soil in the eternal sense of the word—the place of birth and of death. It is the place where forefathers toiled and sowed their sweat in the same land they would one day pass on to their sons. *Khawk* is holy and it is pure. If there is no water available when an Afghan cleanses himself for prayer, he is permitted to use the dry soil. *Khawk* is the core of an Afghan soul.

While my husband wept on that windswept ridge, I did not know if he was mourning his homeland or his abandoned lover or his fear of what lay ahead. I did know that I was as much a part of this land as he. We had abandoned our souls when we moved to the city and now we had returned—two wayward and ruined hearts—to the soil of our father and our mother. I realized, in a rush of clarity, that this would be my chance to rebuild our love. He walked again in the enduring earth of his homeland. He would not be vulnerable to the enchantment of foreign ways and foreign women. The curse of his wandering had been broken and now he was back where he belonged, under the magical spell of horses and sacred earth and starlit night.

The destruction of our dear land saddened me, too. I could not possibly comprehend the scene below us. If not for my husband's emotion, I would not have known that we were gazing down at what had once been my home. The fertile fields that had surrounded the compound were sown in land mines and as barren as a dry riverbed. Only the front wall of the compound remained. The gate, still intact, had become a peculiar passage from one hellish field to another.

Gone were the horses, the houses, the luxurious grass compound, and the fountain courtyard. It all was but a memory. I could make out a few one-room dwellings nestled against the backside of the front wall. It appeared as though someone had stacked stones from the rubble to build pitiful little hovels. I could see at least five kilometers from where we sat and I saw nothing but endless barren fields of stone.

I sat a little distance from my husband and watched him curiously. He wept for a long while, which continued to embarrass Zemar. For the first time since I discovered his betrayal, I yearned to comfort him and to hold him and perhaps even to love him. For the first time since that day at the InterContinental, he seemed human. I saw a dream-shattered man. Every reminder of every memory was rubble in the bomb-leveled fields below. I felt that somehow his inscrutability and invincibility made him inhuman. As long as he was inhuman, I found it difficult to forgive him. I could not forgive a callous, belligerent, self-absorbed man. But a hurting man was more like me. Hurt and disappointment I could understand.

I wondered how he would rise from his weeping. Would he vow his revenge? With the Russians gone, where would he vent his fury? Would he join the feudal lords and become like one of them? Would he slake his thirst for vengeance on his Afghan brothers like some dysfunctional uncle in the national extended family, or would he become a healer to a broken land? I almost laughed aloud at my simplicity.

He is Afghan, I thought. He will rise and declare his anger. He will blame the Afghan communists and vow to crush them with his bare hands. He will join Massoud, and out of his valley he will descend in rage on Kabul. His pride will allow no other alternative.

While I gazed on his trembling shoulders I heard troubling accusations within myself against my own hypocrisy. How could I ask him to forgive his enemies when I could not forgive him of his sins?

I argued with those voices that it was not the same. My pain was personal. He had singled me out and betrayed my trust. His pain was from the wound of an enemy. My pain was from the wound of a lover.

No knife cuts as deep as the one held in the hand of a lover, I thought. The wound of a lover is fatal. There is no recovery from such a wound. And the accusing voices quieted. As my husband sank into his own dark well of sorrow, I struggled to resolve my wordless contradictions. There is no one left to forgive an unfaithful lover, I thought. Because the one who must forgive is dead—she is dead and she is forgotten.

And still, the voices were silent.

A butterfly killed one of my young cousins. The Russians scattered them by the millions from helicopters. They were tiny mines, shrouded in plastic wings and exquisite in their descent. They fluttered soft to earth like beautiful clouds of maple tree seeds and landed without detonating in fields and forests and city streets and court-yards. The Russians tinted them for camouflage. They had colorful plastic wings—green for forest, yellow for sand, and white for snow. They were small and easy to overlook, but fascinating play-things to a child who had no toys. They maimed and killed our children by the thousands.

Those horrors from above took the hands and feet of thousands of Afghans. Many more lost their lives to septic infections in the wounds those tiny bombs inflicted. In a country where medical care was nonexistent and antibiotics unobtainable, even a small wound was life-threatening. A butterfly wound, in many cases, began in the horror of a lost foot and ended in a slow, agonizing, fever-ridden death—the stench of the wound a final insult to human dignity.

My little cousin was six when he found a butterfly lodged in the low branches of a tree near his home. He climbed the tree and lost a hand and part of his face when he reached out for the bright yellow toy. His mother bound the stump as best she could, but within days, a tenacious infection set in. He died in agony a month later, on the way to Kabul, where his mother had hoped to find antibiotics.

She buried him in Kabul and stayed with us for a week before returning. I tried to console her, but she would not be comforted. She wept for days and would not eat.

On the fifth day, I found her in the garden sipping a cup of tea. I sat across from her and said nothing. She looked at me for a long, sorrowful moment and with fresh tears said, "I forgive them."

She astonished me. "Afghans do not forgive," I said. "We find revenge."

"How can I get my revenge?" she said. "Will I kill a Russian? And which of them should I kill? The one who dreamed of this demonic weapon? And where might he be? Should I kill the man who made it? The man who dropped it from his helicopter? The pilot? The commander who gave the order? How will I get my revenge?"

I knew she was right. I even believed the same. I had said what I was expected to say. I spoke with the voice of our culture of reprisal. I did not believe in retribution either, but I found forgiveness difficult to grasp. I simply looked at her, aghast.

"I am not forgiving my enemy for his sake, but for my sake," she said. "I cannot even comprehend why he is my enemy and why he has done this to me. I am not forgiving him because I understand him, but because I cannot understand him."

She was right, I knew, but even my educated mind had trouble grasping her concept of complete forgiveness. "How can you forget what has happened?" I said. "How can you forget your son?"

"I did not say I would forget," she replied. "I said I would forgive. I can never forget and I will always grieve my loss. And I will carry the loss of my son with me to my own grave."

"You are Muslim," I said. "How can you speak like this?"

She looked at me until I felt embarrassed. I averted my gaze to stare across the garden. Finally, in a gentle voice she said, "You know you are not a true believer."

In that moment, I treasured her as I have treasured no other woman but my mother. Perhaps her grief had made her reckless, perhaps even insane. She had the courage to voice what I suspected many of us thought, but none of us dared to speak aloud.

As my husband shook on that hillside, overlooking our wasted compound, I realized he had become my enemy. I had coexisted with him, but I had not understood he was my adversary. He was not my friend and he was not my lover. He was my foe. I found no reasonable explanation for his betrayal, no understanding of his motives, no excuse for his lies. He was beyond comprehension. And if I could not understand him, I found nothing left to do but forgive him. My rage was destroying me. My fury had driven me to madness. And if I were to be healed, I supposed, I must also forgive—not for his sake, but for mine.

I do not understand why he did this to me, I thought. Nor can I forgive him.

And still, the voices were silent.

Chapter 25

Touch—

My husband rose from his place without a word and began the descent to his ancestral land. I could not judge his sentiment by his inscrutable face. He strode with a pace neither determined nor reluctant.

He worried me. If he turned to anger, I would lose him to the war. The Russians' departure did not mean the end of the war. The power struggle between the mujahideen and the Afghan communists would be violent. He would ally with the mujahideen along with the rest of his clan—but without the relative safety of Kabul. He would fight alongside his son. More than likely, they would die together.

If he turned to depression, he would waste away among the ruins of his inheritance. It would be a long, agonizing descent into a silent hell and I would sink right along with him. If madness gripped him, I did not know what he would do. I saw nothing but ruin ahead for us.

How odd, I thought, that I should even care what happened to him. I despised him, but at times, I cared for him. I needed him for my very survival. In the end, I had tolerated my life with him.

As I watched his shoulders quiver on that ridge overlooking his home, my heart went out to him. I did care about him. I cared that things turn out well for him. I cared that he live beyond this war, not just for my sake, but for his. I hoped that he would not be drawn into bitterness and anger and violent rage. I knew the end of that path.

The distance between us seemed insurmountable. I wondered whether I had brought irreparable damage to our relationship with my self-centered madness. But I suppose my insanity had to run its course.

As he absorbed the trauma of the destruction of his homeland, I knew that he also must be grappling with the knowledge that his indiscretions were no longer secret. I had not been very reasonable over the past week, giving him little opportunity to speak to me. How could he open his heart to a madwoman who laughs at corpses and defies the whine of bullets?

It seemed to me that if I had the capacity to care for him, I should also have the capacity to forgive him. And if I had the capacity to forgive him, I should also have the capacity to love him again. I decided, on that descent to the remains of our compound, for the sake of my own survival, I would try to find a way to forgive. But I did not care about living; I cared for my heart. For twelve years I had survived without love. I had not lived. As I trudged behind my husband, careful to walk in the pathway to avoid the mines that were strewn about, I felt very small and very insignificant and very vulnerable.

We entered the compound through the gate, which I found peculiar. I suppose he was following the path of habit, but it seemed bizarre to pass through a gate from one unwalled field to another. Though the lock was broken, the gate was still attached to its hinges. It groaned when my husband leaned into it and I suspected it had not been opened since the compound was leveled.

The gate's moan brought a stir from one of the tattered hovels built against the front wall. It had a low roof and a tiny door that required stooping to enter. I recognized the flat, thin stones in the wall as the flagstones that had once lined our elegant courtyard. The brittle, bluish-gray slate had been wedged off the mountainside in large, irregular sheets and shaped with iron mallets and chisels into paving stones. In their second life, they had been broken in half and stacked without mortar to form the walls of the miserable little grottoes my husband's family now lived in—or at least what remained of his family.

His father had been killed early in the war when he rushed a Soviet platoon on the back of one of his gritty little horses, shouting *"Allahu Akbar."* The Russians unceremoniously mowed him down with their Kalashnikovs and he became one of the first great martyrs in the struggle against the foreign infidels. Now, according to true believers, he is enjoying the fruits of heaven, no doubt surrounded by nubile virgins who serve his every desire.

A thin, stooped woman emerged from the little stone house, shading her eyes from the afternoon sun with an age-spotted hand. I had never seen such an emaciated figure. Her cheekbones protruded sharply in an aged face weathered to the texture of cured leather. Large crevices defined her skin in a crosshatch of irregular triangles. Half-moon patches as dark as indigo marked the skin below her eyes, giving her face a freakish masklike appearance. A threadbare burka hung straight from her bony shoulders like a sheet hung out to dry. No swell of breast or curve of hip shaped her figure. Her long, slender fingers were as fragile as a drafter's pencil. I gasped in shock when my husband greeted her as his mother.

Could this scrawny creature be Huma? I could not believe she had survived the war. I had been concerned about her health when I first met her—the day she and Mother planned my wedding. Somehow she had outlasted all her rival wives and most of their children. She clung to my husband and whimpered. I thought grief would seize him again, but he held her stoically, patting her as he stared across the leveled compound. I could tell by the look in his eye that he was planning its rebuilding.

This is good, I thought. He is thinking about the future. I knew he would throw himself into the reconstruction of the compound and the restoring of the fields. I was proud of him in that moment. In spite of my disappointment in him as a husband, I was proud of his strength and his vision. I knew that he would carve a life for us from these war-ravaged fields.

We drank acrid, unsweetened tea made from poppy seedpods. The bitter tea was difficult to swallow. Since I was unaccustomed to the narcotic effect, I knew to take only a small amount. Huma drank hers easily. She served the tea in chipped porcelain cups salvaged from the wrecked compound. My cup had no handle. As I cradled it in my hand, I recognized the pattern from my mother's teacups. I remembered how we had carelessly thrown two such cups against the mantel of my childhood home the day my husband had insulted me and ridden off in a furious rainstorm. I had bought a set with the same pattern when I set up my own home after the wedding. They were common cups. I had wanted them not because of their value but because they reminded me of Mother. And here was a relic of my former life, safeguarded in my hand. I asked Huma if I could keep the cup and she smiled knowingly.

"Of course, child," she said. I marveled at how quick her mind still seemed to be.

My husband went through a long list of relatives with her. Who was living? Who was dead? How had they died? Who had fled to Pakistan and who was fighting with the mujahideen? While they sorted through an endless list of clan members, I found myself, to my surprise, thinking about Ivana.

My week of madness in some unexplainable way had cleared my mind, or I suppose more accurately, had reset my mind—like some crude shock therapy I had heard was used on the insane. And while my husband dreamed of rebuilding his family compound, I dreamed of rebuilding my marriage. Hope is such an extraordinary thing. It emerges when you least expect. And on that weary day, I began to hope again.

I wondered what had happened to Ivana. Why had she helped us to escape at great personal risk? Out of love? Out of guilt? And if so, did her guilt emerge from her love?

If she loved my husband, I suppose that she would sacrifice herself for him. She must have known that she had no hope for a future with him. She gave up what little she had with him to give him a chance at another life.

If guilt motivated her, she would sacrifice herself to somehow repay her debt and gain her deliverance for the marriage she had wrecked. But guilt was also love. She could not feel guilt if she did not feel love.

Shame comes from hurting someone or something you love, I thought.

Perhaps she was ashamed because she had hurt love itself. Perhaps she understood the preciousness of love. Perhaps she understood her debt to love and her debt to me. Perhaps she understood that she had stolen love and now she must return what she had taken.

She sacrificed herself for love, I thought. And in a way, I am indebted to her.

I was torn between jealousy and respect. I understood self-sacrifice. Before my husband betrayed me, I would have sacrificed myself for him without thinking. After his betrayal, I would still have sacrificed myself—to escape my misery, not to preserve his life. But that would not have been a sacrifice; it would have been giving up.

I understood love. It was worthy of sacrifice. I was willing to die for the sake of love and I was willing to die over its loss. But unlike Ivana, I did not have the courage to abandon hope and forfeit myself voluntarily. It was one thing to be willing to die. It was quite another to be a willing offering for another.

A numbing fatigue stole over me as the poppy-seed tea took its tender toll. I sagged against the rough, irregular wall, resting my head on my husband's thigh. And I thought, as welcome sleep wafted over me, that I had not touched him for many, many years.

Chapter 26

Forgiveness—بخشـــش
Spring 1989

There was little food in the valley. My husband had money, but there was nothing to buy. Most of the able men were either fighting against the tribes with the mujahideen or trying to survive. He could not find laborers to help reconstruct our compound. He spoke of going to Pakistan, where he said he could continue working with the American CIA to bring in supplies and weapons for the mujahideen. The Americans wanted to have a hand in who came out on top. He foresaw many years of struggle. Though I was not happy about him working with the foreigners, I did want him to go to Pakistan. We had not heard from our boys since we left Kabul and I was eager for news from them.

We started by building a little cottage. It was a simple matter to stack the strewn rubble into basic shelters. Most of our roof timbers had been stolen or used for firewood, but he salvaged enough timber to build an earth-covered roof. With practically all the trees destroyed by the war, timbers had become a precious commodity. I worked alongside him, carrying stones until my hands could no longer grasp them. We talked little. He told me where to put the stones and I obeyed in silence.

By the end of the first month, we had a small, tidy little cabin built against the front wall of the compound. He plastered the walls inside and out with clay and earth that we dug from the fields. Nights, I fell into a numb, dreamless sleep, but days, I thought constantly about forgiveness. Day after day, I would think to speak to him, but day after day, I put it off. I thought of a thousand ways to start the conversation, but nothing seemed right. And I still did not know if I was even capable of forgiving.

I could not imagine how to begin. Should forgiveness be based on how I felt, or should it be something I did without emotion? Would some compulsion inspire me? Would my desire to forgive happen of its own accord or would I need to force my heart to submit to my will?

In Afghanistan, the women teach their daughters that love will come to them after they are married. What else could they say? When the family arranges the marriage and the girl has little input into the decision of her future mate, there was no other way for love to come. "You will grow to love him," they would say. And the frightened girl would wipe her tears in private and hope that her life would not turn out like most of the women she knew.

I wondered whether forgiveness was similar. I wondered whether I must first make the decision to forgive him, and my heart would follow after. I wondered whether the return of my love would come after that. I did not know.

What I did know was that I did not love him. At least not the way I had when I first saw him at the edge of my poppy field. He had been magnificent, and noble and beyond my reach. He was the grand vision of my gullible dreams. He was royalty. Even on that day when he negotiated with my family to marry me and he had insulted me, I still loved him. On that day when I saw his displeasure in me, I still loved him. And later, when we were married and I learned of his impatience and his temper and his jealousy, I still loved him. I had been willing to overlook his flaws because I loved him. But my admiration and my respect had been dashed on the gleaming marble floor of the InterContinental's pristine lobby. And now, sitting in the dusty remains of his shattered fortress, he was no longer a prince worthy of awe. I was no longer in wonder of him. He was defeated and broken and sad. There was little to esteem.

Yet, as he threw himself into the rebuilding of our compound, I found my appreciation returning. It had been many years since his hands had been callused by hard labor. He had grown soft and spoiled and even a little fat. Our long trek through the mountains and the work of rebuilding had begun to harden his body and I saw the man he used to be emerging. I saw the man I once knew—strong and resilient and commanding. I saw a man determined. I saw a man with the air of a noble. He inspired me again.

He worked endlessly, restacking the stone walls, clearing the compound of rubble, and building our house. One evening, as he labored on a section of wall well after dusk, I took him a pot of tea and some fresh chapattis. We sat on the ground, facing one another, sipping the tea.

"I admire what you are doing," I said hesitantly.

"What do you mean?" he replied, with a hint of suspicion in his voice.

"I mean, throwing yourself into rebuilding our life, caring for your mother, taking care of me—having hope." I had been looking down at the ground while I spoke, but I looked up when I said the word *hope* and caught his gaze. For some reason, it embarrassed me and I looked back to the ground.

It felt wrong to feel ashamed, but I felt ashamed. I felt ashamed that I had abandoned hope. I felt ashamed that I had slapped him that day in the car as we drove through the battlefield. I was torn between my constant smoldering anger and my desire to move past my hurt. My heart was ripped in two pieces. And one piece said, I hate you for what you did to me, while the other piece said, I want to forgive you, and I want you back again, and I want to love you.

I did not know how to forgive him. The night came quickly, moonless and overcast. I began to cry. He could not see my tears, and I did not sob or choke. My tears flowed gently, without resistance and hushed.

"I am sorry for my behavior on that day we left Kabul," I said. "And I am sorry I cursed you."

I could not see his face in the dark, but I could feel his intent gaze on me. I smiled that I had puzzled him. It had not been my intention. I had meant what I said. But to know that I caught him off guard amused me and I almost laughed aloud.

We sat in awkward silence, neither of us knowing what to say or do. I had not been surprised by joy in quite a long while. I could not remember the last time I was even vaguely happy. But here on this dark, overcast night, with my befuddled husband peering at me through the thick darkness, I felt raw, uncultivated joy. I felt alive for the first time since that dreadful day at the InterContinental.

The conflict bewildered me. I could not understand why I felt the obligation to apologize. After all, he had betrayed me. He had slapped me. He had shamed me and sullied our love. I had been faithful, yet I felt guilty. As far as I could tell, he felt no guilt, no regret, and no disgrace for what he had done. I sat in the thick darkness, pondering what to do next. The dark night gave me a sense of privacy. As I spoke into the dark, I knew he was listening intently and without distraction.

"I have been angry with you for many years," I began. "I have cursed you in the times when my anger overwhelmed me. And once, while you were sleeping, I stood at the foot of our bed and I thought of ending your life where you lay. I thought of taking your pistol from the drawer by your bed and murdering you as you slept. But I did not have the courage."

His silhouette moved slightly and I cringed, thinking he was about to strike me. But the blow never came. In some ways it unsettled me to speak to a dark, unresponsive shadow, but in some ways I found it comforting. It emboldened me to continue speaking. In the past, his unspoken cues managed our conversations. His raised eyebrow, or frown, or deep breath would paralyze me in fear. Not knowing his thoughts liberated me. My heart poured out in an unrestrained rush.

"I have hated you with a spite I did not know I was capable of," I continued. "I have hated you for humiliating me and making a fool of me. I have hated you and plotted my vengeance in a thousand ways. I met with your lover. I called her a diseased whore and I wished her to hell. I hated her even more than I hated you.

"But I am not angry at her any longer. I am sad. I feel sorry for her and I feel sorry for you. She may have sacrificed herself for you and even for us. I do not know how that makes you feel. I do not know if you love her or even care about her. I suspect you do, or at least that you did. I do not suppose a person can enjoy the intimacy you enjoyed with her without feeling some sort of deep affection."

I paused again, thinking he might have something to say about Ivana. Instead, his silence swathed a thick blanket around me. It embraced me, comforting and soft and inspiring.

"I am weary of my anger," I said. "I am weary beyond words. My hatred has eaten the life out of me and I have become an empty shell. I once loved with a reckless abandon. I once believed in love and in dreams and in desire. I once had hope, but I have lost all. I have abandoned the values my mother taught me. I have disappointed her and I am ashamed. I am ashamed and I am sad and I grieve my loss."

In the safe cocoon of darkness, a stream of confession poured out of me, warming and cleansing my soul. Though I spoke to my husband, my heart spoke to the darkness. I felt as if someone wise and caring were listening in on our conversation. As my confession flowed, I became nauseous, but I could not stop the torrent of words spilling out of me.

"I want to forgive you for what you did to me," I said. "Not because you have done anything to deserve my forgiveness, but because my bitter heart is driving me mad. My hatred is a cancer within me. I can feel my anger eating away my soul. I am lost and I am alone and I am afraid.

"I hold you accountable for my heartache," I continued, "but not for my hatred and my anger. I welcomed the bitterness to come and live in me and now that I have lived with him for so long, I do not know how to live without him."

My words startled me. Was my anger a personality—some malevolent visitor living in me at my own invitation, some impish spirit?

When I was thirteen, a spirit possessed one of my cousins. In our villages, people commonly fell under spells. Sometimes an enemy had placed a curse on them, other times they fell prey to an evil eye. Most of the villagers wore charms to protect themselves from evil eyes. My mother scoffed at their superstitions.

"They are ignorant," she would say. "They have no way to explain the things they do not understand. Their torment is mostly psychological. They are mindless sheep, driven by their ignorance and their traditions and their fears. What they cannot comprehend, they credit to spirits and demons and witchcraft."

But my cousin's condition seemed real enough to me. She lay catatonic for two weeks. She would not eat and scarcely drank. About the only thing her mother could give her was thick, sweet tea, which she spoon-fed to her. Her family burned *espand* seeds nightly to ward off the effects of the evil eye. I had seen the practice many times when I visited relatives. They would toss a handful of the seeds on a bed of coals and the seeds would pop and hiss and release a wonderfully fragrant incense. Sometimes the head of the household would wave the burning incense before each family member, offering an inhale of the spicy, sweet smoke.

My mother would not allow me to visit our relatives during such rituals. My cousin's sister told me later about the visit of a holy man to their compound. He came to cleanse her sister of the charm that had been placed on their family. He taught them that a person who is jealous or envious or angry toward another person could have an evil eye. And if they wished ill toward the person they despised, that person could fall under a curse. "Someone," he said, "had cursed her. Their envy gave power to their curse, but they will pay a price for their wickedness. A person cannot hold fire in his bosom and not be burned by the fire. Those who send the fire will suffer along with those to whom the fire is sent."

My cousin said the holy man came as the sun was setting and put all the children out of the house. They sat on their haunches with their backs against the front wall of the home and listened as the ritual took place, first in the compound, then inside the house. The holy man walked through the entire compound chanting as he waved a censer of incense. He recited a prayer over and over.

Espand, espand
With King Naqshband's blessing
Bind the curious eyes

Eyes of desire
Eyes of hatred
Eyes of jealousy
Eyes of evil
Burn in this glowing fire

My cousin lay still in her bed as the holy man chanted through the compound. When he completed seven trips around, he entered into the house, holding a tiny silver box covered in red and blue sapphires in his hand. Its top was open. My cousin screamed and sat up in her bed, her eyes wild and her hair in disarray. In a few minutes she calmed and asked for something to eat.

The holy man left not long after, holding the silver box carefully in front of him. A plaited cord of seven strands from the tail of a black mare bound the box firmly shut.

From that night, my cousin improved. Within a few days, she was back to normal. Within seven days, a young teenage girl in a nearby village fell into a well and died. She was nearly the same age as my cousin, which convinced my aunt that she had been the source of the evil eye. The girl was jealous, she said, that my cousin was about to marry the man she wanted.

I did not know if I believed in the evil eye or in evil spirits or in the power of holy men. I did know that I could not deny the rising bile that choked me and gave me the sudden, overwhelming urge to vomit. I determined to finish speaking into the darkness to the silent figure who sat across from me.

"I forgive you," I said. "I forgive you and I wish you well. I do not know if I can ever love you again, but I hope I will find a way. And I hope you will find a way to love me in return. If you do not, and if I do not, I still forgive you."

The nausea overwhelmed me with a sudden rushing vengeance. I scarcely had time to turn my head as a violent stream gushed out of me. I rolled from my sitting position onto my hands and knees and retched until there was nothing left but gasping, painful heaves. My hair hung down along the sides of my face, drenched with the vile, sour contents of my stomach. I felt a sudden chill and shook uncontrollably.

I swayed on my hands and knees in fear of fainting as I felt the warmth of his rough, callused hand on the small of my back. For a long moment, he rested his hand there. As his heat spread up from the small of my back, I felt as if

I could care for him again. I heard his breathing and I knew him. He was not heartless. He had failed me, but he still cared for me. He had not apologized and perhaps he never would, but he cared. And in my desperate need, I felt that was enough for me to begin with.

We walked back to the tiny house he had built for us in silence. I was too weak to speak. I suppose he, too, was dumbfounded. He helped me clean up and helped me to bed; then he left quietly. I hoped he would go out into the darkness and sit alone and think deeply about what I had said.

I had little from our life in Kabul. On that night when we fled, I had packed only a change of clothes and my diary. I had not written in that diary since I discovered his betrayal, but I could not part with it. It was my only meaningful possession. It was my story. The hands of my father had once caressed its leather binding. When we had fled from the car, leaving it to be crushed under the treads of a Russian tank, I had the presence of mind to snatch my handbag as I ran.

That night I took out my diary and stared meekly at the weathered leather binding. I caressed its soft edges and I thought I would write again. I wrote, but not as I had before. My bitterness had stolen my expression and nothing remained but hollow, weary verse. I wrote anyway. And I hoped that grace would one day return to me.

Espand

Something bitter entered me
It feeds upon my soul
And sabotages our love
I do not know if the fault is yours or mine
I only know that I am dying
And dragging you along

Chapter 27

Naked—عريان

I awoke early the next morning, embarrassed. I lay still on the simple rope cot my husband had made for me. He lay on the floor nearby, snoring softly. In the predawn, the tight little cottage was dark. He had entered not long after I had closed my diary and snuffed the kerosene light. We did not have much fuel, but I had desperately wanted to write. I suspected he had waited outside until he saw the light extinguished before coming to bed. Perhaps he was embarrassed, too. In all our marriage, I had never been as honest with him as I had been the night before. I do not suppose I had ever been that honest with anyone, including my mother and perhaps even myself.

I remembered our first morning together. After making love, I had put on my nightgown, timidly dressing beneath the covers. He had slept shirtless in a pair of soft cotton trousers. In the morning, I had awoken to his movement in the bed and he had teased me by lifting the bedsheet and peeking under the covers. I had pretended to protest and feebly tried to pull the sheet out of his hand, but his grip was strong and he was playfully determined. He had persisted until I released my grip on the sheets and let them slip from my grasp. He had gazed at me until he was also embarrassed and had gently lowered the cover. I never forgot the blushing thrill of his eyes on my near-nude form. It was a sweet intimacy that I had never known. I had not thought of that first morning with my husband for many years.

In a very real way, this morning was similar. I had exposed my heart the night before. He had seen a part of me that I had kept hidden from him since the day at the InterContinental.

He awoke not long after me and groped his way through the darkness to the door. I heard him urinate against the compound wall and a few moments later he rummaged for his clothes. I got up and wordlessly began the morning tea and chapattis routine. In the damp, cold morning I shivered as I struggled to start a fire in the outdoor kitchen with the faint embers that remained among the ashes. I finally managed to get a cheery blaze going. While the kettle was warming, he emerged from the cottage, bumping his head on the low door frame. He cursed, then looked sheepishly at me and smiled. I smiled back and moved aside, allowing him a place by the fire. He stood close to me, warming his hands, saying nothing.

We stood side by side for a long while and I understood. He was too proud to confess his wrong. If he felt ashamed, he would never tell me.

I knew him. I knew he would pretend as if nothing had happened. But I also knew that his eye contact and his boyish smile meant he was glad I had spoken to him. I knew he was not angry.

I served his tea, hot and sweet, the way he liked it, and I rolled small balls of dough between my palms for the chapattis. He stood beside me and cradled the hot cup in his hand, blowing softly across the surface of the tea. There was something comforting in the repetitive task of making chapattis in the predawn quiet. As a little girl, I had loved rising early and making breakfast. It was still a special time for me, a time of quiet ritual. I loved mixing the flour and water together and I loved kneading the sticky dough until it was smooth. I loved the feel of the soft, cool dough between my palms and I loved the dry, dusty sensation of flour on my hands. My mother taught me how to make chapattis. We had spent many quiet, intimate mornings standing side by side at her wood-fired stove. I learned to be quick and I could make a stack of thin, evenly sized chapattis in a matter of minutes. But on this morning I made them slowly, enjoying the comforting soft dough and the warm fire and the smell of my husband's tea and the soft whisper of his breath across the top of his cup. My emotions were still raw, and placid tears formed in the corners of my eyes. I was relieved when he moved away from the fire, turning his back to me. I did not want him to see my tears. I did not want him to think I was angry or disappointed. I was neither.

I wiped my eyes and watched him while I finished the last of the chapattis. He gazed into the soft mist that rose from the ground toward where the sun would soon emerge. It was the direction to Pakistan.

"When do you think you might go to Rawalpindi?" I asked.

My question seemed to relax him, and he looked relieved as he spoke. "We need to decide what to do about the boys and I need a business. The boys are not boys anymore. They are men and they can help me. The Pakistanis will want to control the money the American CIA is giving to the resistance fighters. I do not know which group the Americans will support. If they support Massoud, I will be able to make good business, but I will have to work around the Pakistanis. If they support another faction, it will be difficult. I suspect they will support a number of groups in the beginning. Later they will throw their weight behind whoever seems to be winning. I need to be careful. I will need someone I can trust in Rawalpindi and in Peshawar. The boys need some way to survive. I do not want them here."

"Do what you think is best," I said. "I trust your judgment."

He looked at me quizzically. I knew my words surprised him, but I could not have been happier. I wanted him to go. I wanted desperately to see my boys, but I was afraid for them to come home. I did not want to lose them to civil war.

"The sooner I leave, the better," he said. Dawn emerged and the fog diffused the early light into a soft yellow-orange glow. "I would like to leave tomorrow morning, early."

I thought for a moment before answering. If I protested, he would wonder why. I had no objection, but I did not know where we stood. The best thing might be to leave things as they are for now, I thought. It would take him at least three days to reach Rawalpindi. Three days to think might be good for him and it would give me time to decide what to do next.

For the first time in ten years, I felt hopeful. I wondered why. I felt released from a cage and I could not tell if that cage was of my making or of his. I supposed we both had a hand in its construction.

"We have some millet, some lentils, and some flour," I said. "I'll make cakes and I can make more chapattis."

He grunted his approval. "I suppose you know I have foreign currency from my business with the Americans," he said. "I have quite a lot. It would be dangerous for me to travel alone with so much, but Massoud has agreed to give me safe passage to the Khyber Pass. His men in Pakistan will not dare to hinder me. I will have to pay bribes, of course, and I will have to deal with the Pakistani trucking Mafia. I will need to spread money around, but I will still have enough to buy a transport truck and to fill it with supplies. I will have to sell at prearranged prices to Massoud. What I siphon off to sell to the locals will double our profits. Within three weeks I will return with all the supplies we need and I will have news from the boys."

He had never shared the details of his business with me and I understood this was his way of returning intimacy. I smiled to myself at his feeble attempt to open his heart. It was a man's way and it was almost laughable, but I understood. I hoped more would come later.

I knew he still kept many things from me. I was no longer a simple young girl. He would be supplying munitions to Massoud and he would smuggle opium out of the country and into Pakistan. I knew he would never tell me those things and he had no idea I knew of his involvement in the drug trade when we lived in Kabul. But I welcomed his openness as a good beginning. Perhaps, in time, he would be honest about everything. For the first time since I discovered his betrayal, I had hope for him. Hope that he could change. Hope that he could be the lover I once knew.

I wanted him to know things were different and when I handed him a warm chapatti, I touched his hand and looked into his face. He met my gaze and held it for a long moment before staring back toward the east. I wanted to hold him, but I decided to wait for him to make the next move. I did not know how long that wait would be.

I wanted him to think about us and our future. I wanted him to think of what he would tell me about why he had betrayed me. I had shown him my heart and I wanted him to show me his. I wanted to know how and why and for how long and with whom. I wanted to know if he loved her, if he still loved her, and if he cared about what might have happened to her. I wanted to know what she had that I did not have. I wanted to know how they made love and if it was different with her than it was with me. I wanted to know what I could have done differently and what was my fault and what was his. I wanted to know why my love was not enough for him, why he was not satisfied with me, and why he felt that he had the right to a secret love. I wanted to know if he thought she was prettier than me, or if she was a more adventurous lover or a more interesting person. I wanted desperately to understand.

But I knew he was calculating how much he could make from his first truck and how many trucks he could buy this year and where he would find his drivers. I will need to be patient, I thought. He may never understand my need to understand.

Why?

Why? I asked
And you replied, I do not know
Was it me? I asked
And you replied, I do not know
Was it her? I asked
And you replied, I do not know
What do you know? I asked
And you replied, I do not know
And after many years I understood
That you did not know
But still I hoped
You would uncloak your heart

Chapter 28

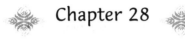

Lonely—تنهــا

B y midday, I had fried hard little cakes of millet and dal and mustard-seed oil. I spread them out to dry while I washed a change of clothes for him at the river near our compound. I washed my face and hair by the river and when I returned to the compound, I drew water from the well to bathe. I hoped he would notice.

The compound had taken shape. We completed our little cottage and we reconstructed Huma's little hut. It was neat and weather tight. Though the tiny lean-to was only a few meters from our cottage, she did not like sleeping there alone and she begged my husband to allow her to stay with us. I lobbied with equal enthusiasm for her to have her own quarters. Thankfully, my reasoning prevailed.

The outhouse on the backside of the compound had filled with rubble, so my husband and I dug a new latrine near where the old one stood. I was glad the well had not filled in. Just digging the shallow pit for the latrine had taken us four grueling days. The ground was stony and we did most of the digging with a heavy steel axel shaft salvaged from a destroyed Russian truck. My husband used its flattened end like a pick to pry out the stones and would hand them up to me to carry off. To dig a new well would have been impossible.

We built a stone enclosure beside the latrine where I could bathe. It had high walls for privacy, but no roof. It felt good to wash and stand drying in the warm afternoon sun. Since we left Kabul, I had bathed only once each week. I detested going to bed without washing, but we had little soap and I was usually too exhausted to trudge to the well and draw water and haul it to the latrine. Most nights, I would wipe myself as best I could and fall into a dreamless stupor on my cot.

That afternoon, my husband went into the village to get the information he would need for his trip. Massoud's men controlled our valley and he needed to speak to the area commander to ensure there would be no confusion. Tomorrow morning he would walk for one day to a village where Zemar was to meet him with a squad of his men. From there they would travel by truck down our valley to the main highway leading up to the Khyber Pass. Zemar would journey with him to the border and once he crossed into Pakistan, it would be a simple matter to catch a bus or a truck into Islamabad or Rawalpindi. A significant American presence remained in Peshawar near the Afghan border, despite the fact that the CIA-funded training camp in Badaber had been destroyed in an uprising. Though he did not say, I knew he would seek out the Americans. He was convincing and his English good. He would work to find a way to build on his connections with the foreigners from Kabul and he would find a way to make money. He would buy supplies in Rawalpindi and coordinate through our sons and the Afghan refugee community there. He had arranged for a relative to stay at the compound to protect us while he was gone. The man was armed, illiterate, and proud. He watched me carefully and he was intolerable, but I felt safer with him there.

We had managed to buy a few chickens from the village and I had six eggs. I cooked them with some noodles and leeks and that night we had a simple meal. We finished eating at sunset and when he had wiped his plate spotless with the last of the chapattis, he picked up the bucket and headed for the well. I could hear him drawing water as I cleaned up after our meal.

The air chilled and I went inside our cottage to prepare for bed. We had not done any hard work that day and for the first time since we had returned to the compound I felt rested. I would have loved to read for a few hours before sleeping, but I had no books. I slipped into a threadbare cotton gown and crawled into my cot, resting on my back. He entered about an hour later and in the dark, spread his blanket on the floor beside me. He smelled of soap.

I lay for a long while, hoping he would say something, but he was quiet. I could tell by his breathing he was not asleep. I felt as nervous as I had been on our wedding night. I decided that since I had made the first move to sleep apart from him on the cot in the sitting room of our Kabul home, that I would make the first move to return to intimacy. He was lying with his back toward me. I reached timidly out in the darkness and touched his shoulder. He rolled over on his back and I let my hand rest palm down on his chest.

He rested his hand over mine. My heart pounded in my ears and I was glad when he did nothing more. After a long moment, I tugged gently on his shirt and he sat up. I could not see him in the dark, but we were face-to-face. I slid my hand along his collarbone to rest against the side of his face and kissed him on the mouth. He responded, warm and tender and cautious. I was glad he did not say anything. My mouth was dry and I could not have answered.

My thoughts swirled in a rush of conflicting arguments. I could not just abandon twelve years of bitterness. I felt my body responding to him and I wanted him desperately, but my mind and my heart argued persuasively against my body. They were saying the same things they had said all these years. That he did not love me. That he was a liar and that he could not be trusted. I did not know which voice to believe. I chose to kiss him more deeply, pulling him up and toward the cot. He responded to me by removing his shirt and trousers. The little cot groaned under his weight as he lay down beside me, and I knew there would be no turning back. I did not want to turn back.

The intensity of my arousal surprised me. I unleashed twelve years of pent-up desire. I helped him remove my clothes with an urgency I had never experienced. I wondered, for a moment, if I was competing with Ivana. I had always imagined that their lovemaking had been more passionate and more fulfilling for him. Why else would he have been involved with her for as long as he had?

I realized with deep sadness that Ivana would always be a part of our marriage. He had opened our secret life to her. She had shared in his past and now she was a part of my past. I would always compare myself to her, and sadly, I would never forget her. I felt as if she were in the bed with us, there to mock me, to mock my beauty and my ability to captivate him. She was there to whisper that she was more interesting, more alluring, more desirable. She was everything I was not.

The urgent demands of my body prevailed. I abandoned myself to the overwhelming flood of desire, and in that brief moment of mindless urgency, banished Ivana. But in the warm and gentle afterglow she returned, as persistent and as demanding and persuasive as ever.

My husband had always been an attentive lover. I suspected that was rare for an Afghan man. He understood my need to be touched and he held me, lying precariously along the edge of the narrow cot. Finally, he became uncomfortable and after a few moments of restless shifting of his weight, he kissed me gently and rose from the bed. As he dressed in the dark and I fumbled to find my clothes that we so carelessly abandoned, I wished he would lie with me through the night. I thought of joining him on the floor, but decided to take one step at a time. Maybe, when he returned from Pakistan, I would ask him to build us a wider bed.

I lay long into the night staring up into the darkness, and Ivana lay beside me. I was not angry with her anymore, but I resented her intrusion. I suspected that in time she would be less of a presence during my secret times with my husband. But in that moment, I could not ignore her. She had trespassed into my life and she had hurt me deeply, in a way no other person could. I decided, on that vigil through a cold and dark night, that I would forgive her, too. Though

I might never forget her, I would not let her rule my heart.

I lay there in the dark, content but lonely. It felt right to be moving away from my season of bitterness. Forgiving him was the beginning of my mending, but I would always feel somewhat alone. Even as he lay there beside me, he remained unreadable. My forgiveness had not unlocked his heart. I still had unanswered questions and unspoken fears. I suppose I was willing to live with those questions. I had returned to him for myself as much as I had returned for our relationship. I would live with him and be faithful, but I might never know him. I would always have questions. I would always have doubt. I would always have fear. I would always feel lonely.

Along the riverside near our compound, where I wash our clothes, there is a solitary oak. It stands alone, proud and resilient. Its trunk is scarred with gouges and carvings and a diseased section near the roots. There, a cavity has opened and in the rot, tiny larvae tranquilly feed in the debris that sloughs from the rotting heart of that majestic tree. A lightning strike had ripped one of the larger limbs away from the massive trunk and it lies partially severed along the riverbank.

The limb is still connected, but its boughs lie broken along the ground. The leaves that remain are yellow and unhealthy. Where a grove of trees once lined the riverbank, the land is now barren. War and famine and desperation have cleared the restful shade and the sun now bakes the rocky riverside.

Lonely

The solitary oak stands
Scarred and broken and cancerous
And in its branches pigeons rest
And in its shade women meet
to wash their clothes
And chatter through the afternoon

Chapter 29

Hope—امیـد

My husband left before dawn. I had drifted to sleep sometime in the early morning hours, but I awoke the moment he stirred. I lit the lantern near the head of my cot and watched him dress. He had packed his bag the night before and had little to do but lace his boots. He was ready in minutes. He lashed his blanket to his pack and started for the door, then paused and looked back at me. I was sitting cross-legged on the bed with my blanket wrapped tight around me to ward off the chill. I smiled weakly. He stood for a long moment with his hand on the door, confused. After an awkward pause he said, "I'll bring some books for you when I return."

He turned and banged his head soundly on the door frame. He cursed, slammed the door shut, and stomped off into the night. "Watch your head!" I called after him and he cursed again. I thought I had irritated him and my heart skipped, but he laughed aloud. As he roared back at me from the dark, I giggled on my cot. I wanted to call out to him that I loved him, but my timidity overruled my courage. After his laughter died, he stood near the door, just outside the cottage. He did not make a sound, but I knew he was there. It comforted me to know he was just as mystified as I was. After a long while, I heard the wistful, fading crunch of his boots on the stone debris of the compound. When I could no longer hear his footfalls, I wept.

The next three weeks tortured me. I experienced radical mood swings, one day feeling hopeful for our future and the next day sinking into despair. This pendulum of emotion confused me. I had expected to move past the haunting memories of that day in the InterContinental. But the more I thought about our future together, the more I remembered the past. When I despised him, as I had for the past twelve years, he did not matter much to me. The past did not matter because the future did not matter. The only thing that had been important to me had been my children. But now my children were gone and my husband was gone and I had no one but Huma and a sullen bodyguard.

I dreamed several nights in a row that I was in the hallway on the sixth floor of the InterContinental, crumbled on the carpet near the door of the room he and Ivana had entered. As I tried to crawl away from the door, the hall became an unending tunnel. Ivana's throaty laugh echoed down the hallway, haunting me and mocking me and jeering my failure. I would awake from the dream and sit upright in the bed and shake in anger. I once struck the wall beside the bed with my fist and ruptured a vessel in the heel of my hand. It hurt for days. I could not banish the sound of her voice from my head. It taunted me as I went through the motions of endless day after day.

Sometimes depression embraced my imagination and I would picture what had gone on behind that door. I imagined her in his arms and them in bed together. I could neither deny nor control the powerful, intrusive images. I would rage within myself against Ivana and against my husband and against my lack of self-control. But the next day I would grieve and weep and wonder what was wrong with me.

About a week after my husband left, Huma fell sick. She lay in her bed for three days, listless and unresponsive. I could not coax her to eat. Finally, I was able to get her to drink some black tea. She revived a little, but still refused to eat. I moved her into my cottage. It would not have been appropriate to ask the bodyguard to help me, so I simply scooped her up in my arms and carried her. With my small frame, I was not sure I could manage her but I lifted her with ease. I stood so quickly in the tiny room that I nearly fell backward. She could not have weighed much more than thirty kilos. She felt little more than an armful of firewood.

I had trouble squeezing through the narrow doors of the two tiny cottages. When at last I lowered her to my bed, she seemed to appreciate what I had done. She drank tea and even ate a piece of chapatti before sleeping for the rest of the day.

She weakened over the next few days. She mostly slept. When awake, she spoke softly, sometimes incoherently, and she ate little. She drank tea occasionally, but seldom drank any water. She hardly had use for the bedpan under the cot. She did not have any bowel movements during her first week in my cottage and she urinated only once each day, barely more than half a cup. Her skin was as dry and brittle as a fallen leaf.

About ten days into her illness, she began to recover. I spoon-fed several cups of weak tea to her in the morning and she ate a small piece of a boiled potato. By early afternoon, she was alert. It was pleasant that day and I opened the door of the cottage to let in some of the bright afternoon sunshine. She seemed to enjoy the fresh air and I helped her to sit upright in the bed.

Except for the time when she had been suspicious of my desire to spend time alone at my poppy field, Huma and I had enjoyed a respectful relationship. We had drifted apart during my time in Kabul, but I had never forgotten her thoughtfulness. She had endured a difficult life, living in a compound with two cantankerous women who competed for their husband's affections.

It broke my heart to see her wasting away in the aftermath of the loss that surrounded her. I suspected she would soon die. I knew my mood swings had made me particularly vulnerable, and caring for Huma did nothing to ease my anxiety. I could not imagine what I would do if she died while my husband was away. I was very afraid. There was no one with medical experience who could help in the village. The old women would do more harm than good with their home remedies and superstitions. Most of them would prescribe a small ball of raw opium to swallow in the evening with a cup of bitter herb tea. Kabul would be the only place where we might find help. The capital had become relatively peaceful with the coalition government in place, but Huma would never survive the trip.

I was sitting with her in the warm sunshine, lost in my thoughts when she said softly, "You have been good to me. And you have been good to my son. I am grateful."

Her clarity astonished me. She looked directly at me, smiling, bright eyed, and alert. I remembered how much I had appreciated her on that day when we first met. We had sat together, her and Mother and me, on a day much like this one. We sat in the warm sunshine in this very compound and arranged the details of my wedding. She and Mother had talked animatedly through the afternoon while I had dreamed of a life that was not to be.

The memory was difficult for me. The ruined compound and the ruined marriage and the worn-out body that lay on the cot near me were more than I could bear. I turned my head away from her so that she could not see my tears.

"I have many regrets," I said.

"I have none," she replied.

I did not say anything more. How could she not have regrets? I thought. She had married a stubborn, violent man who had dominated her life and forced her to share her love. She had lost her family to a fathomless war and her possessions lay shattered around her. The only thing that remained of her life was her firstborn son and a broken-down daughter-in-law.

"I know you have been disappointed," she said after a long silence.

Again, I could say nothing. I wondered what she knew about me, but I was afraid to ask. I suppose I did not want to hurt her. She seemed so fragile and so vulnerable. I was afraid I might say something out of my despair that would cause her grief. I feared that she would not be able to endure that grief—that it would send her to her grave and that I would forever feel responsible.

My quarrel, I decided, was not with her, but with her son. She had done the best she could.

"You were such a hopeful little thing, on that day when we first met," she said. "You were young and dreamy eyed and intelligent and beautiful. I knew life would be difficult for you. You knew too much and your expectations were too grand. You know your mother ruined you."

I looked at her quizzically. She did not seem vindictive or critical. She seemed respectful of my mother.

"She ruined you by giving you hope," she continued. "I have no regrets because I know I have done the best I could with the opportunity life gave me. I wish things could have been different, but I understood the limitations of my people.

"Your father dashed himself against this stubborn land. And he planted a romantic dream in your mother that she passed along to you. It was an impossible yearning."

I wanted to argue with her. I wanted to say that I believed in love, but I knew I would have been dishonest. I was not a believer anymore. I felt instinctively that this might be our last real conversation and I did not want to interrupt her. In some ways, I agreed with her; in other ways I did not. But out of respect for her I kept silent and listened patiently.

"I do not know what he has done to you, but I know my son has disappointed you. I am sorry you have suffered. I have always respected you. I love your curiosity. I love the way you have raised your children. I love your fighting spirit and I love your vulnerability. I love you as if you were my own."

And as those gracious words poured out of her ancient, trembling lips, I wept as I have seldom wept. I could not understand what was happening to me. I did not feel sad or depressed. I felt as if I were being healed. And my tears were not tears of sorrow, but of renovation. My vigil over this frail, aging woman was renewing me. And though she chastised my adolescent dream, she rejuvenated hope within me.

"Find a way to forgive him. Find a way, not for his sake, but for your own. He may be stubborn, like his father, but there is also a part of me in him. Perhaps someday that part of him will emerge."

She smiled warmly. Most of her teeth were missing, giving her a comical smile, but it was genuine and affectionate and filled with bright-eyed wit. I laughed and held her weathered hand against the side of my face. And my tears wet the back of her hand. And as she closed her eyes and sighed and drifted to sleep, I felt love like I have never felt. It was a love born of respect and admiration and honor.

That night Huma died quietly in her sleep. And by the light of the candle I kept burning near the bed, I watched her take her final tender breath. And I did not mourn when she passed into that night. I had no more tears. And as her body chilled, I lay my hand over hers and I swore to her that I would forgive her son. I swore that I would not give up my hope.

Guardian

On the night that Huma died
I sat in reverent vigil
And memorized each crevice
Of her leathered face
I caressed the fragile skin
With tender gratitude
And felt the gentle comfort
Of an ancient watching me
Like when I stroke the darling soft
Of my father's tattered diary

Chapter 30

Noble—شـرىف

At dawn, I sent the bodyguard to one of Massoud's outposts, about a day's journey. From a field phone, he called our relatives in Pakistan and let them know about Huma. Some of my husband's family, who lived in the village, buried her that day.

My husband arrived a week later in a Russian-built truck that was missing a door and fender on the passenger side. It swayed precariously under the load of goods stacked on its bed. Half a dozen men sat on top of the towering cargo, armed with AK-47s. They were not men, but boys, most of them scarcely fifteen years old. One carried a grenade launcher in his lap and appeared to be their leader. My husband sat in the passenger seat, caked in dust.

I could not remember the last time I had been happy to see him and I stood in the door of our tiny house smiling warmly. Not knowing how he had taken the news about Huma, I was unsure of how to approach him. He seemed preoccupied with the business of unloading the truck and organizing the unruly group of boys. Within three hours, they emptied the truck and stacked the goods near the compound wall, covered with a tarp. One of the boys butchered a healthy sheep that had been strapped to the top of the truck and soon the compound filled with the delicious smell of roasting flesh and seasoned rice and fresh naan.

My husband brought a portion of the meal the boys cooked to our cottage and we sat on a mat just outside the door, sharing tidbits of the lamb. Though we did not feed one another, as we had done when we were young, our sharing of a single plate reminded me of those days. But everything reminded me of those days. The nostalgic thoughts sometimes comforted me and sometimes disturbed me. I found this one especially comforting.

My husband talked endlessly through the evening about our relatives in Pakistan and about his business, but he spoke mostly of the boys. Babur was now twenty-four and Padsha twenty-six. They both had fallen six years behind in their schooling because of the war, but they had done well. He had decided to allow them to continue their studies rather than include them in his business. They had finished at an English medium school in Rawalpindi and he had been impressed with their command of the language. Both of them wanted to attend the University of Lahore and he had approved. He felt his business would be developed in a year or two and that he would be able to afford the tuition. He gave them enough money to enroll for their first year.

I mentioned Huma, thinking he might want to talk about her, but he was dismissive. I thought it was strange that he did not want to reminisce over her. It seemed disrespectful. Perhaps, I thought, it is just a man's way. His manner of dealing with losing her was so different from mine. I needed to grieve, and remember, and keep her alive in my heart. He preferred to move along with hardly a backward glance. Someday, I thought, what he has rushed past will catch up with him. Someday he will grieve with a vengeance.

As he prattled on and on, I found myself daydreaming over what Huma had said—that I should find a way to forgive him. He was making it easier for me with his boyish enthusiasm. But I was not a fool any longer. I knew his business was distasteful. His smuggling meant bribes and lies and risk. I knew that he was hiding things from me, and I wondered if he was faithful. But I could see that he wanted me to share in his life and I was ready. Forgiveness might take me months, even years. I did not think I would ever be able to forget.

As we shared the last tidbits of the lamb, I remembered an experience I had in Kabul about three years before we left the city. My husband had a friend there who owned a beautiful Afghan hound. He and his wife lived in our neighborhood and we would visit them from time to time. I never understood what sort of business the man was in, but his wife was an instructor in the medical school at Kabul University. When my husband and I visited, she and I would sit in the courtyard of their home and drink tea while our husbands talked outside in the garden or went into the city together. I enjoyed her company as much as anyone I knew in Kabul.

They had a splendid hound. Most of the village men kept fighting dogs rather than hounds and I had only been familiar with the village breeds. They were muscular and savage. As a little girl, they frightened me. I had seen the village dogs tangle with one another and I was deathly afraid of them. The village men took good care of their animals, especially the ones they used for sport. They showered dogs and cocks and falcons with more affection than they gave their wives.

The Afghan hounds were not at all like the village fighting dogs. The lean and rangy dogs had a long, graceful stride and could cover huge expanses of ground in a short time. They had beautiful silky coats that flowed like robes when they trotted. Afghan and Iranian kings had bred them as hunting dogs and they carried themselves regally, as if they knew their royal lineage. My husband's friend pampered his dog and fed it by hand with scraps from their table. The dog would not take food from anyone but his master.

His daughter had a pet rabbit that she kept in a cage in the back of their garden. During one of our visits, the rabbit somehow got out of its cage. The hound bounded across the garden and killed the rabbit before anyone even realized the animal had escaped.

Our friend flew into a rage and thrashed the animal with a heavy stick. For the next hour, the dog cowered in the corner of the garden. We continued our visit, but it was very awkward. The mother spent most of the hour in the house consoling her hysterical child. My husband and his friend continued their conversation across the garden from me, out of earshot. Sitting alone, I embarrassed myself by drinking three cups of tea and eating an entire plate of sweets.

But a remarkable thing happened as I sat alone in that garden, watching my husband and his friend talk quietly. The hound rose from the corner where he had cowered and walked purposefully over to where his master sat. I remember admiring the animal's noble bearing. His long, well-kept coat gleamed black and glossy in the afternoon sun. The dog carried his head high and walked with such a solemn dignity that he seemed almost human. He reached the place where his master slouched, drawing on his hookah, and sat near the arm of the man's chair, looking straight ahead, his head well above his master's arm. I watched in amazement as the hound laid his head on the arm of his owner and rested there, unmoving. And I thought, what a gracious beast. He forgave this man of his anger and in a splendid act demonstrated his submission without ever losing his dignity. The owner rested his hand on the animal's head and stroked the dog's long, elegant hair.

The hound's well-mannered civility moved me. An aristocrat living in the home of a commoner, the dog had the largesse to rise above his own offense and extend forgiveness to his owner.

I thought of the hound as my husband and I talked long into the night. As the wick burned down to the base of the candle, he produced a small bundle wrapped in a Pakistani newspaper from his pack.

"I hope these are good," he said shyly. "There are more in one of the bags. I'll find them tomorrow."

I opened the package slowly, cherishing the moment. Inside there were two books of poetry by Hafiz, one by Rūmī, and the first volume of an illustrated copy of *One Thousand and One Nights* in Persian. I hugged them to my chest and thanked him. He did not know that my mother had used a copy of *One Thousand and*

One Nights exactly like this one to teach me to read Persian. The old folk tales had captured my imagination. She had avoided the more salacious passages, but when I was older, I read and reread every word of the ten-volume set.

I doubted if he had ever read *The Arabian Nights*, as they were known in English. I found it ironic that he had chosen this particular book for me. I guessed he had gone to a book market in Rawalpindi and asked for some good books for his wife, or maybe he picked it because of the illustrations. The artwork was very well done and the books were good copies, but he could not have known the story.

An ancient Persian king named Shahryar discovered that his wife was unfaithful to him and ordered her to be executed by beheading. He decided that all women were unfaithful and married a thousand virgins, beheading each of them the day after their wedding night. His last wife, Scheherazade, told him a story on their wedding night, but as dawn approached, she ended her telling of the story without finishing. The king was so curious that he delayed her beheading for one more night to hear the ending. The following night she completed the story, then began another, stopping again before dawn in the middle of her telling. She kept the king's interest for a thousand and one nights. Through the course of the legends, the king fell in love with Scheherazade and made her his queen.

My husband pointed to the *Arabian Nights* volume and said proudly, "This is part of a set of ten books and I have the rest of them. I'll get them for you tomorrow."

I smiled and said softly, "How would you like it if I read you one of these stories each night? You might find them interesting."

"I would like that," he replied.

We lay for a long while on the cot that night, talking. I told him about Huma's final words to me, that I should find a way to forgive him. And I told him how grateful I was for all he had done for me. He listened quietly, but said nothing. I wished that he would have said he was sorry. I wished that he would have said he forgave me, too. I wished that he would have asked for an opportunity to prove his love again, but he said nothing. I would have given him anything he had asked for that night, but he did not ask and I was determined not to prod him. If he expressed any remorse, it would be at his own volition.

I was disappointed, but not desperate. I was beginning to understand what it meant to forgive, and though I knew that I could not trust him, I was willing to accept what he was giving me. I hoped that someday he would give me the apology I needed. In hope of that day, I would give up my bitterness and my anger and my hatred. I would find a way to be content. As he stirred, restless on the narrow cot, I asked him if he could build a larger bed.

"Of course," he said. And in the dark I knew he was smiling.

The next three years were chaotic. My husband's business grew rapidly. Within three months, he had six trucks running between Peshawar and the Panjshir. He hired nearly thirty men and by the end of the year, he had rebuilt the compound wall. By the end of the second year, his fleet had grown to twenty trucks and our compound resembled a military camp. The back of the compound, where the stables once stood, became a noisy, filthy repair shop. Security was an obsession for him. He stationed armed men along the walls and he wore a large pistol openly. War-hardened men slept in open barracks-style buildings along the wall opposite our cottage and storage buildings lined the adjacent wall. They filled the buildings with rice and dry goods and weapons and probably processed opium. I pretended not to notice.

From 1989 to 1992, the communist-backed government deteriorated. Najibullah, the Soviet-installed leader, stubbornly resisted the mujahideen factions and it became impossible for him to manage the country. Ancient ethnic rivalries proved too resilient. Finally, in March of 1992, three months after the Soviets stopped their financial assistance of his government, he resigned.

Three million refugees lived in Pakistan. During the war against the Russians, the refugee camps there had been staging grounds for the various insurrection parties. Now that the Russians were gone and the Najibullah government had collapsed, seven major parties divided along ethnic lines and geographic regions fought to gain control. Pakistan backed the Hezbi Islami, a Pashtun faction. The Pakistanis continued to demand that all foreign funding through Pakistan be directed through their secret service. They seemed determined to establish a radical Pashtun-led government in Kabul. Most of the

American CIA funding went through them, as did the Saudi money. I overheard a conversation between my husband and one of his top men and deciphered enough to understand that he was helping Massoud by working with his CIA contacts to siphon American funds without the Pakistanis' knowledge.

The political environment became increasingly volatile. Rival political groups formed a coalition government, and in April of 1992, created the Islamic State of Afghanistan. The process was chaotic. Hamid Karzai, the new deputy foreign minister, spoke hopefully of a new nation that would stand on its own, proud and strong. He spoke of a nation that would honor the traditional values of our people and at the same time allow the progress of democracy. My husband told me it would never be. "The parties of the coalition are too divided," he said. "They are biding their time, gathering their weapons and planning their strategies. There will be a fight for Kabul and the winner of Kabul will rule the nation."

As the country continued to deteriorate, ambitious petty dictators emerged almost overnight. These warlords did more damage to the country and killed more of their own countrymen than the Russians ever did. Processing opium became their principal method of funding and poppy fields sprang up in every valley. Many a young boy lost a leg or a foot to land mines as they cleared the fields for the poppies.

A saying emerged in Afghanistan: *Jangsalaran Jangsalar Hastand*. It means "Warlords are warlords and they will always be warlords." It served as a fitting commentary to the endless drudgery of our lives. We were serfs to the lords of war. And as they raged against one another, the innocent and the ignorant and the powerless were crushed between them.

I realized one cold December day, while a group of men were huddled within our compound in heated discussion with my husband, that he had become a lord of war. He was loyal to Massoud, as were all the men in our region, but he was also opportunistic. Massoud needed him to ferry goods and weapons into the Panjshir and for his CIA connections. He needed Massoud for protection from rogue bandit groups who roamed the mountains and from the foreign Arabs working with the Pakistanis to establish a pure Islamic state. And he needed Massoud's credibility.

I had never met Massoud, but everyone in the country knew about him. He was a living Afghan legend. A young soldier once tried to assassinate him and fired on his car from only three meters away. He missed and Massoud told him, "Friend, you are not accustomed to shooting at a man. Your hands are trembling." Incredibly, he let the young man go free.

The French adored him and he won their hearts by engaging French reporters in their own language. When he occupied a village, he would immediately set up an administrative overseer and provide benefits for the elderly, the disabled, and the widows. He had an engineering degree and was known as a philosopher, but he was also a devout Muslim and his wife wore a veil. He was publicly against the opium trade, yet poppy fields dominated the valley. He preached against terrorism and treated his war prisoners honorably, but his soldiers were illiterate tribesmen. Although they reverenced his noble principles, in the passion of battle, they reverted to their primitive instincts.

Some said Massoud's philosophy kept him from baser inclinations. They said Massoud fought for higher motivations—for human rights and independence. He embodied the mystical lore of Afghanistan.

I did not doubt his earnestness, but I knew from my own experience that noble intentions could be swept away in a moment of passion. It seemed to me that something exists within us all that is not subject to reason. Royalty is not an easy thing.

In my own attempt to be largehearted, I sometimes succeeded and sometimes I failed greatly. I struggled daily to be gracious. I tried to rise above my hurt and fear and disappointment. I tried to be an aristocrat. But still, I felt the fever of jealous wrath when I remembered Ivana. After all the years, my heart still palpitated when I imagined her with my husband. I still felt a certain undeniable rage against his lies. I often remembered my abandonment to insanity when self-righteous zeal consumed me and stole away my sensibility and my education and my values. Passion made me an animal. I suspected that even someone as noble as Massoud fell subject to passion's capricious guile.

Lord of War

My lover is a lord of war
And filled with haughty worth
He bows before a bloodied altar
To the god of violent earth

And on that abomination
I place a humble dove
And hope that in the afterlife
I might find true love

Chapter 31

Slavery— یبردگ

Spring 1992

Spring in Afghanistan is the time when kings go to war. It has been the time of war for as long as we can remember. The men, restless from their winter of inactivity, rush to spill the blood of their enemies onto the rain-softened ground. And I imagine the soil drank their sacrificial offering more out of necessity than desire.

In the days of my childhood, the pungent ripe earth would rouse from her winter sleep and groan in urgent birthing. Green grew soft and lush on the mountain slopes and in the freshly tilled ground. The smells of new beginnings filled our valley. Farmers spread ripe, sweet manure in the fields and wheatgrass sprang up overnight. Fields would carpet in days and within six weeks, the grass flowed like waves as afternoon storms rushed down from the mountains and swept along the valley floor.

But in the days of war, the hopeful wonder of spring was a hazy memory. The rains still came and the streams still swelled to violent torrents, but the trees that had preserved the soil on the mountain slopes had fallen to Russian bombers. And the white water of spring rolled unmolested down the slopes and stripped the land to barren stone. The fields that once undulated in luxurious waves of grass were sown in land mines and rubble and the broken machines of war. The few cultivated fields that remained were small and pitiful. They were more likely to be planted in poppies than in wheat or barley.

April of 1992 marked the beginning of the most heartbreaking period in the history of our people. I doubt we will ever recover. We lost something in that season's perverted razing of Kabul that forever sullied our heart. Our land had endured the rape of foreign invaders for three thousand years. But in the spring of 1992, we ravished ourselves in an irrational frenzy.

On April 18, the British Broadcasting Corporation reported that Massoud had amassed forty thousand troops north of Kabul. I did not think that Massoud had that many men. My husband had been increasingly absent with the organization of the spring offensive. His convoy of trucks between Kabul and Peshawar shuttled supplies and weapons twenty-four hours a day. He told me that for weeks they did not shut off the trucks' engines. They would simply change drivers when one became too weary to continue. One truck had been lost off the side of a mountain, no doubt because the driver had fallen asleep at the wheel.

The BBC also reported that twenty thousand troops loyal to Gulbuddin Hekmatyar, the leader of the Hezbi Islami party, were positioned south of the city. Hekmatyar was a clever politician who had studied engineering at Kabul University. Though he did not complete his degree, he was known as Engineer Hekmatyar. He formed his Islamic Party while he was in exile in Pakistan in the 1970s. There, he established a relationship with the Pakistani leadership that led to millions of dollars in foreign aid. The pipeline of money that had flowed from the United States and from Saudi Arabia during the war with the Soviets continued to flow to Hekmatyar during the battle for Kabul.

General Abdul Rashid Dostum, the warlord leader of the Uzbek community, controlled the airport with about five thousand troops. He allied with Massoud in the fight for Kabul. Dostum was a thug with a grammar-school education. He fought with the Soviets against the mujahideen and then switched sides after the Soviets departed. I disliked him immensely. To me, he represented all that was wrong with us. I suppose the educated leaders were no better. If anything, they were worse. They were enlightened. They understood the advantages of development and education and reason. But their education could not free them from their mindless ambition and greed and tribal arrogance.

With my husband gone for weeks at a time, I spent long nightly vigils following the battle for Kabul on our shortwave radio. Just as he had said, the city became the focal point of the ambitions of Afghanistan and of the meddling nations. The fight for Kabul continued to escalate through the spring. In June, Hekmatyar began shelling Kabul, raining rockets and artillery down on every area of the city. Various mujahideen factions controlled different parts of the city and fought one another for strategic advantage.

Hamid Karzai, in an interview with a foreign reporter, seemed to be extremely distressed. "I do not know what is going to happen," he said. "We are killing one another. It is senseless."

On a late-summer afternoon, I was in my garden gathering a few eggplants. I had worked hard on my little plot. It stretched along the wall of our compound near our cabin. My husband had built a low wall alongside my garden that separated it from the main compound. It blocked the morning and evening sun from my plants, since there was such a narrow space between two walls, but it gave me privacy from the constant comings and goings of men in the compound. There was a cistern in the far corner of the garden and one of the men would fill it from the well each morning. I had everything I needed and I seldom left the little area of the garden and the cottage. It was suffocating in the summer, and I wished I had some shade trees, but my life was far better than everyone around me. I was grateful for what I had.

I heard the clamor of a truck entering the front gate of the compound. Its dry brake pads squealed nastily and its exhaust spewed black clouds of diesel smoke skyward. The bark of men shouting and the rude bellow of the air horn announced the truck's arrival. It annoyed me that the drivers blasted their horns at every opportunity, particularly when they pulled into the compound. It seemed important to them that everyone within a kilometer knew that they had arrived. I ignored the ruckus until I heard the gate to my little area groan open. Startled, I looked up and saw my husband in the gateway, holding a young boy in his arms. He walked across our little courtyard and laid the boy on a cot in the shady outdoor sitting area in front of our cottage. In the bright sun, I could not see the boy clearly, but he appeared to be wounded.

I walked over to where my husband stood, dropping the eggplant in a basket near the cottage door. As my eyes adjusted to the shade, I made out the boy's features. He was a frail, beautiful child of about twelve or thirteen. His wounds were serious. One of his legs ended midthigh in a bloody stump. The bandages were filthy, encrusted in dark, dried blood and yellow discharge. His left leg was intact, but heavily wrapped below the knee with another grimy bandage. He groaned on the cot and mumbled something I could not understand.

"Who is he?" I asked.

"He is one of my distant relatives," my husband replied. "I owe his family a favor. Do you think you can help him?"

We had some antibiotics from Pakistan and clean bandages. I had antiseptics and everything I needed, but it was unusual for my husband to bring one of the young men into our living area. Many wounded men had been treated in our compound. The men were all familiar with battle wounds and usually took care of themselves. We had no doctors. Most of them were hiding in Pakistan. I felt inadequate to care for someone with such serious wounds. The boy appeared to be near death.

"Can't the men take care of him?" I asked.

"It would be difficult in the case of this boy," he said.

I looked at him curiously, expecting him to say more. How was caring for this boy any more difficult than caring for the others who had come here? If it were because of the seriousness of his injury, why would he want me to care for him instead of the men? If it were difficult for them, it would be far more difficult for me. And even though he was a relative, it was unacceptable for a woman to tend to a male in such a way—even a young cousin.

"It will also be difficult for me to care for him," I said.

"He is a dancing boy," my husband replied.

They call it *bacha bazi*, playing with boys. It is a practice that everyone in the country knew about, but never discussed. Destitute fathers would sell their sons to a wealthy man to be trained as an entertainer, knowing that the boys would also be used for sex with the men they entertained. The money was difficult to refuse. I had seen them dancing for the men at weddings in Kabul. Women were forbidden to dance before men, so young boys took their place. They wore women's clothes and mascara. They moved gracefully among the men who encircled them, mincing their steps and flirting openly. Most of them were slim and attractive.

But wedding dances were not the same as the dances that took place at late-night gatherings in grimy meeting halls. In those places, the men would clamor for the attention of the dancing boys, fawning over them like lovesick juveniles. If a wealthy man owned him, the boy would not be available at any price. But a boy owned by an entertainer would leave with the man who offered the most money for his sexual partnership.

During the war with the Russians, men would be away from their wives for months at a time. The dancing boys substituted for women. With bells on their feet and willowy, seductive movements, they mesmerized the men. Fights commonly broke out among the men driven to jealousy by their lust for the boys. And often, suspicious lovers murdered the boys. Many of the field commanders kept boy lovers.

I looked at my husband for more information, but I could tell he would give me none. My immediate thought was to refuse. Most Afghan men would never allow their wives to refuse their request. There would be no discussion and there would be no request, really, just a command. But neither would any Afghan husband ask his wife to care for a boy such as this one.

I looked at the boy and felt pity for him, but also curiosity. Even though he was filthy, he was very pretty. His long hair hung gracefully along the sides of his delicate, chiseled face. He had flawless pale skin and lithe arms. He groaned as he shifted on the narrow cot. In that moment, I made my decision.

"I will help him," I said.

And with that choice, a strange companionship began. My husband excused himself to take care of something with his truck. I made hot, sweet tea and mixed it with raisin alcohol. The boy drank it in one gulp and asked for more. I knew that cleansing his wounds would be painful, so I gave him several large glasses of the potent drink. Within about thirty minutes, he slumped against the side of the cottage in a stupor.

I fetched some water and antiseptic and removed the bandage on his lower leg. I began with his intact leg, thinking that I would be better able to stomach the horror of the injury. But when I unwound the cloth from his leg, the seriousness of the wound startled me. His leg was gashed open from his knee to his ankle. I could see the entire length of his shinbone, visible and unevenly broken. Fragments of bone and metal adhered to the bandage when I removed it. Other fragments stuck out of the wound like the splinters of a broken tree limb. Someone had bound the wound without even bothering to wash it.

The flesh was not yet putrid, but I knew that if I did not treat the wounds immediately he would have little chance of survival. This boy will never dance again, I thought. Maybe this is the best thing that ever happened to him.

I found my husband in the main compound. "I need more antibiotics, antiseptic, sutures, and gauze. And I need opium."

He studied me for a moment, then without a word turned and walked toward one of his storage buildings. I went back to the cottage and sat on a low stool near the boy, waiting for him. When my husband returned, he handed me a large packet of medicines bound in a cloth and about one hundred grams of opium paste wrapped in a single sheet of Pakistani newspaper. I hefted the little packet in my hand and looked at him with just a bit of a smirk. He made no response.

I made more tea with cinnamon bark and added the raisin alcohol. When the boy stirred, I gave him the tea and a pea-size ball of opium. He swallowed the opium and drank four cups of the tea, which I worried might be too much. Within a few minutes, he fell asleep again.

It took me six painstaking hours to pick the bone and metal fragments out of his legs and suture his wounds. I amazed myself by setting his broken leg. Since his leg was splayed open, I could see the break clearly. The bones had not yet fused, so I aligned them in place and bound the wound tightly. I stitched him with a suture kit from my husband's medical supplies. I lay several thin strips of wood along the length of his calf and bound it tightly, forming a simple splint. I was quite proud of my work.

I nearly vomited when I removed the dressing from his horrid stump. I began by covering part of the stump with the loose flap of skin that had remained intact, but I did not know how to suture it. Something large and sharp had sliced his leg neatly, as if a surgeon had cut it. I did the best I could to clean the stump and hoped there would be no infection. At least we had antibiotics. Without them, he would never survive.

By the time I finished dressing the wounds, it was well past midnight. I removed his kurta and washed him. I had already cut off his trousers, a scandalous act that would have led to a beating or worse by most Afghan husbands. I wondered what my husband would have said had he returned to see me bathing a young boy covered with nothing more than a cloth across his abdomen. I did not much care. He was just a boy, hairless and pale, his skin as smooth as a woman's.

I dressed him in a pair of my own billowy Afghan trousers and a clean shirt and left him on the cot at the cottage entrance to sleep. I was exhausted, but found myself rising throughout the night to check on him. He stirred a few times and groaned, but mostly he slept. The porch on the outside of our cottage was covered, but if it rained, the boy would have gotten wet, so the next day my husband moved him to Huma's old cabin. He said nothing about the fresh shirt and trousers.

The boy slept for three days, waking only to drink more tea. I gave him the opium about every six hours and slowly reduced the amount of the alcohol. On the third day, he vomited and I knew he needed to take food. Eating raw opium with nothing more than tea and raisin alcohol was taking a toll on his stomach. The cinnamon bark I added to the tea helped with the nausea, but raw opium makes a person nauseous, even without alcohol. With great difficulty I persuaded him to eat a plain chapatti. On the fourth day, he ate noodles. By the fifth day, he was eating eggs.

With my husband gone again, I busied myself caring for the boy. I was surprised by how much I enjoyed his company. Looking out for him gave me something to live for, I suppose. It was rewarding to watch him improve. It was four weeks before he could move from the bed and even then, only with great difficulty. My husband had one of the men fashion him a crutch, but the boy could not endure the pain of putting any weight on his intact leg. His wounds were healing nicely, with no signs of infection. I kept a bedpan nearby, but he and I were both overjoyed when, a few weeks later, he could make his way to the toilet. I have no idea how he managed squatting in that crude outhouse on one leg.

I read aloud to him in the evenings and we had long talks, usually about what we were reading. He was illiterate, but very intelligent. He had unquenchable curiosity. I was curious about him, too, but he said very little about himself, or the life he had lived. I thought often of how sad the life of this beautiful, articulate child had been. He could have been anything he wanted, given the opportunity. But war and lust and greed had enslaved his soul and stolen his potential.

His name was Shayan and as the days began to cool, I fell in love with him. I suppose he became a surrogate son to me, but he was so unlike my own boys. My boys had been bright and inquisitive, but their father had captivated and manipulated their curiosity. Shayan loved the things I loved. He had no interest in kites or horses or guns or knives. More than once, he wept as I read moving passages from love stories. The questions he asked were the questions a young girl would ask. I would have expected a boy like him to repulse me, but oddly, his feminine sensitivity drew me closer to him. But when he asked for my mascara, I refused.

He asked constantly for opium. I suspected that he was accustomed to it long before he came to me. I had never used the drug. The villagers often gave it to their children whenever they were sick and sometimes just to quiet them or help them sleep. Mother abhorred the practice. I had seen her more than once get into arguments with the local women about giving opium to their children. "They have no idea of the harm they are doing," she would say.

I began giving him smaller portions and worked him down to once a day. For several hours after taking the drug he became especially talkative. I am ashamed to admit it, but I began giving him a larger dose in the early evening, at the time when we would read.

One evening, I read a passage from *Shahnameh*, the Persian Book of Kings. We were reading about Afrasiab, a mythical king and enemy of the Iranians. Shayan remained quiet when I finished reading. I knew he was thinking about his own war experience.

"What happened to you in Kabul?" I asked.

He looked at me carefully. He had washed his hair that afternoon and it hung long and soft on his shoulders. In the gentle light of the lamp, his beautiful eyes darkened. He peered at me through narrowing slits, as if I had threatened him personally. For the first time he seemed angry with me.

"I am not your enemy," I said quietly.

He looked away from my gaze and stared up at the ceiling. I watched his face soften and after a long moment, he sighed heavily and told me his story.

"My master lived in west Kabul, in Qargha. Hekmatyar was shelling the city every day and there were so many bodies in the streets that the people did not bother to remove them. Some families had no one left to bury their dead, so the dead lay bloating in the streets. We were not fighters. We were just trying to survive. Most of the dead had not been fighters. They were women and children and old people.

"Sometimes," he continued, "rockets dropped without warning on an apartment and an entire family would disappear. Once, I was buying some tomatoes from a man on the street when a shell hit nearby. It hit a man selling okra. He vanished. Pieces of his flesh plastered onto the building near where I stood. His blood spattered my kurta all along my left side. I just stood there. The man selling the tomatoes asked me if I still wanted them. I bought them without saying a word. I gave him his money with hands splattered in blood.

"I remember thinking, as I rode my bicycle back to my master's apartment, that hell could not be a worse place than Kabul. I saw the bodies of some fighters tied to trees. Each of them had been shot in the temple. They were Hazaras. I saw a child sitting in the street near the body of a woman. He was about three years old. He was not crying. He stared off in the distance while he patted the woman's head.

"In the apartment building where I lived, there was a little girl about my age. She was beautiful. We were friends. Her mother had been wounded and her father killed in a mortar attack. She went for water one morning and never came back. Some of Dostum's men caught her and raped her. They cut her throat and left her body in a bombed storefront at the end of our street.

"We could not identify the enemy. The mujahideen were fighting one another and we were caught in the middle. They were insane. The fighters would kill anyone who was not of their own ethnic group. Sometimes they did not care if they killed their own."

His voice trailed off and he stared a long moment at the ceiling. I thought he was finished, but he took a deep breath and continued.

"I had gone out to buy flour for chapattis. We had all learned to wait until there had been a heavy barrage of rockets and mortars before we ventured out. When the soldiers tired of loading their mortar tubes, they would take a tea break. That was usually in the late afternoon. During the lull I would go out.

"I left on my bicycle to take the road toward the Paghman district. I was not more than a few blocks from my apartment when a rocket hit behind me. I thought it might have hit my apartment building, so I turned back to check on my master when another rocket hit near me. I awoke to my master's slaps and the sound of him calling my name. I passed out again and the next thing I remember was waking up in a tent.

"My master was not a bad man. He treated me well most of the time. We had a friend in Massoud's army, north of Kabul. He had been one of my lovers. My master took me there and our friend must have given me to your husband. I was only there one day and I do not remember much. But I do remember that the trip in the truck to this place was the longest day of my life."

His voice trailed off again and I said nothing. I took his hand and held it for a long while. How I hated what war had done to my land. And though I had little nostalgia for the city of Kabul, I was sorry for the devastation of the only civilized place that remained in our country. I regretted that my husband was playing an important role in this madness.

"I know you are curious about me," Shayan said. "You want to know about my life as an entertainer. If you will find an opium pipe for me and allow me to use it, I will tell you everything."

The next morning I took one of the wives of a man who worked for my husband with me to the market. She helped me to find what Shayan wanted and what I needed.

The Fall of Kabul

The widows of Kabul
Beat their breasts
And throw dust upon their heads
And lament their fallen husbands
They bury their toddlers in shallow graves
To the moan of wayward rockets
They hastily fill the narrow pits
With stubborn shifting pebbles
And wish that they had never known
The urgent suckle
Of a greedy child

Chapter 32

Liar—دروغگو

That evening I brought the opium pipe to Shayan. He smiled, and thanked me and touched my hand with the flair of a courtesan. "We have been reading too many stories about Iranian kings," I laughed.

I do not think he understood. He smiled again and took the long, slender pipe in his delicate hands. He kept his nails clean, carefully trimmed long. They made his slender fingers appear even more fragile. I envied those womanly, soft hands. His movements were intriguingly feminine, yet also comical. I tried to imagine his training as an entertainer. I found it difficult to understand.

How could a man teach a boy to behave like a woman, then use the boy for his own pleasure? I could not understand how a man could so blatantly misuse and degrade a child like that for some unimaginable fantasy. How, in God's name, could a human being be so callous? I suppose that was why this child's story captivated me like no other—and repulsed me like no other.

Some cunning man had patiently taught him feminine mannerisms and exaggerated sexual innuendo and suggestive dances. Someone had taught him to sing, mimicking a female voice as only a prepubescent male child can. Someone had taught him how to entertain an older man and satisfy his sexual desire. Someone had formed this child into a curious creature who, even though now free, insisted on the familiar patterns of his feminine charade.

How could a man be satisfied in a relationship built on such a pretense? This poor counterfeit could never be a woman. But some man found contentment in a relationship with this boy. Though this child sang coyly of love, he knew only of love based on deception. He knew only selfish desire. Lust had consumed his life, his hope, his dreams. Yet as he lay on the cot in Huma's cabin with one badly damaged leg and a useless stump, he clung to the very behavior that had ruined him.

The opium pipe had a long, slender tube with a removable porcelain bowl attached to the end. There had only been a few in the market, crudely constructed of reed stems and clay bowls, but one old man had a beautiful Turkish pipe with tapered bronze tube. The blue porcelain bowl was decorated with tiny white stars and a crescent moon. The old man had dug it, undamaged, from the rubble of a wealthy man's home. I bought it thinking that Shayan deserved at least one elegant possession. The boy seemed to appreciate the gesture.

Shayan placed a tiny ball about half the size of a pea in the pipe bowl and lay prone on the cot. He asked me to remove the globe from the kerosene lantern and he rested the opposite end of the pipe stem on one of the metal clips that held the lamp glass in place. As the porcelain bowl rested near the lantern flame, a pungent, sweet, incense-like aroma filled the room. He asked me to light a pine splinter and hold it over the pipe bowl. As he drew on the pipe stem, I watched the flame suck down into the pipe bowl and kindle the ball of opium into a glowing ember. Smiling contentedly, Shayan handed the pipe to me. I placed the globe back on the lamp and lay the pipe under the cot. He rolled over onto his back, put his hands behind his head, and smiled.

I waited for a good while, saying nothing. He lay still, gazing glassy-eyed at the low ceiling. After awhile, he turned to look directly into my eyes with a dreamy expression.

"Sing me one of the verses you used to sing when you entertained," I asked.

He took a deep, wistful breath and sang in a clear, beautiful falsetto.

I am tender and shy and delicate
My flesh is white and yielding
I am like a valley flower
Fresh and open and sweet

You are strong and dark and dangerous
Blackened by the sun
You paw impatiently
Like an Arabian stallion

I tremble when I am near you
And confused by my desire
I kiss your roughened hand
And yearn for you to crush me

He sang a haunting chorus between each verse—a repetitive couplet about valley flowers crushed under the flashing hooves of an Arabian stallion. The song disturbed me, but as he looked at me with those dreamy eyes, I knew he wanted my approval. I wanted to pull him to my breast and tell him that I was sorry. That I wished he could have had a different life. That I wished he could have known love—a love that gave as much as it took. I fought back the tears and said not what I wanted to say, but what he needed to hear.

"You have a beautiful voice," I said. "You have the voice of an artist."

He smiled at me again, but I could not tell if his contentment was from the opium or from my compliment. For the first time, I understood the allure of opium. It had the power to make someone happy, regardless of the circumstance. It was a poor substitute for love, I thought, but certainly much easier to find. For the first time in my life, I desired the drug for myself.

"Did you have many lovers?" I asked.

"More than I can count," he said. "Some of them were kind to me, but most of them were cruel. Some of them would beat me after they made love to me. Some of them would beat me while they were making love to me. Some of them beat me when they were unable to become aroused. Some of them made love with the intention of hurting me. Most of them were angry and impatient and difficult.

"One of Hekmatyar's commanders told me that he wanted me to come and stay with him. He told me that I would be his only lover. He said he would kill me if I went with another man. I did not like him. He was impossible to please. My master was not willing to sell me to him. We had to hide from him for some weeks until he left the city and returned to his men, south of Kabul.

"I would stay with a lover for an hour or so," he continued. "My master would usually wait for me outside. They would not take me to their homes, but to a borrowed or rented room. Sometimes they would want me to spend the night, but my master would not let them unless they paid more money. I did not like to spend the night. Those were the times when I was most likely to be hurt.

"If I were beaten, my master would take good care of me afterward. He would speak kindly to me and tell me he was sorry it had happened. He usually gave me a special meal or a little money. Sometimes, he would buy me a new outfit. He would let me rest a day or two. If my face was bruised, he would demand more money from my lover."

"Your master was also your lover?" I asked.

"No," he answered. "He never touched me, but I was very afraid of him. He had a bodyguard who was always with him. The man was huge, with a thick forehead. He would stare at me and sometimes touch himself. My master told me if I ever disobeyed him, or if I ever tried to run away, he would give me to his bodyguard."

"Do you remember your family?"

"Yes, of course," he answered. "I could even visit them, but they were ashamed of me. I did not like to go to see them. They would not say much and they would not look me in the eye."

"Perhaps they were ashamed of themselves," I said.

"Perhaps," he said thoughtfully. "They were very poor. What else could they do? We were all starving. I do not regret that they let me go with my master. My life was much better with him. I had food every day."

I had to step outside. I stood in the courtyard near the little cottage and watched a half-moon crest over the mountains. Tears streamed down my cheeks and splashed noiselessly in the dry dust at my feet. He is a child, I thought. When he is a man, he will understand. When he is wise, he will realize his loss. He will be enraged when he discovers he has believed a lie. Everyone wants revenge for the unfairness of abusive love. Everyone hates to be deceived and lusted upon and used.

Some of my tears were for the boy and some of them were for myself and some of them were for love. I mourned for love. I mourned that something so pure and so fragile and so rare remained so desperately out of reach. I mourned over the lies I had believed and over the lies I had not known were lies. I mourned that I could not tell when lies were lies and when truth was truth.

I wept because I could not tell the difference between lust and love. I wept because I did not know whether I even knew the difference myself.

My husband had charmed me and charmed my mother and charmed our family. He made promises that he did not intend to keep, or could not keep. He bought me with a dowry and a house and a future and a dream. Like an imprudent child, I had believed it all. My mother had believed it all. And now I did not know whether he was faithful to me. I did not know if he intended to bring another wife into our home. I did not even know if he had some boy like this one, hidden away in Peshawar or Kabul.

I wept because I was afraid. I feared my own heart. Perhaps I, too, had lusted. I had wanted to be swept away in romance by a powerful, wealthy man. I had desired him that day in the forest when he sat on his lean horse and looked on me with interest. I had lusted for him as earnestly as he had lusted for me. I had desired a house and servants and respect. I had lusted for the things I saw on that first visit with my mother to my husband's compound. I had dreamed of how I would live in that compound and become an enlightened and benevolent queen to the illiterate villagers who lived nearby. I had gotten my desire. And now I stood in the shattered ruins of that very compound and sowed my tears in the very ground I had lusted for as a young girl.

Everyone lies, I thought. Everyone desires. Everyone uses everyone else. Everyone pursues his own lusts. And everyone pays for his sins.

Liar

My lover is a liar
A master at his craft
He deftly works a shuttle
Across his tapestry

I watch his nimble hands
And admire the cunning weave
As intricate patterns surface
On the budding cloth

His loom begins to groan
As the taut and artful plait
Bows the heavy frame
And distorts the fragile vision

I watch the self-destruction
In weary resignation
And vow I'll not fall victim
To his cunning

Chapter 33

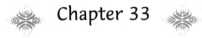

شـهوت—Lust
Summer 1992

That summer was a lonely, dusty trek. My husband disappeared for two or three weeks at a time. I was a prisoner in my garden within the compound. Shayan continued to improve and we grew close. I enjoyed him, but a child is no substitute for adult conversation. I missed Huma.

In October, when my husband returned from one of his trips, I told him that I wanted to keep the boy. I did not ask, as I suppose I should have. I simply told him. He said nothing, but gazed at me with a kind expression. His look surprised me. I had expected protests and excuses. When he did not say anything, it threw me off guard. After a few moments of awkward silence I blurted, "What is it like in Kabul?"

"It is very difficult to understand," he said. "You would not recognize the city. It is in shambles. Everything the Russians built has been destroyed. A mujahideen unit occupies the school the boys attended, but it is just a shell of a building. The mujahideen are fighting one another and all of them are heavily armed. Artillery shells rain down on the city day and night. It seems the supply of rockets is unlimited. I knew this would happen. I knew there would be a fight for the city, but I never dreamed I would see our people destroy one another like this. It is very sad."

He brooded, looking into the distance. I had never seen him like this, so melancholic. He schemed endlessly of how to make more money and how to have more trucks and how to improve his supply chain. I had never seen him stop to consider the consequences of his work.

"The boy told me about his life in the city," I said. "He told me many unsettling stories."

"We will never be the same," he said simply. "We have entered into the mouth of hell."

I could not comprehend this rule of malice in my land. What inspired us in our insane rush to self-destruction? I wondered whether our misery was punishment for our ambitious greed. But the foreigners were equally greedy. Who would punish them? The Russians, the Americans, the Pakistanis, the Iranians, the Arabs—all of them determined to conquer and rule Afghanistan. Ambition and covetousness drove them to undermine one another for the privilege of possessing us. Among us, the tribes had fought one another for the right to lead the war against the foreign invaders. Now that the foreigners were gone, we spilled our lust upon ourselves. And while our children died, the men schemed endlessly, dreaming of power and control and possession.

It seemed to me that the tribes were pawns in a great game of desire. And the powerful nations that manipulated our greed were simply more dominant pieces in the same endless scheme. But beyond the craving of men, there seemed to be another unseen ambitious force. A force determined to do more than dominate—a force determined to destroy. To destroy all that was good and right and noble and hopeful. The more I witnessed evil the more I believed in evil. I did not know where it lived, or what it wanted, but somewhere I knew an intentional and determined and unseen force was the enemy of all living things.

My mother believed every human being was born pure. She would look into the fresh face of a newborn and say, "Look, little one. There is nothing in those bright eyes but curiosity and love. They do not covet. They do not desire. They do not take. They only give. For a brief moment they are innocent."

She believed that life corrupted children. She believed that they were born from God himself and polluted by the world they graced. "It is so sad," she would say. "They bless us with their purity and we corrupt them with our greed. By the time they are two, they will learn scheming from their mother, pride from their father, and selfishness from their brothers and sisters."

Her way seemed reasonable. I could not deny that life seemed to corrupt itself. Innocence is quickly lost. I learned from my cousins at a very early age that all children are scheming. Some children are more deceitful than others. Some are insatiable. And some are spiteful beyond imagination. As a woman, I had learned that some men are cruel and some only seemed not to be cruel. Some men lie openly and some only appeared to tell the truth. In all my life, I had not known one man who could be trusted and I knew only two or maybe three women. Mother told me that my father was a man to be trusted, but I never knew him. I suppose if I had known him, I might be a more optimistic person. But the more life disappointed me, the more suspicious I became. I did not believe in anything. I did not trust anyone. And I trusted our religious leaders least of all.

The mullahs believe that some people are born with immoral intentions. "The foreign unbelievers," they say, "are deceivers and hypocrites. They cannot be trusted. They seem to have good intentions, but they are the instruments of Satan. They will perish in hell for their sins. They are destined for annihilation at the hand of Allah's holy warriors."

The mullahs say that the unbeliever, who refuses to submit to Allah, should be destroyed because he has given himself over to Satan. In rambling sermons, they teach about a malevolent spirit who works tirelessly in the unseen world to undermine the acts of their merciful God. They call him *Iblis* and believe the unenlightened foreign infidels are his minions. I cannot understand how a merciful, all-compassionate God could endorse, and even command, war. To the mullahs, the holy cause justified their self-righteous violence.

Most of the village religious leaders were illiterate. Many of them memorized the entire Quran to qualify as a leader. The impressive task took years, but they memorized it in Arabic, which they did not even understand. To me, that was the height of ignorance. Illiterate, stubborn men dared to teach me right from wrong, wicked from pure, from a book they could neither read nor understand. And they vowed their allegiance to a vengeful God of endless contradiction. It was mindless.

I had known many foreigners during my days in Kabul. They did not seem at all to be devils. But the mullahs were right about one thing. The foreigners were unfaithful. They flirted and seduced one another with reckless disregard for the pain they caused their lovers and their children. They were infidels. But the foreigners were right about the mullahs.

Both seemed driven by an unreasonable blindness to the suffering they caused. The infidels destroyed love with their lust and the mullahs destroyed life and joy and hope in the name of the All-Compassionate One. The foreigners lusted for pleasure and the mullahs lusted for blood. It seemed to me that some intelligent force manipulated them all for its intentions. I could not understand why. What does evil have to gain in its constant struggle against good?

My mother taught me about the faith of Islam when I began to ask questions about God. She thought there were some good things to be learned from the teachings in the Quran, but there were also things she could not accept. "I will never believe," she said, "that it is just to take the life of another human being. We are the darling of creation. There is nothing more sacred than life." I so missed my mother's sensibility.

I was weary of the compound. For three weeks, I had not been out of the little enclosure around our house and garden. A delightful late-afternoon cool drifted down from the mountains and I asked my husband if we could take a walk. We strolled down to the river, taking my favorite path that meandered between barley fields past the ancient threshing floor. The stone walls that once lined the path lay scattered across the field. Walking among the ruins of my former life, I had to be careful not to be nostalgic. It would have ruined a pleasant evening.

My husband seemed unusually quiet. I let the silence rule as we walked along. When we reached the river, he sat down heavily under the oak tree where the women came to wash. The river water murmured softly. He sat for a long while, staring across the vacant river. The sun was setting over the mountains and I knew the air would chill. I wrapped my shawl tightly around me, more out of anticipation than discomfort. My husband startled me when he spoke abruptly in an agitated voice.

"I do not understand what is happening to our people," he said.

"It's the war," I replied. "It's difficult to see the destruction and not be affected. You see the ruin everywhere and you remember what the land once was. It wears you down."

"It's more than that," he said. "It does trouble me that we have lost so much. It also troubles me that our people have lost their way. We are devouring one another."

Though I wanted to speak, I kept quiet. I was curious to hear what he would say.

"I do not understand why we are killing one another," he continued. "I sat with Massoud's captains and listened to them strategize over Kabul. I watched the daily demolition of a city I once loved. We reared our boys in that city and we watched them become men. We had a good life there."

I fought mightily to keep silent. I had no pleasant memories of that time. It is ironic, I thought. He remembers the wealth and the status and the influence he had in Kabul. I remember my suffering and my shame and my disappointment. I found it very difficult to swallow my hurt.

"What we are doing is wrong," he said. "It is not just foolish, it is wrong. The stories you have heard from Shayan are only a small part of what is happening across the country. Our people are consuming one another. It is senseless. I have seen field commanders trade young boys like Shayan with one another as they might trade a sack of rice for a garment. The boys are nothing to them. I saw five of Massoud's men take a young Hazara girl into an empty building. I heard her muffled screams and I did nothing. The girl's mother and sister came the next day and carried her body away. No man was there to help them. They screamed at us and they cursed us and they threw stones at us and they condemned us to hell. Most of the men mocked them."

I knew he was ashamed. My husband was a strong, resilient man. That was what I fell in love with as a young girl. I remembered admiring his burly hands and I remembered my fascination with the scars on his hardened body. I remembered my desire for his vigor. I remembered how I delighted when he picked me up off the floor and laughed at my feeble struggling. I had hungered for his power and his independence and his zeal.

Now, as we sat in the fading light along that murmuring river, I saw a different man. He was fragile, like me. He sat cross-legged on the river-bank with his elbows on his thighs and his hands loosely clasped over his ankles. His head hung low on a weary neck, his shoulders hunched, his face sagging. I have underestimated him, I thought. Perhaps Huma was right. There was a part of her in him but a stubborn world had stolen away that fragile piece of his heart.

He had quivered on our wedding night—trembled like a skittish lamb under my steeling hand. When I was swollen with our first son, he wept on my belly and dampened my gown with the hushed flow of large and precious tears. He heaved in grief when he sat on that barren stone and gazed on his father's wasted compound. He had wept as a man weeps—with great pent-up, weary springs unleashed from deep, mysterious caverns. A man's tears rupture like a storm on a wasted desert. They awaken dormant seed and the barren hills burst overnight in ravenous bloom. A man's tears are rare and generous and overwhelming. Though he did not weep as we watched the summer river flow, I understood that rare moment. His heart springs were near the surface.

I rested my hand on his forearm and waited. I shivered in the cool air. "I suppose we should go back," he said quietly.

In the dark walk home, I struggled between my disappointment and my hope. Though he had not apologized to me, he was beginning to understand his wrongs. He is grappling with things important to me, I thought. I should be patient.

Desire

I possessed my obsession
The intention of my dream
And it has pounded me
To ruin

What I hungered after
Is no longer my desire
What I craved
Has consumed me

I cannot seize your love
Like some cherished plunder
I cannot own you
Or command your will

Love is its own dominion
Love cannot be possessed
Love is a kingdom without law
A land without frontier

I cannot purchase love
Or acquire it like some property
But love can buy me if it chooses
If love finds me worthy

I long that you might purchase me
With the currency of love
The coins of brokenness
And humility

Chapter 34

Dreamer—نــــدہیب خواب

Spring 1994

The struggle for Kabul dragged. For two years, the mujahideen sniped one another and for two years, my husband profited from the transport of weapons into Afghanistan—and opium out. In a short time, he became a very wealthy man with nowhere to spend his money. He stored duffels of cash under our bed. I suspected that he hid most of his profits in Pakistan. That would have been the prudent thing to do. He visited the compound routinely, two weeks home and two or three weeks away. He visited Pakistan about every two months and brought letters from the boys.

I poured myself into Shayan. I suppose pity and fondness and boredom motivated me. But

I also felt determined to pass along my mother's values to someone. My husband had sabotaged my efforts to form those values in my sons. And even though I could not wean the boy from the opium pipe, I found him bright and inquisitive. One day he read aloud a Persian translation of a poem that Suleiman the Great had written about Hürrem Sultan, the Slavic harem girl who eventually became the sultan's legal wife. He began weeping.

"My life is ruined," he sobbed.

"What do you mean?" I asked. But I knew what he meant. He was fifteen years old. Thin wisps of hair had formed at his temples and on his upper lip. Stories of military generals fascinated him and he read everything I could find on Alexander the Great and Suleiman the Great and Mohammad Akbar the Great, the third Mughal emperor. He no longer groomed his nails and he cut his hair short. Most of his feminine mannerisms had disappeared, yet he still had a certain female sensitivity. Some days he was moody, some days angry, some days sullen, and some days weepy.

I had known this day would come. "Something will work out," I said. But my words came out hollow and without conviction. I understood the disillusionment of stolen dreams.

My father had been a dreamer. The title of his diary, my most treasured possession, was *My Dream—My Reality*. I had long ago translated the twelve pages he had written in his elegant French script. The lines were filled with hope and ambition and love. They spoke of my mother and of the mountains and of the intriguing beauty of our people and of all the things I also cherished. They spoke of love, as love was supposed to be.

I, too, once dreamed like my father, but I abandoned my dreams. Sometimes I would read the pages I had written in that weathered book during the early days of our marriage. I had filled them with innocent presumptions. And though I had begun to write again in my diary, the words I placed on that ancient, fragile paper lacked the sheen of my early sentences. I wrote phrases cloaked in cynicism and self-doubt. And though I did not write openly of my disappointments, my words betrayed me. My words could not hide my secret shame. In those early days of vision, I framed my thoughts in hope. But in these days of reflection, my sentences hinted darkly at my regret and my mourning.

I often wondered whether my husband ever bothered to read my diary. I did not leave it in the open, but I did not hide it. He had seen me write in the late evenings, but he never once in all our married life asked me what I had written. I was glad that he allowed me that privacy, but disappointed that he never took an interest in the opinions of my heart.

As I watched Shayan weep I agonized over what I should do. I wanted to give him hope, but I knew the danger. Nothing can unsettle a person more completely than broken dreams.

I had once been a hopeful person. I had deferred to my mother and dreamed that I would one day be like her. I dreamed that I would be intelligent and beautiful and independent and confident. I dreamed that I would find love. I wish I had been less ambitious. If I had never hoped, I would never have been disappointed.

I could not ask this young boy to abandon hope. My life had not turned out as I expected, but that did not mean that his life would also be a disappointment. I still clung to hope—that one day my husband would become my love. I hoped that he would one day open his soul to me and ask my forgiveness. I despised what hope had done to me, but I could not bring myself to tell Shayan to abandon his.

In the first year of our marriage, my husband took me on a three-night trip up into the mountains southeast of our valley. We traveled with two saddle horses and a stocky pack pony. Afghan women do not ride horses. I had worn billowy trousers and hidden my hair as best I could under a men's cap. We left our compound before dawn and reached the mountains by sunrise.

I was apprehensive, especially when we began a series of steep switchbacks that traversed a sheer ridge. My husband laughed at me as I clung white-knuckled to the saddle. To stay on, I had to straddle the animal like a man. I was so sore the next day I could scarcely move.

We camped in tall pines near a hot spring that welled up from the ground and flowed through a series of shallow pools before joining a clear, deep stream. The water smelled faintly of sulfur and the steaming rocks that surrounded the spring were stained with an ocher tint. The water was scalding at the spring's mouth, but where the overflow entered the stream and mingled with its cold, clear water, the temperature was perfect. Someone had stacked large stones in the streambed to form a protected pool and we sat in the steaming water for most of the morning. The hot soak eased my aching and I rested there until my skin shriveled.

We talked more than we had ever talked that morning. Something about the isolation and the gentle whisper of the pines and the warm, penetrating soak loosened my husband's tongue. He spoke mostly about his business plans and his hope to begin building a compound adjoining his father's. I remember very little about his schemes, but I recollect everything he said about the building of our compound. His ambitious plans overwhelmed me. But mostly I remember carefully watching his sun-darkened face and valuing the passion he possessed for his dreams. I remember marveling at his ability to see years into our future with such hope and confidence and courage.

His visions were contagious. When he finally quieted and rested in the warm spring waters, I began to dream my own dreams. I imagined our children and our life together and our own family compound. I imagined growing old with him. I thought that someday, when our children had families of their own, we would visit this place again. And we would sit in the warm cocoon of these mineral-laden waters and reminisce over our life. We would talk of all the good things we had experienced together and we would comfort one another's sorrows. We would rest our aging bodies and we would be content.

Just above the soaking pool lay a tiny meadow filled with wild roses. The uncultivated vines crowded the sparse soil of the rock-strewn field. The small, vibrant flowers emitted an exotic scent in the dry mountain air. My husband gathered a few dozen of them in his shirt and tossed them into our steaming pool. I lay back in those fragrant waters and thought that all my dreams would come true. I thought that my life would be happy and content.

Now I labored to hide my regret. I wondered how others dealt with their disappointments. I found it ironic that the one person I knew who was somehow able to discover his dream was my husband. It seemed unfair that he prospered in everything he chose to do, as if some providential hand guided his every decision. Within just a few years of fleeing Kabul, he was a wealthy and powerful man again. He no longer talked of his regret over the destruction of our homeland. He no longer spoke of his guilt over the atrocities he had seen in the battle for Kabul. I admired that in him, but I also resented it. I resented that I could not leave the past behind as easily as he had done. I resented that he did not seem to be ashamed of his sin. I almost wished that he would not find such success in his business. He left Kabul broken and tender and remorseful. But his new success emboldened him and made him cocksure. He had no interest in my opinions.

I suppose he was eager to leave his past while I was still trying to understand our past. I thought of his betrayal nearly every day, obsessing over every detail. But the more I devoted myself to understanding, the more resentful I became. I resented that he was carefree while I was trapped in an endless cycle of questions with no answers. Most of all, I resented that he had stolen my innocence and my hope and my dreams.

I understood why Shayan wept. "You must give up your desire for revenge," I told him. "You will never get even with them for what they have done. You must forgive them."

Shayan looked at me and through clenched teeth said, "I will never forgive them for what they did to me—never!"

I felt such sadness for him. I remembered my oldest son's anger when my mother died at the hands of the Russians. He still vented his rage now, against his own people. I vowed that Shayan would not become what my son had become. I would not allow him to follow the reckless path of revenge and anger and self-destruction. I would not allow him to become like me.

"I understand how you feel," I said simply.

"How could you ever understand?" he spat. "You have lived a protected life. Your husband is a warlord. You live in a walled compound. You have never known suffering. You have never been used. You have never felt dirty. You have never been betrayed, or lied to, or cheated. You will never understand."

I thought for a long while before I spoke. I could see myself in Shayan. I did understand his anger and his thirst for revenge and his disappointment. Most of all, I understood his broken heart. I knew that before he could dream again he would need to give up his right to get even. Revenge would never slake his rage.

I sighed and decided to take an enormous risk. I told him my story. The words poured out of me with a clarity and passion that startled me.

At first, he seemed skeptical, but as my tale tumbled out of my soul, he listened intently. I spoke for three hours and I wept often. It seemed surreal to be speaking all my secrets aloud. As I told him my story, I felt as if I were standing outside my body, watching a stranger tell the riddles of my life.

It comforted me to know that someone who cared about me understood my suffering. For once, I was not alone in my grief. I experienced a profound cleansing as I exposed the secret shame of my failed love and my disappointed heart. Even though he was only fifteen years old, he had the wisdom of an adult. Shayan had lived three lives in his short time. He listened with an intent focus that calmed my soul. For the first time in my life, someone understood. He wept with me and we held one another and we grieved together. We grieved over our broken hearts and our stolen lives and our abandoned hopes. We vowed that we would not give up our dreams. We vowed that we would rediscover love. We vowed that we would forgive our enemies. And we vowed that we would forgive our lovers.

That night I dreamed of my father. I often dreamed of him in those days. I suppose it had something to do with my aging or perhaps my years of melancholy. In my dream he held me like I imagined he would have held me had he lived to enjoy my childhood. He held me close and warm and comforted. He smelled of tobacco and leather and forest. And as I lay my head along his broad shoulder, he stroked my hair with his roughened hand and whispered to me in French-tainted Persian. And though my dream did not possess the clarity of language, I knew that he understood my sorrow. And that he was proud of me. And that he wanted me to be content.

My Enemy

My enemy is my lover
And in the muddy trenches
We lob the weathered stones
Of our mothers and our fathers

We desecrate the land
And sow the fields in salt
We cut the trees and fill the wells
And make slaves of our own children

And in the waylaid rubble
We sit in deep regret
And wait upon the other
To repent

Chapter 35

Order— نظم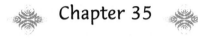
Summer 1994

Alocal governor in the Kandahar region kidnapped two teenage girls in July of 1994. His men shaved the girls' heads and took turns raping them in their camp. Mullah Omar, a wounded resistance fighter teaching in a local religious school, organized fifty of his students and freed the girls with only a dozen or so rifles. They hanged the warlord from the barrel of a tank. Inspired by Omar's bold leadership, students from around the Kandahar region joined his movement by the hundreds. They called themselves the Taliban.

Later that year, two commanders in the same region got into a fight with a group of local men arguing over a young boy whom both groups wanted to sodomize. They killed several of the civilians in the fight and the militia commanders took the boy for themselves. The Taliban, growing stronger by the day in number and in moral zeal, freed the boy by force.

I felt a strong foreboding when I heard of the growing Taliban legend. In some ways I welcomed the stability they would bring. The entire country longed for peace. But I feared that they would take law to an extreme that might be worse than chaos. In many other regions of the country, lawlessness and civilian abuse had become intolerable. I understood why the people longed for protection. They had endured war too long. Everyone had lost someone. Many had lost everything.

We enjoyed a certain sense of order under Massoud's command in the Panjshir Valley. For the most part, the fighters in the valley had exercised restraint. I feared what might happen if Massoud were assassinated.

I was grateful for the order in my little world. My trees produced succulent fruit. My vegetable garden gave me far more than Shayan and I could consume, and when my husband was home, he gorged himself on the fresh produce. I knew that while he traveled he ate mostly meat and flat-bread. When he left, he would always take a few melons and a sack full of cucumbers and tomatoes. If I had a field where I could grow grain and mustard seed for oil, I would need nothing.

Shayan helped me with the garden. Even with one leg he was stronger than me and he easily doubled the amount of work I could do. We fell into a routine, rising early to work in the garden and resting in the afternoons. At night we would read. Sometimes we would talk for hours about what we had read.

We seldom touched one another, but at times, when we sat together drinking tea, my need for companionship was so great that I had to refrain myself from reaching across the mat to caress his face. He slept in Huma's old cabin, while I slept alone in the cottage. There were times when I nearly asked him to sleep on the floor of my cottage. There were times when I felt so lonely I thought I could not bear it. I was grateful, though, for my tidy world. I knew that not more than a day's journey from us, people lived in the tyranny of chaos.

Early one summer morning, as I pulled the ripened tomatoes from their vines, I noticed that something had stripped the leaves from the entire bottom quarter of one of my plants. Only barren stems remained. I looked for the caterpillar culprit, and found him stretched along the bottom side of the next leafy stem, happily munching on the tender leaf above. I mindlessly plucked him from the stem and crushed him under my sandal. I felt a grim satisfaction at the feel of him popping under my foot and a mild annoyance as his soft, green innards gushed out to soil my opposite ankle. Shayan laughed.

Later, as we sat together in the shade and rested, I thought of the necessity of power. "Someone must take charge," I said to Shayan. "Someone must bring judgment and discipline. Without order there can be no life."

He stared at me curiously and seemed perplexed. "What brought that on?" he asked.

"The caterpillar," I replied, and he laughed.

"You're going mad," he teased.

It took me the rest of the day to understand what I was trying to say to him. I was grateful for the order that my husband had created around me. The walls and the armed men who loafed in the larger compound shielded me. In the safety of my shelter, I had my books and my garden and my companion. I had everything I needed.

Love has a certain sense of order. Love has rules. Those rules provide stability. The promise of faithful love establishes a trust and a sense of calm. But broken promises unleash chaos. Love cannot exist without security. Trust builds security. Promises kept build trust.

I was grateful for all the things my husband had provided for me. I knew he did those things out of love. But I longed for not just an ordered world; I longed for an ordered heart. I wished he could bring order to our troubled past.

In some ways, it was unfair of me to expect so much from him. He could have taken a second wife or abandoned me, but he had not. I suppose I should have been content. It had been twenty years since he betrayed me. I was nearly fifty years old and I still longed for something that would never happen. I was grateful for the serenity of my garden, but I still held him responsible for the enemy that continued to consume my soul. A fat worm had been eating away at my heart for twenty years. Only barren stems remained.

The Taliban swept through the Kandahar region, seizing the territory of one local commander after another. In most cases, the warlords surrendered to them without a fight. They captured Kandahar city and the surrounding provinces. By early 1995, they were shelling Kabul in an attempt to take control of the capital and defeat Massoud. Despite the heavy losses the Taliban suffered from Massoud's entrenched fighters, they continued to grow in their influence across the country. Through the course of 1995, they garnered significant financial aid from Saudi Arabia and military support from Pakistan.

My husband fretted over the growing Taliban influence. Foreign money and military logistical support increasingly steered toward the Taliban and his business out of Pakistan began to suffer. The situation deteriorated and by mid-1996, the Taliban gained majority power in the country. On September 26, 1996, Massoud retreated from Kabul. The next day, my fiftieth birthday, the Taliban marched triumphantly into the city and established the Islamic Emirate of Afghanistan. By the end of the year, the Taliban controlled three-quarters of the country. Massoud still commanded the northeast quadrant, and Dostum the northernmost regions, but the rest of the nation was Taliban.

The Taliban went to work immediately, setting up the most austere Islamic government in the world. They closed movie theaters, banned music, and burned books. They would not allow men to shave, keep pigeons, or fly kites. They required women to wear a burka. Unless a male relative accompanied them, they could not appear in public. They could not attend school past the age of eight and even that little education was limited to the study of the Quran. Anyone caught educating a female beyond the age of eight faced a severe beating or execution without a trial. Women could not visit a male doctor unless accompanied by a male chaperone, and female doctors did not exist. The Taliban required women to cover the ground-floor windows of their homes so that passersby could not see them. Taliban enforcers roamed the street and imposed immediate judgments. They beat Kabul women with rods for wearing heels, or for laughing, or for being caught in public without a male relative. In the villages, life remained less restricted, and in the Panjshir, life changed very little.

Days in my garden prison languished to months and years. My husband spent a great deal more time in Pakistan. I saw him about once a month. The Panjshir remained under Massoud's control while the Taliban in Kabul issued their petty decrees, regulating the mundane details of every issue of life. I would not have been allowed to have my books in Kabul. The Taliban raided stores and homes to destroy any books or magazines that contained pictures. Since most of the enforcers were illiterate, they ignored books containing only text. They considered anyone who loved literature, or film, or education, or music, or art their enemy. I would not have fared well in Kabul.

In 1998, the Taliban defeated Abdul Dostum, the commander of the northern provinces. He went into exile, leaving the Panjshir Valley and the northeast region the only area of the country outside their control. Our region of safety slowly shrank and everything hinged on Massoud. He was the remaining voice of sanity in the country.

At nineteen, Shayan had become surprisingly agile on his one leg. I supposed his years of training as a dancer helped. He would sometimes entertain me by dancing with the use of one of his crutches. I would clap my hands and sing a traditional chorus and he would sing and dance on one leg, sometimes pirouetting two full circles as he balanced on his crutch. He could leap from a squatted position on one leg, and with his crutch held high overhead, do a full twist in the air to land as nimble as a cat. He had amazing comical skill. I was the only one he felt comfortable performing before and my gales of laughter always seemed to make him happy. He was the only person who could make me laugh.

In early November 1999, Shayan traveled to Kabul to visit his family. He returned near the end of the month and swung gracefully on his crutches into the compound. He smiled when I greeted him, but I could see that his smile was forced and insincere. I assumed that his family had not been happy to see him. I prepared a fresh pot of tea, and we sat together on a mat near the compound wall, enjoying the warm sunshine.

I let him brood for a while and finally asked, "How was your family?"

"They're doing as well as could be expected," he replied. "Kabul is a little better now that the war has ended, but everyone is afraid. The Taliban are vicious. I saw them cut a man's hand off right in the street. They accused him of stealing. There are many foreign Arabs among them."

"Is that why you seem disturbed?" I asked.

He shook his head and stared into his tea. The sun had warmed the compound wall and I leaned against it, letting the warmth soak into my back. I decided not to push him. He would talk when he was ready. I drifted off to sleep. As I relaxed, my empty teacup slipped from my hand and glanced off my ankle. It startled me and I jerked awake. Shayan was staring intently into my face.

"You are fortunate to live here in this protected place," he said.

"It is my prison," I replied.

"Yes, I suppose it is a prison, but all of Kabul is a prison. You have more freedom in your prison. Here, you can think what you like and speak what you like and behave as you like.

"I should not have gone to Ghazi Stadium," he continued. "She was my neighbor and my family knew her." He grew quiet, staring again into his cold, unfinished tea. When he finally spoke, it was deliberate, through clenched teeth.

"She was accused of murdering her husband, of killing him with a hammer while he slept. She had seven children. My family knew her. They said she had two beautiful teenage daughters. Her husband would beat her and her daughters every night. He was a police officer. She put a sleeping pill in his food, but when she went into his room to kill him, she lost her nerve. Her oldest daughter killed him with a four-kilo hammer, one blow to the head. The Taliban arrested the woman and beat her until she confessed. She told them that she had killed him herself. She protected her daughter."

Shayan looked directly into my eyes, then lowered his face, staring unseeing into the milky surface of the tea he had ignored drinking. "I am ashamed I went to the stadium," he said. "My family and all their neighbors walked there. I went with them. The stadium was full. I think we have seen too much war. It has been three years since the Taliban took Kabul. I think we were thirsty to see blood."

He began to cry, then to sob, then to heave in grief. I kept quiet, not knowing what to say.

"The Taliban drove her into the stadium in the back of a Toyota pickup truck," he continued. "Two women police officers, both wearing a burka, helped her down and she walked slowly toward the center of the field. The women Taliban walked beside her. She would take a step, then pause, and then take another step. The stadium fell silent. It seemed to take forever. When she reached the middle of the field, she stopped and knelt. After a moment, she stood up and ran, but one of the women caught her and forced her to kneel.

"A Taliban soldier moved close behind her. He aimed a Kalashnikov at her. His first shot caught her square in the head. I saw blood spray from her face and I saw the bullet tear into the ground a few feet in front of her. She fell forward and he shot twice more."

My heart sank. I felt deeply for Shayan. I reached across to touch his arm but he pulled away from me. "I am so ashamed," he said again.

I leaned forward and gently took the cold cup of tea from his hand. As I stood and turned away, I tossed the untouched tea into the garden.

"Her name was Zarmina," he said simply.

Somehow, hearing the woman's name touched me deeply. "I am sorry for her," I said.

I sat back on the mat. The warm sun felt good on my face. The wall radiated its healing warmth deep into my back. I felt comforted resting against the thick earthen surface. After a long rest, Shayan looked at me.

"Do you love me?" he asked.

For a moment, I was speechless. "Of course I love you," I finally stammered. "I love you like I love my own sons."

"Why do you love me?" he asked, his eyes expressionless, his face passive.

I squirmed against the wall, feeling awkward. "I do not know why I love you," I replied. "I could say that I love you because you are bright and intelligent and interesting, but I did not know those things about you when we first met. I could say that I love you because I appreciate your courage and your sense of humor but when we first met, I only felt sorry for you. Even then, I loved you."

"I love you because of what you have done for me," he said. "I love you because you cared for me when I was dying. I love you because you have educated me, and have been my friend. I am very grateful for you," he said softly.

"And I am grateful for you," I answered. "I would have gone mad without having you here as my companion."

I realized, as I leaned against that sun-warmed wall, that I loved him before I knew who he was or who he could be. I loved him without knowing that he would return my love. I loved him out of pity and out of compassion. As I taught him, he had become more like me and I had become more like him. We had shared the past seven years together and we had changed together. I had not known that he would inspire me. I had invested love into him not knowing what I would receive in return. I was grateful for that day when my husband brought him to me, shattered and broken and lifeless.

"Do you think God loves us?" he asked.

"I do not know," I said, somewhat perplexed.

"I think God must love us," he continued. "But I think he must be disappointed in us. I wonder if he is grateful for us. I wonder if he is happy with what we have become."

"I do not know much about God," I said. "I do not know what he thinks of us."

"Do you love your husband?" Shayan asked.

"I do not know," I said. "I once loved him, but he has disappointed me."

"Did you love him when you first met him?" he said.

"I did," I answered. "I remember it as if it were yesterday. I loved him instantly."

As Shayan gazed at me, I understood. I had loved my husband before I knew who he was. I had loved him in hope. I had invested my love into him in the hope that he would return that love to me. And for some years he had loved me in return. In those years, I had been happy. Perhaps if I loved my husband as I had in the beginning— perhaps if I loved him with the same hope I had in those days—perhaps he would return that love to me. Perhaps he would be grateful.

I thought for a long while about what Shayan said. He was right, but he was young and inexperienced. He did not know the disappointment of broken hope and broken dreams.

"It is difficult," I said simply.

"Yes," he replied. "It is difficult."

My Forgotten

In the corner of my garden
I sowed a night jasmine
And through a lonely winter
I forgot that it was there

I forgot the nightly visit
Of frail scent
I forgot the delicate hush
Of tender hope

And on a tearful evening
In the season of my sorrow
I caught the elusive fragrance
Of my forgotten

And I remembered in my mourning
The sweetness and the wonder
Of summer dusk
And jasmine

Chapter 36

Hear—شـده درک
Spring 1999

It took me five years to establish my little garden within our compound. My pomegranate tree began to produce. The apple trees had grown well above the height of the wall. Their thin, pliant branches hung heavy with small, sour fruit. I did not have enough room for many trees, but I was pleased. In a few more years, I would have all the apples, pomegranates, and plums I could want. I even had an almond tree in the corner. It was one of the first trees I planted, and now it was producing well. I worked hard to fertilize the trees with manure and I watered them daily. My husband was amazed at how quickly they grew.

In the vegetable garden, I grew onions and leeks and garlic. I planted rows of eggplant and okra and tomatoes. Thick heads of cabbage and leafy greens lined the area near the wall and I even managed to grow some purple carrots that grew half as long as my forearm and as thick as my hand. When I cooked them with ghee, they were sweet and rich and irresistible. My husband loved that dark, heavy dish and he would eat them until he could not move. I would not pull the carrots unless he was home.

Under the almond tree, I placed a stout wooden bench with a backrest. A carpenter in the village had carved it by hand from the remains of an old roof timber. He had carefully sanded the gnarled surface as smooth as wax. I would sit there every morning with my tea and rub my hand along the soft, rounded edge of the weathered timber. It reassured me to touch that antique wood. I imagined the thick timber must have been more than a hundred years old. It had endured season after season supporting the heavy, packed earthen roof of someone's home. I pictured it shattered by a Russian bomb and pulled from the rubble by an enterprising carpenter. And though it had been sawed into smaller pieces, it felt ancient and resilient.

In the crotch of my almond tree, a tiny pair of finches built a nest. I watched them through the spring as they fretted about the compound, gathering grass and twigs and leaves. In a short while, they constructed a tight little home. They were bright little birds with brilliant red breasts and heads. Their melodious song made my heart overflow. When they completed their nest, the female stood on its edge and sang through the morning. She stood as straight and tall as her little frame would allow. She strained her neck skyward and warbled a lilting melody that filled the courtyard. I imagined that she was singing, "Look what I have done. Notice me." I laughed aloud and embarrassed myself over my unfettered appreciation for that bold little bird.

Everyone has the need to be noticed, I thought. Everyone wants to be heard. Everyone wants to tell his story. Everyone wants his life to count for something. Everyone wants to be appreciated and understood and desired. I lived a shrouded life in the corner of a walled compound in the midst of a wasted, dysfunctional land. My walls were my veil and irrelevance was my prison. My children were men, two of them fending for themselves in the chaotic, bustling streets of Lahore and Rawalpindi. Only God knew where Zemar was.

I assumed he was involved in the siege of Kabul. Their letters were less frequent and much less personal. My husband roamed the war-ravaged land with scheming, violent men who greedily devoured the sad little crumbs the foreigners had left behind. I sat in obscurity on my little bench while events beyond my control ensnared me in my pleasant prison. If not for my books and for Shayan, I would surely have gone mad.

I suppose the need to be heard was what touched me so deeply when I shared my story with Shayan. Somehow, it helped to know that someone understood me. Someone knew of my suffering and my disappointment and my shame. In a strange way, I thought, Shayan is a more intimate friend to me than my husband. I realized, in that coherent moment in my garden, that love is much more than living with someone and having his children and sharing his dreams. Love is honesty and transparency and a sense that your lover understands you.

My husband knew of my frustration and my anger, but he did not understand. He might never understand. His shame clouded his perception just as anger and disenchantment clouded mine. The humiliation of my failure as his wife had trapped me in this secret life of suffering. My life counted for little if no one understood.

My husband was my companion and my lover, but he was not my confidant. I suppose that the only confidant I ever had was my mother. I had wanted to tell her about my husband's business and his treachery, but I could not because of my embarrassment. I regretted that shame had paralyzed me from intimacy with her and I mourned that I had never enjoyed such intimacy with my husband. Perhaps that sort of relationship was possible between a man and a woman, but not in Afghanistan, and not in my marriage.

How I wished I could stand on the edge of my nest like that little finch and ring out my clarion song. It would not matter to me whether that song was exquisite or melodious. It would only matter that someone heard it and took note.

In a sudden rush of memory, I recalled a time when Mother and I saw a woman slap her little girl in the market. The child had stolen a pear and slipped it into her pocket. The fruit was large and impossible to hide. But the little girl was young and she thought that if the pear could not be seen, it would not be noticed. Her mother slapped her on the cheek and wrenched the fruit from her hand. Tears spilled down the child's cheeks and she cast her gaze down toward the dusty ground.

"That woman will break her child's spirit," my mother had commented quietly. "She will berate her and ridicule her and demean her until she has no sense of value for herself. The poor thing will marry a man who will dominate her and she will live her life in mindless obscurity. She will vent her frustrations upon her own daughter."

I was too young to understand my mother's cynical prophecy, but I remember looking up at her and admiring her wisdom. I remember thinking how fortunate I was to have a mother who did not slap me and who would listen to me and reason with me and care for me.

"Everyone wants to be understood," she had continued. "Even a child wants her life to count for something. Even a child is embarrassed when humiliated. We all want our life and our story to have meaning. This is a deep human compelling. We need someone to understand our story and appreciate our value.

"Someday you will have children. I hope you will be grateful for them in the same way I have been pleased with you. I hope you will see their value and that you will help them to know how much they mean to you."

I understood, as that little finch bellowed with all the shrill bluster her little lungs could marshal, that gratitude was an important necessity to love. I did not think my husband was grateful for me. He needed me to look after the compound while he was gone. He needed me to cook for him and wash his clothes and fulfill his physical need. But I did not think he was grateful for me. If I were honest, I had little appreciation for him. If I were honest, I blamed him for my malaise. I admired his strength and his determination and his intelligence, but I did not respect him. I was not grateful for him.

I was grateful for Shayan. I thanked God that I had someone to confide in. But how I wished that person could have been my husband.

When the finch laid five dainty blue-speckled eggs in the nest, the male fed her. He would flit to the edge of the nest and regurgitate seeds into her open mouth, then disappear for more. When after two busy weeks her brood hatched, he continued feeding her, retching into her open mouth time after time. He had endless energy.

She, in turn, would regurgitate the twice-digested seed into the ever-open mouths of her young.

I watched them morning after morning and marveled at their persistent cooperation. This was not their time of love, I thought. It was their time of labor. But their love carried them through their labor and they served their hungry brood tirelessly. I wondered whether duty or desire motivated the little male. It seemed, for the most part, that they were too busy to be concerned with desire for one another. I once counted thirty-seven trips he made from outside the compound to the nest. I lost interest and lost count. He continued through the day diligently feeding the female and fretting over their nest.

I was certain that he served her out of obligation, but I was equally certain he served her out of love. They were grateful for one another. Sometimes, in the evening, they would sing together. Their harmony would lift above the evening chorus of crickets and frogs and above the clamor of the larger nearby compound. The male would sit on a branch and crane his neck and bellow a clear, warbling call. Sometimes she would answer him and sometimes she would sing along with him. They adored one another.

Shayan laughed at me when I told him about the birds. He called me sentimental, using one of the new words he had learned. His developing vocabulary pleased me and I made no comment. But I did touch the side of his face, as my mother had done to me as a child. I told him that I was proud of him. I told him that I could not ask for a better friend. I told him that I hoped he would find someone who would respect him and listen to him and understand him. I told him that I hoped he would have a meaningful life.

Listen

One night I held my pillow
Tight around my face
And into that downy bosom
Poured silent tears

And when my sorrow spent
I lay in the quiet roar
And listened to the night
In weary vigil

My lover lay beside me
His breathing murmur soft
Soft and placid
And careless

Chapter 37

Creation—نشیآفـــر
Summer 2001

I bought a pregnant ewe from a village shepherd and kept her in a little pen in the back corner of my garden. She had an injured hind leg and the shepherd did not think she could deliver her lamb. She favored the leg and bleated pitifully. Her cries annoyed my husband.

A few days later, Shayan held her down while I fitted her with a splint. She bellowed through the ordeal and struggled mightily against us, but once she was free, she stood on all fours, her heavy belly suspended on a sagging back. A conspicuous quiet fell over the compound.

"That's better," my husband said, smiling. He had watched us from my garden bench in stoic skepticism, flipping his cigarette butts over the garden wall. "She might make it after all."

Sometime in the night about two weeks later, she delivered a little male. He did not bleat in the night, but we awoke in the early dawn to his impatient fuss. I ran to the pen and watched as he furiously suckled, butting his head upward into his mother's udder to stir the milk's flow.

I let them both loose from the pen and they wandered about my garden. It was late summer and I had harvested most of it. The few remaining plants were dry and past bearing. I let the ewe stray at will and she grazed contentedly. The lamb danced around the compound on spry, stiff legs, the remains of his umbilical cord still attached to his belly.

He wandered from the ewe and panicked, crying pitifully, searching for his mother. She bleated her reply, but he had not yet learned to follow her voice. He scampered about, confused by the echo within the garden walls.

My husband sat cross-legged on a mat in front of our cottage, drinking his tea and enjoying the warm morning sun. The lamb found him and nestled its face between his back and the cushion he had leaned against the wall. It butted angrily, searching for an udder. My husband laughed so hard that he spilled his tea. With a tender smile, he lifted the lamb, his wide palm under its belly, and carried it to its anxious mother. He watched contentedly as they rejoined. Peace was once more restored to our little world.

"That was kind of you," I said.

He looked at me with a soft expression that I recognized from the time of our courtship. I did not know whether I had been blinded to it, or whether he had lost the capacity for that gentle look somewhere along the way. I only knew that it moved me to see it once again.

"I should have carried you to your mother like that, once—long ago," he said.

"I suppose I should have bleated more persistently," I said with a warm smile.

He looked at me for a long, heart-still moment. A sudden sadness hung about him, gloomy and heavy, like a water-bucket yoke across his shoulders. He just stood there, tired and aged.

Embarrassed, I turned back toward the ewe. The lamb's tail wagged anxiously as he continued his tireless search for nourishment. The ewe stared across my thirsty garden, contemplative and still. I could not help but smile.

My husband left for Rawalpindi the following day.

When I was a child, I thought only of the day. I never considered the day past or the day to come. I did not think of weeks or months or seasons. I did not plan and I did not regret. I did not fret the future and I did not grieve the past. I lived for the day. As a woman, I thought of seasons and years and decades. In the summer of 2001, I entered into the season of my reflection. It was to be a brief season.

I was working in the compost pile the day I fell ill. Each morning, one of my husband's men would bring a quota of five buckets of fresh manure that he had collected from the field near our compound. We no longer cultivated that field and the grass was thick. Young boys grazed their sheep there and the droppings were plentiful. The man who brought the manure was old and sullen. He resented his chore. I gave up my attempts to befriend him.

Shayan and I covered the manure every morning with a layer of earth and straw and clippings from the garden. When the fruit trees cast their leaves, we would pile them near the compost and mix them into the pile until they were depleted.

We turned the pile every evening, working in the sheep manure. We watered the pile and layered the top with fresh straw to keep the odor down. The soil underneath was rich and dark. In the pungent rot between the soil and the upper layer of fresh compost, a healthy colony of earthworms thrived. Sometimes, in the cool mornings, I could see a faint cloud of steam rising from the compost.

The day was warm and the sun relentless. Shayan and I had finished turning the top of the heap and I stood leaning on the handle of my turning fork. I felt dizzy and dropped to the ground, resting on my hands and knees. In a moment, Shayan was at my side.

"Are you all right?" he asked.

I did not answer. My strength had simply drained away. I thought at first it was from the exertion of turning the compost, but this was something I did every morning. I struggled to rise, then sank back to the ground. It took a good twenty minutes for me to regain enough strength to hobble back to my cottage. I walked trembling and bent over with a sudden and urgent pain in my right side. Shayan swung easily beside me on his crutches and helped me lie down inside. I did not have the strength to rise until the next day.

The sharp pain lasted a few days, and finally subsided into a dull, distracting ache. The weakness stretched from days to weeks. By the end of June, I was jaundiced. My skin and the whites of my eyes were the color of milk tea. My urine was as dark as old blood. Shayan fretted over me like a nervous young mother and began to annoy me with his smothering. I snapped at him often, and then felt guilty over my sour disposition. He ignored my irritations and my apologies.

After six weeks, the jaundice had not cleared. By the time my husband had returned from Rawalpindi, I knew the illness was serious. I somehow knew that I would not live much longer. I did not merely have hepatitis; I had something far more serious.

My husband was shocked when he saw me. I had lost at least ten kilos and scarcely had the strength to make it to the toilet. He surprised me with smothering worse than Shayan's. I did not know how to respond. I was grateful for the attention, but it perplexed and embarrassed me. I was still ashamed of him. I still resented him. I was unprepared for his kindness.

I did not fear dying; I welcomed it. The burden of my sorrow made me weary. I thought it would not be such a bad thing to lie down to rest.

The imams taught that God took seven kinds of earth and from it formed the first man. He breathed into the man and he began to live. God named him Adam and from his side he took the substance to make the first woman, Eve. I thought it would not be such a bad thing to return to the place of my origin. I would go back into the earth, like the dead plants and dung in my compost heap. I would give my life back into the source from which God made it. I did not know if the paradise the imams spoke of existed. I hoped it did. I only knew that I was weary. I was weary of my unanswered questions. I was weary of my struggle. I was weary of my disappointments. I was weary of it all.

I thought that cabin would be my final resting place. As I lay there, very little in my life remained that mattered to me. I loved Shayan. I loved my boys. And I was beginning to love the man who so earnestly tried to serve me. I wanted to tell him that I loved him and I wanted to tell him that I had forgiven him, but I could not bear the emotional toil. I was simply too weary.

I wanted to close my eyes and slip into a silent coma and drift away. I wanted to die in my sleep, peacefully drifting off to the paradise that I hoped existed. My husband wanted to take me to Islamabad, where they could run tests and possibly cure me. I dreaded even the thought of that impossible journey. I told him so, but my protests were weak and meaningless. He would do what he felt best, regardless. I no longer had an opinion. Someone else now made my decisions.

I began taking small doses of raw opium. Shayan gave them to me without my husband's knowledge. I did not know if he would approve or disapprove, but I did not have the energy to argue with him, so I did not risk bringing it up. I took one little ball every morning with my tea and though it made me nauseous, it greatly eased my pain. It also constipated me. Shayan told me that I should use the pipe to avoid those complications and to make the opium more effective, but I was reluctant. I had railed against opium all my life and it seemed hypocritical to take the drug. But my pain became unbearable at times and I could scarcely function without it.

In late August, we left for Islamabad. My husband made a simple cot for me and rode with me in the back of one of his trucks. I remember the journey up to the Khyber Pass as if I were seeing it through the eyes of someone else. The jostling of the truck was unbearable as I passed in and out of consciousness. I remember the truck lurching as the driver shifted gears on the steep switchbacks. I remember the whine of the weary transmission as the truck labored up the mountain. I remember my husband's face peering down at me from above. It was a kind face, etched in concern.

The opium and the pain and the disorientation of traveling a long distance in a vehicle without windows made the journey miserable beyond description. I desperately wanted the voyage to end. But in brief moments of coherence I saw my husband's face marvelously illuminated by a flickering shaft of light that sliced into the truck. A tarp stretched across the back opening and it flapped noisily, allowing sharp bursts of light to pierce the dark interior. Those focused strobes etched his face deep into my memory, as if my eyes were a camera and my mind were the film.

This is not the face I remember from my young dreams, I thought. It was softer and longer and tired. It was a kind face—a face that had traveled a long and difficult journey. Weary, haunted eyes sunk hollow and deep into that weathered face. It was a face filled with regret, I thought.

"I love you," I said feebly.

But I do not think that I spoke aloud. I heard the words in my mind and I think my lips parted in speech, but I do not recall hearing the sound of my voice. I could not tell if he heard me. I hope I do not die today, I thought. I hope I can remember this moment and remember this face and remember what it is I want to say.

I wanted to say, "I forgive you."

A line of trucks, stretching for miles, blocked the Khyber Pass. My husband sent the truck back home. He and one of his men carried me through the pass. It took four hours, but the journey was so much better than the riotous clatter of the old truck. Wrapped in a thick blanket, I swung gently between them on the loosely hung canvas stretcher and watched the sun set over the mountains. I watched the stars appear one by one out of the deepening sky and I thought of my husband's weary and craggy face.

"Please God," I whispered. "Do not let me die just yet."

Creation

I wish I could remember
The dawning of our love
Oh, that I had captured it on canvas
Or described it on parchment
Or chiseled it in stone

I wish it were as pure
As the day it formed
I wish it were sharp
And lucid and undisturbed
In my recall

I wish that I could give you
What we had in the beginning
When we were innocent
And childish
And trusting

Chapter 38

Legacy—مـيراث
Fall 2001

I awoke in a sterile, unadorned room in a private hospital in Islamabad. My husband slumped in a chair in the corner, snoring. Mildew and water stains stippled faded green walls that at one time were probably intended to be soothing. The room smelled of disinfectant and old urine. Noise from a busy street filtered through the rusted screen of a small window high on the wall. An IV bag hung from a metal rod stand and a clear plastic tube ran from the bottom of the bag and disappeared under a wide piece of tape on the inside of my right arm. I tried to speak, but could manage only a dry, raspy croak from my parched throat. My husband stirred at the sound and I managed to squeak out that I was thirsty.

It took him a few moments to comprehend what I had said. In a groggy stupor, he brought me a small plastic water bottle. I gulped greedily from the bottle and coughed, spraying the sheet with the cool water.

"Easy. Easy," he said.

"How long have I been here?" I asked.

"Two days," he replied. "The doctor has run some tests and he should have the results tonight."

"I want to go home," I said as I sank back into the heavy fog of sedation.

When I awoke again, it was dark and the street noise had subsided. My husband was speaking to a tall, lean man in a white lab coat in the corner of the room. I could not see the man's face but I could see my husband's. He was frowning.

I strained to hear what they were saying, but their voices were low and their words did not make sense. By the time I realized they were speaking in Urdu, the fog had settled over me again and I drifted back into the place I had been in my sleep. It was a desperate, confusing place with no water.

I do not know how long I lay in that overly soft bed. At times I awoke to daylight and at times to dark. I did not know if days or hours passed. At times my husband was in the room and at times I was alone. I remember the kind face of a woman who pressed a wet cloth to my lips. I remember the furrowed, contemplative face of the doctor who stood over me and scribbled on a translucent red plastic clipboard.

At last I awoke to a sort of coherence. In spite of my long period of rest, I was weary. Although I was hungry, I could eat only a little. A young, patient Pakistani girl fed me with a plastic spoon. The soft, rich porridge felt warm and pleasant and nearly brought me to tears. I held the gruel in my mouth and tasted deeply of its creamy richness before swallowing. The sweet milk tea that followed soothed me. I left a small portion of the delicate spiced drink in my cup, breathing in the pleasant aroma until it was cold.

I felt increasingly alert through the day and that evening, Babur stepped quietly into the room. He hesitated at the door, awkward and cautious. At thirty-three, he had grown lean and strong like his father. A neatly groomed beard framed his dark face. His freshly pressed, sand-hued kurta whispered as he crossed the room and when he leaned over to kiss me, I caught the hint of cologne. I fought mightily, but could not stop the tear that wedged itself from the corner of my eye and trickled easily down the side of my face.

"You are a vision," I said admiringly.

I wanted to tell him how much he looked like his father, but I did not know if that would make him proud or insult him. I knew his father was not happy with the career Babur had chosen. When he finished college, he had taken a job in the British High Commission, where he worked as a translator. He was fluent in Dari, Pashtu, Urdu, Arabic, English, and French and he understood scores of Afghan dialects. His management skills made the greatest impression, and within a year he was promoted to a position as an administrative assistant. I could not have been more proud of him.

We talked for a while about his job and about his life in Islamabad. He seemed ill at ease and kept glancing back at the room door. He finally interrupted me and said that he had someone he wanted me to meet. He opened the door and a beautiful Pakistani girl stepped shyly into the room. She was tall and thin and graceful. She wore an elegant Indian-style silk top that reached her knees and black slacks. I noticed the pointed toes of Western heels peeping out from the perfectly tailored bottoms of her slacks. Subtle, elegant gold embroidery trimmed her teal top. She wore her hair uncovered, pulled back and bound behind her. Her skin was light and flawless. I looked into her dark, doe-like eyes and loved her instantly.

She seemed unaware of her natural grace. She turned her face toward Babur, her body following the subtle curve of her elegant neck in a slow, sensuous pivot. Her top shimmered faintly and I caught the gentle swell of her pert breasts moving beneath it. She stepped close to Babur, grazing his arm ever so softly with long, elegant fingers, and peered up into his face with searching almond eyes. He held her gaze in gentle reassurance. There seemed to be a deep, almost spiritual bond in their brief look. I wondered if they had made love.

"Hello," I said hopefully.

"Hi," she replied. In a single step, she crossed the room and extended a slender hand to me. Her grip was cool and tentative. Her fragile fingers easily encircled my small hand. I held her hand for a long moment and gazed carefully into her face. Shy, she looked down, nervous and unsure. She was gorgeous.

"This is Farhana," Babur said hesitantly in Urdu.

"She is beautiful," I replied.

I held her hand until she was uncomfortable and after a long while let it slip from my grasp. She took a step back and stood near Babur. He touched her reassuringly and smiled. A long moment of awkward silence followed while we all tried to think of something to say.

I did not want to interrogate her, but she intrigued me. It was obvious they were in love. I did not care whether Babur's father approved, but I knew that her father would not likely consent to her being in the company of a young Afghani man, no matter how successful he might be.

"What do you do?" I asked.

She was a student, twenty-eight years old, finishing a doctorate in medical science at the University of Islamabad. They had met during her first year at the University of Lahore. Babur had graduated that year and moved to Islamabad.

They texted one another on their mobile phones and had video chats every weekend from Internet cafés. We did not have mobile phones in the Panjshir and the Internet was something I had never seen. It sounded like a useful device.

She had moved to Islamabad for her graduate studies. Her father was an army officer and her family lived in nearby Rawalpindi, in the cantonment area. My heart sank when I heard her father was an army officer. He will be furious, I thought, when he finds out about this love match.

"Does your father know about Babur?" I asked cautiously.

"He has different plans for me," she said.

After an awkward silence, Babur said matter-of-factly, "We are in love." He said it with a sense of finality, as if that settled any argument I might bring.

Yes, I thought, you are in love. I smiled and told them how happy I was for them. I told them I knew they were in love the moment I saw them. I told them love would find a way. And I thought of how I adored Babur, my youngest, my baby. Of my three boys, he looked most like his father. But of them all, he was most like me.

He was not pragmatic or cunning or purposeful. A deeper motivation drove him. He was driven by love. He did not care that the medieval engines of family and language and culture arrayed against him. He did not consider the consequences. His irrational commitment to a mysterious obsession made perfect sense to him. He was my legacy.

But I knew the tyranny they would face from both their fathers. I knew that uncles and aunts and cousins and brothers would join the fracas. Her mother would rage and threaten and conspire. There would be thinly veiled threats. It could be dangerous for Babur.

I wanted to tell them that they were not doing a wise thing. I wanted to plead with her to come to her senses and forget about Babur. I wanted to reason with them and tell them they did not understand love. I wanted to beg Babur to let the girl go if he loved her. I wanted to tell him that his love for her would destroy her. But their tender look silenced me.

I beckoned Farhana to the edge of my bed. I pulled her close and kissed her on the cheek. I breathed in the sweet scent of her hair and I whispered into her ear, "Have courage, little one.

True love is a rare gift. Be faithful to it and it will be faithful to you."

And as they left my dreary little room, I felt my heart go with them. I felt bound to them in hope. I could not bear to disappoint them with what I knew they would soon face. I hoped that love would be different for them than it had been for me. I could bear my own disappointment, but I would never be able to bear theirs.

I hoped that the dream my mother had planted so deeply in me would become their dream. I suppose my illness had forced me to think beyond my life. And I thought of the impossible desire that Mother had given me, the longing for faithful love. Though I had abandoned the wish of that love ever becoming mine, for Babur's sake I could not cast off hope.

I had slept too much over the past days and I lay through the night restless and hurting and sleepless. I understood, through that long watch, my mother's hopeful promises when she spoke to me of love. I was thankful I had never told her of my disappointment. I would have broken her heart.

I watched the easy blush of dawn through the dingy window of my room and listened to the sound of the awakening street below. I could hear the hiss of compressed gas as street vendors fired up the burners on their oil kettle cookers. The smell of dough frying in old grease drifted up through my open window and nauseated me. As the dawn became the day, the sound of buses and horns and conversations rose in a blaring crescendo. I wanted to go home. This is not the place, I thought, where I want to finish my life.

My husband visited me midmorning in the company of the doctor. They entered the room grim faced and hesitant. I knew what they would say and I was glad. I was glad there was nothing they could do for me. I did not want to stay in this dreary place. I did not want treatment, or surgery, or medication. I wanted to go to my valley and rest in the hush of my garden. I wanted to join my mother and my father.

My Will and Testament

I have no field to leave to you
No gold or silver or treasure
No home to shelter you
No well to slake your thirst

I leave to you my hope
My dream of faithful love
May it feed and comfort you
And soothe your transient heart

May love be true to you
As you are true to love
May the gift of love
Be your sacred fortune

Chapter 39

Confession—اقــرار

We crossed the Khyber Pass back into Afghanistan on the morning of September 9, 2001, the day the al-Qaeda assassinated Ahmad Shah Massoud. I fell in and out of consciousness and did not comprehend the news until a few days later. Two foreign al-Qaeda members from Tunisia posed as journalists and during their interview with Massoud, they detonated a bomb that had been hidden in their video camera. He died in a helicopter, on the way to a military field hospital in Tajikistan.

I awoke two days later in an unfamiliar room. The thick earthen walls smelled damp. The rope bed I lay on appeared to be newly constructed and it creaked when I stirred. My husband lay beside me, sleeping quietly. In the dim light, I could make out the sparsely furnished room—a table and two chairs, some utensils on a shelf over the table, and a wood-fired clay stove in the corner. The stove bore no charring and seemed unused. On the table, I recognized my little shortwave radio and the dishes on the shelf above the table appeared to be from my cabin. It bewildered me.

My husband stirred and sat up, rubbing his face. "Where are we?" I asked.

He did not answer, but rose and strode across the little room to the simple timber door. He fumbled a bit with the latch and finally opened the heavy door. I knew instantly. Beyond the door, a little meadow flowed down a gentle slope and beyond the meadow, the remnants of a neglected apple orchard. We were in the old cabin. We were in my poppy field.

He stood in the door and turned back to me, smiling like a schoolboy. "You could not have given me a greater gift," I said. I could not stanch the flood of tears. For several minutes I could not speak, or even breathe. He looked concerned and started toward me, but I held my palm up for him to stop. I did not want anything to move. I wanted time to stand still. I wanted to remember him framed in the door by the morning sun. I wanted to remember his boyish expression. I wanted this moment to last forever.

"I gave your uncle the money he would need to rebuild the cabin and told him he could have it and the land when we are finished with it," he said. Then he lowered his gaze. I assumed he was ashamed that he had used the phrase, "Finished with it." I pretended I had not noticed.

"I love you," I said softly. And though my voice was weak, this time I knew he heard me. He hung his head again. After a long, awkward silence, he mumbled something about going down to the village for supplies.

In the little kitchen attached to the side of the cabin, he made tea. He poured it into a thermos and helped me from the bed to a mat he had placed in the sun in the front of the cabin. I leaned against the earthen wall of the little house and watched his figure recede and disappear as he rounded a bend in the trail down into the valley. In the distance, the village was awakening, but it was too far away to hear its stir.

My field was untouched by the war. The tiny house that stood on the foundation of the older cabin was almost identical to the original. It was constructed, like many of the buildings in the Panjshir, of compressed earth and stone, topped by a flat, heavy timber roof. Stone and earth, compacted over the roof timber, formed a thick seal.

The apple orchard was in shambles. I was surprised that any trees remained. Most of the trees in the Panjshir had been destroyed in the war. Even the stand of pines behind the cabin had survived. I thought I would go up into those pines and find the stream where I had first seen my husband, but I was too weak to rise. I knew the meandering path to that quiet little brook by heart and as the wind stirred in the pines, I imagined myself going there. I closed my eyes and pictured the majestic man I had seen that day, watering his horse beside a moss-covered stone.

When he returned three hours later, I was in the same position I had been in when he left. He sat heavily beside me and said, "The lion of the Panjshir is dead."

My heart sank. If Massoud was dead, our valley was no longer a refuge. "What will happen?" I asked.

"I do not know," he said. "But the al-Qaeda is responsible for his assassination. It was a well-planned suicide mission. Life here will never be the same. Padsha and Babur should remain in Pakistan. Zemar will fight with the others to defend the valley. We are fortunate that he was not with Massoud at the time of the attack. My business will be affected, but we will be safe here, at least for now."

We sat for a long while in silence. Our time together in this isolated cabin might be difficult, I thought. We were strangers, stranded and vulnerable and awkward.

"Most of your books and your personal things are in a set of trunks under the bed," he said. "I told Shayan he is free to visit if he likes. I think he will come."

I rested through the day while he busied himself setting up the house. In the afternoon he began gathering the firewood we would need through the winter. That evening, as he sat at the table and I lay on the bed, we heard on the shortwave of the attack on the World Trade Center in New York. We listened together well into the night until finally, wearied of the news, he turned off the radio and lay beside me on the bed.

I could not sleep. When I realized that he was not sleeping either, I asked him if he was in danger from the Taliban.

"There is greater danger from the Americans," he said. "This is a major victory for the al-Qaeda—first Massoud and now a successful attack on the Americans. The Taliban will be energized and they will try to consolidate their control of all Afghanistan. We should expect them to attempt to enter into the valley. I think the resistance will be strong, even without Massoud. This valley is difficult to penetrate and we still have fifteen thousand men. But the Americans have been provoked. They will want blood."

Another long silence followed, broken by his timid, almost inaudible voice. "I have sinned against you," he said.

I lay stunned beside him. I did not know what to say, nor where to begin if I were to speak. I lay still, listening to the persistent pounding of my heart.

"I believe I am being punished for my sins," he continued. "I am ashamed of what I have done. I will tell you everything."

And he poured out his confession. It happened so quickly and so unexpectedly that I could barely

comprehend it. There had been five women alto-
gether—a young, single woman in Rawalpindi,
whom he provided with a house and a living
allowance; two prostitutes; a married woman
who lived on the east edge of Kabul; and Ivana.

I let him speak without interruption. Within a
few minutes, he finished, and the room fell silent
again. I lay stunned. His confession moved me,
but left me with a troubling, unsatisfied feeling. I
had many questions.

He had spoken with little feeling and he left
out most details. He spoke with remorse, but
shed no tears. He had asked for my forgiveness
at the end of it all.

I thought for a long while before I spoke.

"I am willing to forgive you," I said. "But before
I forgive you, I want to understand why. I want
to know why I was not enough for you. I want to
know what I did to drive you away from me. I
want to know if you are confessing to me because
of your guilt or because you love me. I want to
know if you ever loved me. I want to know why
you have waited until now to confess to me."

I cried. The choke welling up in me caught me
by surprise and confused me. I had dreamed so
long of this day, the day he would confess. But

instead of relief, I felt overwhelming sadness. I felt as if I were grieving my loss anew. Most of what he told me I had long ago suspected. Nothing he could say would have surprised me. But it hurt me and angered me. I had many questions.

I wanted to know if the women were pretty. I wanted to know if he loved them. I wanted to know if they pleased him more than I had pleased him. I wanted to know what they had that I did not have. I wanted to know a hundred details about each of them. As I tried to piece together a lifetime of deception, it only confused me more.

He patiently answered my questions at first with as little detail as possible. As I persisted, he told me more and I began to piece together some of our past. But the more I asked, the more irritated he became. I realized, after three hours of interrogation, that I was ruining what little hope there was for our reconciliation.

"I am sorry," I heard myself saying. "I know you want me to forgive you, but I need to understand."

That September night, we began our journey back. In those transparent moments when he did not try to excuse himself for what he had done, I felt closer to him than ever. It felt odd, to hear him tell of things that ripped my heart from my chest and yet drew me closer to him than ever. At times he would slip back into his old habits. He offered evasive answers to my questions and was distant. In those times when he protected himself, I felt myself becoming angry and unreasonable. I learned to allow him to see my hurt without judging him for what he had done. He learned to be honest and transparent and defenseless.

"Have you ever killed a man?" I asked one morning.

We were in our usual sunrise spot on a mat in front of the cabin enjoying the warming sun, drinking our tea. The fall weather had settled in dry and cool. I had wrapped myself in a heavy blanket. He still wore the cotton trousers he'd slept in and a light kurta. Though we sat side by side, I had turned myself toward him, anticipating the question I wanted to ask. I watched his face carefully.

He must have known that I was testing him. I had asked him that question once before, early in our marriage. But still, he hesitated. He rubbed the side of his jaw with his thumb and my heart sank. He is stalling, I thought. He probably won't lie, but neither will he tell the truth.

He remained quiet for a long while, then looked directly into my face and said, "I have killed three men."

"That is a heavy burden for one to carry," I said.

"I have no regrets over two of them. They were common thieves. I caught them during the siege of Kabul, stealing from one of my trucks. They fired at me, turned to run, and I shot them both with a pistol. My men threw their bodies into a dry gorge."

"And the other?" I asked.

"The other was hardly a man, just a boy," he said. "He was thin and beardless, about eighteen or nineteen, and cunning. He was one of my drivers. I had been kind to him and even helped his family when the al-Qaeda killed his father. He thanked me by stealing from my shipments. He had even organized some of the new boys to work with him. They were siphoning off large portions of ammunition intended for Massoud and diverting them to Hekmatyar. I wanted to make an example of him."

I watched him intently, drawn into what I hoped would be the beginning of modest transparency. His face softened and he gazed thoughtfully into the distance, carefully avoiding eye contact. I took it as a hopeful sign.

"One of my men informed on him, and that night I beat him with my fists in front of the men. We were camped at an abandoned school with some of Massoud's fighters. I beat him till he was nearly unconscious, then sat on his chest and put a knife at his throat. He looked up at me and began to cry. I told him to die like a man, and I cut his throat. His blood sprayed my face and the men laughed. In that moment, my rage turned to regret, but I could not let the men see my weakness, so I laughed along with them. I told them that this is what would happen to anyone who betrayed me."

I thought he would weep, but he did not. He stared unseeing at the horizon, passive and troubled and alone. Tentative, I laid my hand over his. His felt cold to my touch.

"Sometimes," he said, "the boy comes to me in my dreams. He looks up at me with pleading eyes and he cries for his mother and his father."

Then he wept.

I let the quiet rule the moment and I felt the gentle warming of his hand beneath my palm.

My field did not have the power to heal me, but it did rejuvenate me for a season. I suppose those virgin tears I had sown in this meadow of my childhood bore a certain fruit in the season of my reflection. Sometimes that fruit was sweet and sometimes it was bitter. Sometimes the fruit brought tears and sometimes it brought resentment. Sometimes we wept and sometimes we laughed. Sometimes we mourned our loss together and sometimes I mourned alone.

I suppose we shared a thousand hours of conversation in that long winter of confrontation. Some nights we sat cross-legged on the bed as a candle burned on the table beside us and we talked until the dawn. I was frail and thin and often in pain. I had no desire for physical intimacy. I suppose he did not find me attractive. But his thirst for conversation was endless. And I remembered with great sadness those early days of our marriage, when young and bursting in bloom, I would bring him his tea. We would sit on our mat together and talk until the moon was full in the night sky. We would make love and hold one another until the heat of our bodies forced us to move apart. We would drift off to sleep with hands and knees touching and through the night, I would feel the caress of a tender hand along the curve of my hip. I remembered those nights with deep, sometimes inconsolable grief.

I could not pinpoint when we lost our love for conversation. Perhaps it happened when I focused on raising our three boys. Perhaps it was when he had begun to prosper, and he diverted his attention to his business. Perhaps it was when my bloom began to fade that he lost interest.

"When did you lose your love for me?" I asked one evening.

"I'm not sure," he said.

He spoke quickly, sometimes answering my questions without pause. I did not recall him ever talking to me that way, even during the time of our betrothal.

"I've thought quite a lot about that," he continued. "I've thought that perhaps it was when the boys began to grow. You wanted them to be children longer than I did. I wanted them to become men. I wanted them to be like me."

I didn't say anything. I had learned, in this season of our intimacy, that the truth was more important than my opinion. I waited while he sorted through our past.

"Sometimes," he wondered aloud, "I think that I never loved you until now. If I had loved you, I would have been true to you. But I remember having affections for you, even when I began to spend time with the other women. Maybe my affections for you were just affections. I mean, maybe I did not have the capacity to truly love any woman. Maybe I was just thinking about myself. I think that love and affection are two different things."

"Did you feel the same way toward the other women?" I asked. "Were your affections for them any different from your affections for me?"

He paused before he answered. I knew he was not trying to misdirect me this time. He was grappling with the truth of his relationships.

"I did feel affections for them," he said. "I know that must hurt you to hear that. But I also know that you want me to be honest with you. I did love them, except for the prostitutes."

That hurt. It hurt to be reminded of the prostitutes, but it hurt even more when he acknowledged his feelings for the other women. I knew that Ivana, the woman he kept in Rawalpindi, and the married woman in Kabul had probably been close to his heart. I suspected that the exotic foreigner had been especially dear to him.

I did not reply. I was beginning to move past my anger. The more open he was, the less anger I felt. I did not cry much anymore, but I did feel an abysmal pain that never seemed to diminish, like the cancer that grew persistent and demanding in my belly.

"I'm sorry," he said.

He apologized nearly every day. Sometimes I felt guilty over that. Sometimes I felt that it was wrong of me to allow him to humiliate himself, but it helped me to know that he was remorseful. His penitence became my only consolation. I knew that someday I would not need the constant reassurance of his regret, but for now it served as a salve to my heart.

"I understand," I answered. "Thank you."

When we sat across from one another on that lumpy cotton pad, and when I spoke to his softened face in the wavering light of an exhausted candle, I understood that there were things about him that only the passage of time could alter. Though I could have done many things differently, I could not have changed him. I had to wait for him to change himself.

I abandoned my formalities in that season and I began to call him Amir. I suppose that addressing him as Husband had been my most grave mistake. As a young woman, I had thought that love was defined by my obedience to the law—the law of husband and wife, family, village, tribe, God. But when the time of lawlessness came, and when order collapsed under the rule of war and hatred, the law failed me. I should not have devoted myself so thoroughly to right and wrong. I should have given my heart to leniency. But how can a selfish young girl understand grace?

My mother had known the way of grace. I had once complained to her about my husband but she had not joined my discontent. She had simply gone quiet. She had never criticized him or taken my side against him. She had a unique gift to straddle the world between right and wrong without choosing sides. But I always knew what she believed. She believed in the way of love.

I wondered if she had ever had occasion to forgive my father. I could not imagine him committing an infidelity but with the wisdom of age, I knew that it could have been possible. I had no way of knowing. I only knew what Mother had wanted me to know about him. I suspect that if she had needed to forgive him, she would have kept it to herself. I suspect she would have preserved the noble parts of him to give me as my legacy. I suspect that she loved me too much to disappoint me. She wanted me to know true love.

In the forgiving light of those candlelit nights, I saw things in Amir that I had not noticed before. Age had softened his face. The pads around his eyelids sagged, making his eyes appear smaller and less intimidating. His piercing black gaze had become more searching, more curious, and sometimes he even looked frightened, as if the inquisitive, unsure little boy had returned to those aging eyes' dark surface—the windows to his soul.

"What could I have done differently?" I asked one afternoon. He was pulling heavily on his water pipe. He had packed the bowl too tightly and he struggled to draw the sparks from a fresh charcoal ember down into the tobacco.

It was about a week after *Eid al-Adha*, and pleasant. I found myself in the constant pursuit of warmth in those days, and I was grateful for the mild weather. Amir had given up cigarettes for me, but still smoked his hookah in the afternoons. It seemed a fair compromise and besides, I enjoyed the familiar gurgle of his old pipe. At last, he ignited the tobacco. He sat back, contented, enveloped in a fresh cloud of dense gray smoke.

"I know you must think that my mistakes were because of something you did or didn't do," he said. "That if you had been a better wife, a better lover, a better mother, things would have gone differently. I know you think this was your fault. I know you blame yourself, but you cannot take the blame for this. I made the choices I made. I did those things, not you."

He had neglected his pipe as he spoke and went to retrieve a fresh coal from the stove. It was difficult to accept that I could not have changed the outcome of our life together. I felt powerless. It was unfair.

"Surely I could have done something," I said when he returned.

"You could have done some things differently," he said. "But that would not have changed me. I would still have been the same person. I would still have made the same mistakes. You have been a good wife and a good mother."

I never accepted that. I could not. Perhaps my stubbornness or my pride would not allow me to surrender. But I could not give in to helplessness. I chose not to argue with him about it. We disagreed on so little in those days that it seemed irrelevant in the light of how he had changed. He had become the man I always wanted him to be. My mother would have liked this man, I thought.

He asked me questions during those days. He mined the deep-heart treasures that I had hidden in my decades of reading. He wanted to know what my mother had taught me. He asked about my father.

In January, a heavy snow fell in the upper reaches of the Panjshir. A deep, pristine blanket covered my field. I had great difficulty staying warm and Amir kept a fire stoked in the little cabin stove. I would often stand in the entrance of the cabin for as long as I could bear. I would gaze across the pure white mantle that graced my field and flowed down the mountain slope to touch the edge of the village below. And I would whisper to the quiet, my gratitude.

My Journey's Rest

I stood in reverent hush
Among the midnight pines
As heavy snowflakes whispered
To the forest floor

And I thought about our love
And of its delicate splendor
And the way its diffused grace
Once captivated me

I thought of all the years
And all the fragile memories
That layered at my feet
Like those pure crystals

And I cast down my regrets
My sorrow and my shame
And swore in that pure moment
To forgive

And those sober towering sentinels
Witnessed my heart vow
And bowed their graceful limbs
In honor

I told them I was grateful
Content to lie with you
And embrace the winter still
The season of my rest

Chapter 40

Bloom—کــردن شــکوفه
Spring 2002

I think it surprised Amir that I lived through the winter. My doggedness kept me alive. I was determined to see the poppies bloom. "They are the flower of love," my mother had said.

The poppies in my meadow did not blossom in profusion. They did not bloom in thick patches like the flowers that dotted the valleys. Sparse and random, they competed for survival with the grass and wildflowers. They were wild and uncultivated and unrestrained. They were as unexpected and vulnerable and frail as love itself. They are the flower of love, I thought. And yes, as my aunt had said, they are the flower of death. I suppose that death is the only thing as persistent as love.

As spring emerged, bright and hopeful, I found myself returning to the days of our beginning. Through that torturous winter, there were times when I thought that love had never been my possession. There were times when I thought I had possessed love, but lost it somewhere on my journey. There were times when I thought I did not know if love existed. And finally, the time had come in that winter of my life that I had discovered love.

I spent long hours in the morning sun, gazing into the distance. I mourned the lost years. I mourned my youth. I wanted to feel that my life had counted for something. I wanted to feel that someone would miss me when I was gone—that someone would mourn my passing. I suppose that I measured the significance of my life by those who mourned me, and the degree of their mourning. I sorted through many memories and many regrets within those memories. I suppose most of all I regretted that I no longer had the time to enjoy what had come to me so late in life. I knew there was little time remaining to enjoy love's contentment.

On the darkest night of that winter, Amir helped me unearth what I had lost. With little to do in those dreamy days, he fell in love with my books. He loved it most when I read to him. One evening, I read aloud from the poetry of Hafiz of Shiraz. As I read the poem "True Love," he began to weep. His weeping became a wail that rose above the song of a winter storm howling through the tops of the pines. And in that keen of mourning, he broke. The burden of a lifetime of regret was finally more than he could bear. He crumbled under the load like an aging, weary pack animal. He tried to rise from the edge of the bed, where he sat with his back toward me, but his legs would not support him. He fell on the mat near the bed and lay facedown on the floor and begged me to forgive him.

"I am so sorry for what I have done," he said. "I am sorry that I robbed you of something so precious."

And in that weakest of his moments, when he was broken and humble and desperate, I loved him more than I had ever loved him. I had loved him in the beginning because of his strength and his mystery. But I loved him now for his humble remorse. It comforted me to know that he had accepted the weight and the consequence of what he had done. When he accepted the burden of my sorrow, he was finally selfless. And when he was selfless, he was true to love.

When he called himself a fool, I knew that he understood selfishness. He understood that giving himself to another woman with no regard for me was the most self-centered and most hurtful thing he could have done. He understood that he had not only betrayed me, he had betrayed his children and himself.

When he pounded his forehead against the floor and cursed his father, I knew that he understood the unfairness. I knew that he understood my vulnerability. I knew that he understood how shameful it was to use someone as an object of lust, with no regard for that person's heart. I knew that he was not just angry with his father; he was angry at the system he helped to perpetuate. He was angry with his clan and his culture and our way of life.

When he wept until the mat was damp with his tears, I knew that he understood my suffering. For the first time in his life, I knew that he was sorry he had hurt someone else. I saw, in that dark of night, that he took my pain upon himself. And as he crumbled under the load of my anguish, he displayed a sorrow beyond expression. He grieved as a woman would grieve and he poured the bitterness of his soul onto the floor of that lonely cabin. When he rushed out into the night to fall on his knees in the meadow, I knew that his tears were joining those that I had sown so many years ago. I knew that at last he understood true love.

On a clear morning, when the poppies had fully bloomed, I asked him to take me up into the pines to the place where I first saw him. Though it was scarcely a hundred meters to the little stream, it was not an easy journey and I leaned heavily on his arm. It was much smaller than the stream I remembered from the time of my virginity, but the water was still clear, and fresh and cold. And as we sat on the edge of that stream I gave him my diary.

He held it in his weathered hands with reverence and I watched a single tear trickle down the side of his face and onto the dark leather cover. I thought of the hands of the man who had fashioned that book—the hands of my father. And I knew that the man who now held my most cherished possession was worthy. He was worthy and he was forgiven.

That night my father came to me as if in a dream. He spoke to me in his native tongue and motioned for me to follow him up the gentle rise of a forest trail. I did not understand his words, but I understood his intention. I understood the language of his heart and his heart called me to come with him. His heart called me to trust him.

We trekked through dark, moss-blanketed rhododendron forest cathedrals, then towering pines, and finally, lush meadows of wildflowers. At first, I followed him without reluctance. I had searched for him all my life. I had searched for that lean face that gazed into my little-girl soul from the black-and-white photo resting on my mother's mantel. I followed that gentle, sun-leathered face with unconditional trust.

But the more we climbed out of the valley, the more reluctant I became. I stopped often to look wistfully back along the trail. He would pause, waiting patiently for me to continue. There was no urgency in him, but neither was there hesitancy. He seemed determined to continue his journey. A deep, mysterious longing urged me to follow him, while a yearning nostalgia beckoned me to return. I could not choose between the want for my father and the want for my husband. Both were the call of love.

Somehow I knew that once I had taken my father's path, there would be no returning. I knew what I was leaving behind, but I did not know what lay ahead. I was content with the love I had known and I wanted to return to that love. But I was attracted to the love I had not known. Perhaps, I thought, there is a greater love than I have known. Perhaps there is a love more true.

As the forest thinned, he continued upward, picking his way among the scattered boulders. The trail vanished as we steadily climbed until finally, we reached an impossibly steep rise. I held to the tail of his coat as he continued the ascent and I felt the surge of his strength. We crested on a snow-blanketed summit and turned to gaze back along the way we had come. Below us, a valley flowed into the distance. Beyond the valley, brilliant peaks stretched to the horizon.

The land was beautiful in the way the aged men of my childhood had described it. The land was beautiful in the way I remembered it in my longings. Thick forest blanketed the mountain slopes and rich, green patchwork terraced the lower hills. In the valley, a strong and clear river descended through fertile pastures.

As I gazed on that land, I knew that my journey had ended. And I knew in the valley below, a man would mourn my departure. And I knew his love was true.

True Love

Place me like a seal over your heart
Like a seal on your arm
For love is as strong as death
Its jealousy unyielding as the grave
It burns like blazing fire
Like a mighty flame
Many waters cannot quench love
Rivers cannot sweep it away
If one were to give all the wealth
of one's house for love
It would be utterly scorned

Song of Songs 8:6–7 NIV

A Word From Carey

I envisioned *The Poppy Field Diary* as an allegory on the principles of love and the journey to forgiveness. I chose Afghanistan because of my experience in the Himalayan culture and my love for those mountains. But I also chose it for the raw and aged wisdom that emerges from that primitive life. I wanted to explore the lost voice of the ancients. As I studied love's tenets, I was profoundly influenced by four nonfiction books: *The Art of Forgiving* by Lewis B. Smedes helped me understand the process of forgiveness; *The Seven Levels of Intimacy* by Matthew Kelly helped me understand the progressive nature of all relationships; *NOT "Just Friends"* by Shirley Glass helped me understand the agony of infidelity; and *Once Upon a Secret* by Mimi Alford helped me understand the paralysis of shame. I highly recommend these books, especially if you've been hurt and need help on your journey to wholeness.

I have a liberal arts degree in philosophy, religion, and English literature. I've traveled in more than forty-seven nations and have enjoyed soul-searching conversations with people from just about every culture—African, Asian, European, Latin American, Middle Eastern, Russian, and tribal—as well as just about every religion: Christian, Muslim, Jew, Hindu, Buddhist, Sikh, Jain, animist, atheist, and agnostic. I've been just about everywhere on this amazing planet and I've discovered that people of every race, creed, and culture experience disappointment in their fellow human beings. I don't know why, but it seems that we can't help but hurt one another.

I hope that you find true love on your journey. And if you are disappointed somewhere along the way, I hope that you find the grace to forgive.

Appendix—The Path of Forgiveness

On August 11, 2013, Harold Knapke, 91, and his wife, Ruth, 89, died eleven hours apart. Their children said, "It was their final act of love." They were nine days from their sixty-sixth wedding anniversary.

Harold and Ruth met in elementary school, romanced through World War II, and married soon after the war. They were inseparable through life. Ruth contracted a rare infection and it became apparent that she would not recover. Soon after, the children noticed that their father's health was also failing. He died three days later at seven thirty in the morning.

When their father passed away, the children gathered at their mother's bedside, and though she was not coherent, they told her, "Dad's up there waiting for you."

She died at six thirty that night. The family laid the couple to rest in a joint funeral.

"Mom and Dad were ordinary people," their daughter Ginny said. "I guess if people can learn from their story it's that there is a love that lasts."[1]

On October 7, 2013, Floyd Nordhagen, 92, and Margaret Nordhagen, 88, were killed in an automobile accident in rural Washington state. The state trooper responding to the accident said he found the couple holding hands.

Their son Marv said later, "They were always holding hands. They still cuddled a lot."

"He would give her a hug and a kiss every day. Whenever they were near each other, he would reach for her and she would reach out for him," said their daughter-in-law Lynn.

The couple had been married sixty-eight years.[2]

On February 27, 1859, on a sidewalk in Washington, D.C., Congressman Daniel Sickles gunned down Philip Barton Key, United States attorney for the District of Colombia and the son of Francis Scott Key. Known as one of the most handsome men in Washington, Philip Barton

Key was entangled in an affair with Sickles's much younger wife, Teresa.

Most of Washington knew of the affair, including President James Buchanan. Sickles heard of his wife's infidelity through an anonymous note that read, "There is a fellow, by the name of Philip Barton Key, who rents a house for no other purpose than to meet your wife. He has as much the use of your wife as you have. With these few hints I leave the rest for you to imagine."

Though Sickles was a philanderer himself, he could not bear the humiliation of his wife's infidelity, and in a jealous rage he confronted Key and shot him three times with a derringer.

The murder trial spun into what many consider America's first media circus and the first use of the "crime of passion" defense strategy. Sickles's defense attorney, Edwin Stanton, who was eventually appointed Abraham Lincoln's secretary of war, argued that Sickles was caught up in a "transport of frenzy." Sickles was acquitted.

Daniel Sickles sent his wife, Teresa, to an isolated country home and visited occasionally. Teresa died of tuberculosis at the age of thirty-one. Daniel lived a long and ignominious life, leaving a trail of seduction, scandal, blackmail, and corruption. With no military experience, he commanded the 72nd New York Volunteer Infantry during the Civil War. He exposed Union rear positions to a Confederate attack with an ill-advised movement of his troops in the battle for Gettysburg. He later served as President Ulysses Grant's minister to Spain, where he had an affair with Queen Isabella II and a tempestuous second marriage to one of Isabella's young attendants. In 1897 he successfully lobbied Congress for a Congressional Medal of Honor for his fiasco at Gettysburg, where he had lost a leg.[3]

The great Jewish philosopher king, Solomon, had it right when he said, "Love is as strong as death." Throughout history, passion has accounted for moving heroism and disgraceful rages, beautiful romances and heartrending betrayals, honorable and dishonorable legacies. There is no cause and effect more prevailing than love.

If love is as certain as death, forgiveness is equally certain. The act of forgiveness is perhaps one of the most misunderstood, yet most necessary, functions of our expressed humanity. Some forgive too quickly and never reason through to the root of the conflict. Some bury their hurt and pretend it never happened. Some think they can forget what happened, and some try to erase the memory by abusing drugs or alcohol.

Everyone, at some time or another, will find the need to forgive someone of a disappointment, an offense, and perhaps even a betrayal. We cannot help but love and we cannot help but hurt one another. And just as everyone will at some time need to forgive, everyone will at some time need forgiveness.

Statistics vary widely, but a 2011 Kinsey Institute study estimated that 23 percent of men and 19 percent of women would have a sexual affair at least once in their marriage.[4] Combining those statistics suggests that at least one partner strays in approximately one-third of all marriages. One-third of all American marriage partners will find the necessity of separation, reconciliation through forgiveness, or keeping a secret from his or her spouse. Those statistics hold true for most Western cultures and are escalating in other world cultures due to rising Western influence, the introduction of women into the workforce, and the increasing connectedness of social media.

Shirley Glass, author of *NOT "Just Friends"*, found that the vast majority of affairs begin in the workplace. According to Ms. Glass, most affairs do not start with sexual infidelity, but with the act of growing closer to someone other than one's spouse. Intimacy, she says, is where most affairs begin.[5]

Everyone, at some point in life, will experience disappointment in another person. It is inevitable. Something exists within us all that drives us to deceive and manipulate. We will all be cheated, stolen from, and made fools of. But when that deception comes from someone we love it wounds us at a deeply personal level that is difficult to comprehend and difficult to overcome.

Love Hurts

People we do not love or respect cannot seriously hurt us; it's the ones we care about who wreck us. The consequences of betrayal are directly linked to the intensity of the relationship.

Betrayal in a business partnership affects earnings and inflicts material loss. It is frustrating and may incite anger, but it's not necessarily emotionally devastating. Betrayal in a friendship or a love relationship, however, is demoralizing. It inflicts emotional, psychological, and even spiritual loss.

We are hurt to the same degree that we are emotionally invested. This is why families and marriages are sometimes dysfunctional. A child feels betrayed when his parents divorce and that sense of abandonment through betrayal will more than likely affect that child throughout his life. According to U.S. government statistics, children raised in single-parent homes are significantly more likely to: use drugs,[6] commit suicide,[7] exhibit behavior disorders,[8] commit crime,[9] perform poorly in school,[10] and be incarcerated.[11]

Adults who experience infidelity in marriage may be forever marred by a deep sense of mistrust. They may find it difficult to fully trust anyone again. A parent who watches her child abandon the family's values is wounded when that child betrays the beliefs of his parents. Loss through betrayal is directly linked to love, friendship, and intimacy.

Everyone Lies

"False words are not only evil in themselves, but they infect the soul with evil." —Socrates[12]

At infidelity's core is deceit. Deceit and broken promises crush affections. Lies undermine the principles of trust, fidelity, and compassion— essential values in healthy relationships. When a person fails in his humanity, he destabilizes those values and wrecks the relationship.

When someone betrays us, we question that person's ethics. From that indignation we question the morals of every person. As we judge human nature, we might move to question the value of life, leading to cynicism and depression. Betrayal might even lead a person to question the meaning and worth of his existence.

Romantic betrayal rouses a sense of loss and disappointment unlike any human experience. There is no life event that shakes a person more deeply. The death of a loved one might move us, but death, unless it is an unexpected one, is something we are psychologically prepared to face. There is nothing that can prepare us for the waste of betrayal, unless we are predisposed to believe that all people are entirely motivated by greed and selfishness. And if that is our conviction, we have already abandoned any hope of human goodness.

Lost Hope

"And though in all lands, love is now mingled with grief, it still grows, perhaps, the greater."
—J.R.R. Tolkien, *The Lord of the Rings*

Love is the foundation of hope. When love is undermined, hope is weakened. People who have abandoned hope through hurt often make generalized judgments, such as, "All men are liars," or "all women cheat," or "all daddies eventually leave." They make judgments because they have given up hope. If there is no hope for goodness, there is little hope for true intimacy. Anything that causes shame, regret, embarrassment, or guilt is not intimacy, but abuse. Lies are abusive.

People who have lost hope often drift into shame or anger. Because they feel unworthy, those who live in shame will accept abuse that others would find abhorrent. They feel, deep down, that they deserve the mistreatment. They often fall victim to angry people who are acting out their hurts. It's amazing how these two seem to find one another. They feed one another's need for unhappiness—classic code-pendency.

Lost Dignity

"Everyone needs a sense of shame, but no one needs to feel ashamed." —Friedrich Nietzsche

In the summer of 1962, Mimi Alford, a nineteen-year-old intern in the White House, lost her virginity to President John F. Kennedy in Jacqueline's bedroom. That event was the beginning of her eighteen-month-long sexual relationship with the most powerful man in the world. She kept the affair secret for nearly forty years, telling only a few close friends. In 2002 historian Robert Dallek published *An Unfinished Life: John F. Kennedy*. His book mentioned an interview he discovered in recently declassified documents that referenced an inappropriate relationship Kennedy had with a "tall, slender, beautiful" college sophomore. In May 2003, Celeste Katz, a reporter with the *New York Daily News*, confronted Ms. Alford regarding the relationship and asked if she had been the young intern. Mimi was sixty years old.

In 2011 Mimi Alford published a compelling and very believable account of her relationship with Kennedy in her book, *Once Upon a Secret*. She describes the public exposure as "liberating."[13]

Secrets have power. They intimidate, they shame, and they paralyze us with a sense of unworthiness. They destroy love. It took Mimi Alford a lifetime to conquer her fear and shame. Her secret crippled her emotionally and destroyed her first marriage. With no sense of dignity, she lived in humiliation, accepting the abuse of a controlling relationship. Through public exposure she found peace and, interestingly, a supportive, healthy romantic relationship.

"When you welcome what you've been running from, your life is no longer shaped by trying to avoid it." —Kim Rosen, *Saved by a Poem*

Lost Intimacy

"I spent my entire life misguidedly cradling a secret and letting it close off, one by one, the doors to my heart." —Mimi Alford, *Once Upon a Secret*

There are many levels of intimacy. Sexual intimacy is the most primitive and the one least significant at the close of life. After the children have gone, and sexual energy has waned, and there is no longer an ambitious career drive, little remains but companionship. If there is no sincerity at that final stage, there is little to keep the relationship meaningful. Secrets may be the reason some elderly couples end their lives in argumentativeness. It is difficult to keep secrets buried for a lifetime. If there are secrets, there will always be a nagging suspicion. Lovers are perceptive.

Counselors have wide-ranging opinions on whether a person who has betrayed another should confess his indiscretion. Some believe that telling the truth, and a willingness to explore the reason for the betrayal with candid discussions, is the only way to reestablish true intimacy. It requires courage, humility, and, in many cases, someone to help negotiate the process. Those who believe in the power of truth believe that intimacy means more than living together, making love, raising children, pursuing a career, or sharing expenses. They believe that true intimacy means transparency.

If a couple chooses the path of truth, however, it must be a wholehearted commitment. Transparency is an all-in game. The offended partner then has the right to know whatever details he feels are necessary for understanding and moving forward to either reconciliation or separation. Many counselors insist on this process. Glass calls it "the story of the affair."

Others feel if there is no chance that the betrayed will find out about the affair, there is no need to confess. But, they caution, if there is a remote possibility that the affair might be discovered, it should be confessed. The problem with this approach is that there is always a chance, regardless of how remote, that the affair will come to light. There is also the problem of making a decision on the behalf of another regarding what is best for that person. Keeping someone in the dark scorns that person's value and belittles his intelligence.

In December 2011, a ninety-nine-year-old Italian, Antonio, left his ninety-six-year-old wife, Rosa. After seventy-seven years of marriage, they became the world's oldest divorcés. Just a few days before Christmas, Antonio was searching through an old chest when he found letters his wife had written to a lover in 1944. She had kept the affair secret for sixty-seven years. Though she confessed everything when Antonio confronted her, he refused to be reconciled. They had five children, twelve grandchildren, and one great-grandchild.[14]

Truth has a way of emerging. It sometimes seems to have a mind of its own. If you hold truth as a core value, or believe in its eternal value, you have no choice but to confess everything. If truth is a principal value to a healthy relationship, then truth will prevail. It may not be easy and there is the possibility that the offended person will not be able to cope with the truth. That is always the risk of intimacy. That is one of love's terrors.

Forgiveness

"Life is about love. It's about whom you love and whom you hurt." —Matthew Kelly, *The Seven Levels of Intimacy*

There are typically three responses to betrayal—forgiveness, dismissal, or anger. As Matthew Kelly points out in *The Seven Levels of Intimacy*, "The opposite of love is not hate but indifference."[15] Dismissal is the ultimate retaliation. Dismissal says, "As far as I'm concerned, you don't exist—you're not even worth my anger." The unfortunate truth about unforgiveness is that it usually hurts the person who has been offended far more than it hurts the person who has committed the offense.

"When we forgive, we set a prisoner free and discover that the prisoner we set free is us." —Lewis B. Smedes, *The Art of Forgiving*

Heartache, disappointment, and a deep sense of personal loss are the unavoidable results of betrayal. No amount of forgiveness will remove those crippling memories. But forgiveness does allow the healing process to begin. Without forgiveness there can be no personal healing and no moving past the bitterness.

Forgiveness also opens the way for the offender's healing. When we forgive, we initiate a process that may help heal the person who has lied to us. Without our forgiveness, the betrayer may never experience a sense of wholeness.

Grief

"I will not say, do not weep, for not all tears are an evil." —J.R.R. Tolkien, *The Lord of the Rings*

Grieving is a natural and healthy experience, and it occurs in predictable stages. It is a process. Because betrayal is personal and can only be inflicted by someone we love, the process must be personal, and it must involve grief. Not grieving over the death of a loved one is abnormal. In the same sense, not grieving over the loss that comes from betrayal is abnormal. Grief is a healthy human sentiment that, if suppressed, may lead to very unhealthy emotions and even physical illness.

When I was a six-year-old, I knew an elderly man who lived next door to my grandmother. He sat through the afternoons sipping bourbon. About an hour before sunset he would drive his vintage Ford to a nearby cemetery to grieve at his wife's graveside and leave a bouquet of fresh flowers from his manicured garden. He would return to his front porch sometime after dark and drink through the remainder of the evening. I never knew his story, but even as a child his grief moved me. He must have loved her. Perhaps there were regrets, perhaps secrets. I don't know. But I do know that he could not move past his heartache.

In 1969 Dr. Elisabeth Kübler-Ross published the book *On Death and Dying*. Her study helped inaugurate compassionate approaches to deal with terminal illness and personal loss such as the death of a loved one. Dr. Kübler-Ross outlined five stages of grief that are consistent with the experience of betrayal.

Denial: "This cannot be happening to me." Denial is an unconscious process that helps protect us from unbearable pain. It takes time for our minds to process emotional loss and one natural protective mechanism we employ, subconsciously, is to deny the facts. We choose not to believe what has happened and assume there must be some sort of misunderstanding. As more facts come to light, we slowly drift away from denial and begin to process those facts rationally. But as we do so, negative emotions begin to surface.

Anger: "Why did this happen to me?" Our sense of fairness forces us to try to find someone to blame. A betrayed spouse will obsess over the details of his partner's betrayal, trying to discover why it happened, or perhaps seek personal blame for causing it. A person who is facing the loss of a loved one to terminal illness will question the fairness of what is happening. A person who has lost a loved one to an unexpected tragedy may question God and, out of anger, even blame God. Anger is a natural response to the unfairness of betrayal, and it occurs during the processing of facts. When we understand and accept the facts of the betrayal, we begin to experience the emotion of betrayal—anger.

Bargaining: "Can we negotiate a reasonable settlement?" A person who is facing death from a terminal illness will often try to bargain with God, making promises in exchange for a few more years of life. A person who has been betrayed may want to bargain with the betrayer, thinking that there was some misunderstanding. But betrayal is not a misunderstanding. It is the result of deliberate choices. The only way past betrayal is forgiveness. Negotiation will not resolve the conflict or heal the wounds.

Depression: "I just don't care anymore." A person who is facing terminal illness will disconnect from loved ones as he begins to understand the certainty of death. This is a natural process and is a helpful part of grieving one's loss. It is unhealthy to remain in isolation, of course, but a time of pulling away and of solitude is a normal part of the grieving process.

A person dealing with betrayal may pull away from the betrayer and say, in essence, "I really don't care what happens to you." Though this may feel necessary for a period, as that person deals with emotional injury, it is not healthy over the long term. Isolation is unhealthy in both grief and betrayal. A person must express forgiveness to his betrayer. What the betrayer does with that forgiveness is his choice. He must live with the results of accepting forgiveness and reconciliation, or rejecting it.

Acceptance: "I am going to be OK." Acceptance does not mean that we are happy with what has happened. It does not mean we have no regrets. Acceptance simply means we have come to terms with our experience and that we are free of bitterness. A person facing death comes to terms with mortality. A wounded spouse accepts the pain of loss and reclaims what is salvageable of the marriage. An accepting person faces the embarrassment of a failed relationship and salvages something of value from the experience.

It's Personal

"The weak can never forgive. Forgiveness is the attribute of the strong." —Mahatma Gandhi

Betrayal is intensely personal. It is a direct assault on our values, our love, our personality, and our sense of self-worth. Because it is personal, it must first be internally processed. We cannot initiate the reconciliation of a damaged relationship until we have reconciled the conflict within ourselves. We must process the facts of the betrayal, process emotions, and process grief. Only then can we attempt to reconcile the relationship. We cannot, however, force another person to reconciliation. We can only extend the invitation for healing through forgiveness.

Reconciliation

"Forgiveness is the fragrance that the violet sheds on the heel that has crushed it." —Mark Twain

Reconciliation is relational. Conflict cannot be resolved without both parties' contributions. Though we might forgive someone of a betrayal, we cannot reconcile with that person unless he is willing. And we cannot move the process forward without humility. We must acknowledge the possibility that we have some share in the blame of the failed relationship. We must be willing to apologize and seek forgiveness for our personal failure.

In his classic book *The Art of Forgiving*, Lewis B. Smedes gives some of the most practical, wisdom-based instructions on reconciliation I've ever seen. He says:

- *The most creative power given to the human spirit is the power to forgive the wounds of a past it cannot change.*

- *We do our forgiving alone inside our hearts and minds; what happens to the people we forgive depends on them.*

- *The first person to benefit from forgiving is the one who does it.*

- *Forgiving happens in three stages: We rediscover the humanity of the person who wronged us, we surrender our right to get even, and we wish that person well.*

- *We cannot forgive a wrong unless we first blame the person who wronged us.*

- *We do not excuse the person we forgive; we blame the person we forgive.*

- *Forgiving is a journey; the deeper the wound, the longer the journey.*

- *Forgiving is not a way to avoid pain but to heal pain.*

- *Forgiving is the only way to be fair to ourselves.*[16]

Letting Go

"*People can be more forgiving than you can imagine. But you have to forgive yourself. Let go of what's bitter and move on.*" —Bill Cosby

I have a blind children's home in Nepal where for a number of years I helped a young blind man named Dhansing. When I first met him, he lived in a remote area of west Nepal, in the Jumla region. At that time it was a three-day walk from his home to a road, and that road was a treacherous one-lane rock trail that was unusable for vehicles half of the year. There was nothing attractive about the young man. He had no one to help him with his appearance and he was very poor. His clothes were usually full of holes, threadbare, and faded. He could barely afford soap, much less deodorant. When I would visit him, he would cook for me. Sometimes the food had grit in it and sometimes I wondered what he put in the pot, but meals with him were magical.

When Dhansing was an infant, he had an infection in his eyes. There was no medical care in his valley. His parents took him to a village shaman who treated him by pouring hot oil mixed with herbs into his eyes. He lost his sight. As he told his story to a group of us, one of the young Nepali men with me grew angry and said, "You should tell us who that man was. He needs to be held accountable for what he did to you." I'll never forget what Dhansing did. Leaning toward the young man who had spoken, he found his arm, rested his hand there, and said quietly, "I've let it go."

It was stunning and I fought back tears for quite a long time. This young blind man had accepted his past and truly forgiven his enemies. He had no bitterness. His life was a thing of beauty.

I provided for Dhansing for more than six years. He finished school, found a job teaching in a Nepali government school, rented a little village house, and married one of the girls in my blind children's home. He was twenty-one and she was nineteen when they married.

In a few months, they were pregnant. On November 5, 2013, Dhansing's wife, Pankali, gave birth to a beautiful six-pound, six-ounce little girl. I was anxious to see the child, hoping that her sight was all right. I should not have worried. The baby was gorgeous! She had clear skin, bright eyes, and gazed with alert and normal vision. They asked me to name the baby, and with the help of some Nepali friends, I named her Rosanie—"guiding light" in Nepali.

It's difficult to describe how moving that experience was for me. I thought of how that beautiful, sighted little girl, even as a toddler, would lead her mother and father through life. I thought of her playing tricks on her mom, hiding as quiet as a mouse in the corner and moving things in the room. And I thought of that bittersweet day when Dhansing and Pankali would give their pair of eyes to a man who would take Rosanie as his wife, a sacrifice of love as in *The Gift of the Magi*.[17]

I have received far more from Dhansing than I have given him. I have learned the beauty of letting go.

Find Your Way to Wholeness

Perhaps you began reading this appendix out of curiosity and continued because it spoke to your heart. Perhaps you've been hurt and unable to forgive someone. Or perhaps you know someone who has been devastated by a betrayal and unable to fully recover. If you're in a physically abusive relationship, get out now. If you're in an emotionally abusive relationship, don't accept it. Find the help you need for your healing. If someone you care about needs help, help that person. If you need counseling, get it. It may be expensive, time-consuming, and even humiliating, but it may save your health, your sanity, and your life. It may even restore the relationship you once had with someone you once loved.

Life is short. Find the path to forgiveness.

Celebrate the Love You Have

My mother, cleaning up the remains of our little tea party, glanced up at me. "True love," she said with a wry smile.

"True love," I said with contempt.

And we began to laugh. And the rain pounded the roof, and I imagined my husband riding home in a miserable downpour. My mother threw a teacup into the fireplace and it shattered, spraying the room with fragments. I followed her lead and hurled a cup of my own, and we laughed until we could not stand. We laughed while the storm thundered down the valley. We laughed at men and guns and dim-witted girls and foreigners. We lay on our backs and held one another's hand and laughed at the ceiling. We laughed until she begged me to stop. And I never loved her more than in that moment.

Glossary

Afghan horse culture

Though much of the ancient lore is disappearing with the nation's modernization, Afghanistan is one of the world's oldest enduring horse cultures. The training and breeding techniques used by Afghan horsemen are based on ancient traditions passed from fathers to sons throughout ten thousand years of nomadic life. Afghan horses are identified more by their national origin than by breed, but they are renown for their endurance, strength, and fearlessness. They are generally smaller than Western-bred horses or Arabians, but they are versatile, and their use in military conflict continues into modern times. During the Soviet occupation, mounted mujahideen may have killed as many as fifty thousand Russians. In 2001, U.S. Special Forces and CIA officers fought from horseback with

Afghan Northern Alliance fighters in the war against the Taliban. Their success in combining modern military technology with the efficient, mobile horseback units of the Northern Alliance is legendary.

Afghan languages

Pashto and Dari are the official and most widely spoken languages in Afghanistan. They are both Indo-European languages of Iranian origin. More than forty minor languages are spoken in the country, and many Afghans are multilingual. Dari is a form of Persian (Farsi), more closely resembling classical Persian. Iranian and Afghan Persian are very similar and mutually understood, with the main differences being some vocabulary and pronunciation.

Ahmad Shah Massoud

Massoud was an Afghan political and military leader and a key figure in the war with the Soviets. A Tajik of Sunni Muslim background, he was born to a well-to-do family in the Panjshir Valley in 1953. He attended Lycée Esteqlal, a Franco-Afghan school in Kabul, where he was a gifted student. He was a brilliant military strategist and political leader and the only Afghan leader who never left the country during the war with the Soviets. He was assassinated on September 9, 2001, two days before the World Trade Center attack, by a pair of al-Qaeda suicide bombers posing as journalists. He is a national hero in Afghanistan.

AK-47

A gas-operated assault rifle designed by Mikhail Kalashnikov and manufactured in the Soviet Union. It is the most widely used assault weapon in the world.

al-Qaeda

"The Base." A militant Islamic organization founded by Osama bin Laden. Members of the al-Qaeda are Sunni Muslims who practice Wahhabism, an extreme form of fundamental Islam. Their intent is to return Islam to its foundation by building Islamic states founded on sharia law.

Allahu Akbar

"Allah is greater" or "Allah is the greatest."

Arabi sheep

A domestic breed of sheep found in southern Iran, southern Iraq, and northeast Arabia. It is primarily bred for meat.

attan

An Afghan folk dance and the national dance of Afghanistan. It is performed at weddings, at celebrations, and as a war dance.

bacha bazi

"Interested in children" (Persian). A sexual-slavery practice dating back to ancient times that thrives in Afghanistan. PBS's *Frontline* aired a comprehensive and informative documentary on the practice in April 2010.[18]

British Lee-Enfield

The Lee-Enfield was a bolt-action, magazine-fed rifle used by the British military in the early twentieth century. One of the finest infantry rifles every produced, it remained in service in the British military until the mid-1960s. It is still used by the Indian army. The rifles' simplicity, durability, and accuracy made them a favorite in Afghanistan, where they are still in service.

Khyber Pass copies of the Enfield models are common across Afghanistan and Pakistan.

burka

An Arabized version of the Persian word *purda*, meaning "curtain" or "veil."

Buzkashi

Literally, "goat grabbing"—an extremely violent game played on horseback, and the national sport of Afghanistan. Opposing teams try to maneuver a headless goat carcass to a central target. The game is of unknown origin, possibly imported to Afghanistan by Genghis Khan's Mongol invaders in 1219. Some have speculated that the Mongols would raid Afghan villages and steal goats and sheep, snatching them as they galloped through. Afghan men would mount their horses and pursue the raiders in an attempt to retrieve the stolen animal. When the invaders left, the game continued.

Eid al-Adha

"The Feast of the Sacrifice"—an Islamic holiday honoring Abraham's willingness to sacrifice his son Ishmael to God as an act of submission.

espand

A west Asian flowering plant used for making dyes, inks, and tattoos. It is used in some traditional medicines and commonly used as incense in magic and religious rituals to ward off evil influence. Its use predates Islam and can be traced to the ancient Semitics.

Hafiz

An Iranian poet, mystic, and scholar born in the early 1300s. The themes of his writings focus on love, faith, and spirituality. He is still the most popular poet in Iran. His works are often memorized in Iran, Afghanistan, and Turkmenistan and used as proverbs.

Hazara

The third-largest ethnic group in Afghanistan. They are also found in significant numbers in Pakistan and Iran. Due to their physical characteristics and cultural practices, they appear to be descendants of the Mongolians. There is some genetic indication of their Mongolian ancestry. As an ethnic group, they have experienced persecution as far back as the sixteenth century. In August 1998, the Taliban massacred six thousand Hazara in the northern city of Mazar-i-Sharif.

Hürrem Sultan

A Ukrainian concubine of Hürrem Haseki Sultan, a sixteenth-century ruler of the Ottoman Empire. She eventually became his legal wife and played an important role in the Ottoman Empire and in Sultan's political relations with Europe.

Iblis

"Satan." From an Arabic root word meaning "he who causes despair."

inshallah

"Allah willing" or "if Allah wills."

Jalāl ad-Dīn Muhammad Rūmī

A thirteenth-century Persian poet, Sufi mystic, and theologian. His works are still popular in the Persian-speaking world and have been translated into many languages.

Jezail

A heavy, long-barreled, Afghan-made musket, very accurate for its time, with a range of more than three hundred meters. It was used effectively against British troops in the Anglo-Afghan wars of the nineteenth and early twentieth centuries.

The Jezail fired a large .50- to .75-caliber projectile, and was a deadly sniper weapon.

jihad

"Struggle."

jinn

"Hidden from sight," "genies." Spiritual creatures who live in the invisible world and may be good or evil.

khawk

"Reverence for the land." Similar to Native Americans' concept of sacred land.

Khyber Pass

A one-thousand-meter pass between Pakistan and Afghanistan and part of the ancient Silk Road. It is one of the oldest mountain passes in the world and of strategic military significance.

King Naqshband

An ancient Persian Zoroastrian king.

kurta

A long, collarless men's shirt worn in southern and western Asia.

Kushan treasure

The Kushans were a nomadic people who formed an empire that included parts of north India, central Asia, and southwest China. Soviet archaeologists, just prior to the 1979 invasion, discovered the Bactrian gold, a priceless trove of gold artifacts, in the graves of wealthy Kushan traders who had plied the Silk Road. The collection was safely stored in a bank vault throughout the reign of the Taliban and remains a national treasure in Afghanistan.

Mon Rêve Devenu Réalité

"My dream has become my reality."

mujahideen

"Strugglers."

mullah

"Master" or "guardian."

naan

A simple flat bread made from flour, water, and salt. It was first used in ancient Mesopotamia when the Sumerians discovered that grains could be ground into flour.

pakol

A round, woolen Afghan men's cap.

Panjshir Valley

"Valley of the Five Lions." One of the richest and most beautiful regions of Afghanistan. It is home to about one hundred and forty thousand people, including the largest concentration of Tajiks, a Persian-speaking ethnic group of Iranian origin.

qabili pilau

The national dish of Afghanistan. A delicious dish of lamb in rice cooked with onions, carrots, and raisins, and seasoned with coriander, cinnamon, black pepper, cumin, cardamom, cloves, and rose water.

Quran

"The Recitation." Islam's principal text, believed to be given to Mohammed by the angel Gabriel over a period of about twenty-three years.

Shahnameh

"The Book of Kings." An epic fifty-thousand-verse poem written around AD 1000 by the

Persian poet Ferdowsi. It contains an account of the Islamic conquest of Persia and the story of creation.

Sherwani

A long men's overcoat worn in south Asia. It originated as a hybrid of the *shalwar kameez*, which is a long shirt worn by men and women in central and south Asia, and a British frock coat. It was originally worn by Muslim aristocrats in northern India, but became fashionable formal dress attire in modern times.

Sufism

A mystical sect of Sunni Islam.

Suleiman the Great

The tenth ruler of the Ottoman Empire. He was a brilliant military strategist who conquered most of the Middle East, much of the North African coast, and much of Eastern Europe. His advance into Europe was halted at the siege of Vienna in 1529. At the time of his death in 1566, the Ottoman Empire was one of the world's foremost powers.

Taliban

"Students." An Islamic fundamentalist movement that spread from Pakistan into Afghanistan in the mid-1990s.

The Arabian Nights

One Thousand and One Nights. A collection of Arabic and South Asian folk tales compiled in the Islamic Golden Age between the eighth and twelfth centuries.

Acknowledgments

Thanks to these crackerjack editors: Sara Brady, Michael Mandarano, Monique Peterson, and Brenda Pitts.

Thanks to these amazing friends—for their enthusiastic encouragement, their insightful ideas, and their thoughtful suggestions: Ann, Anna Joy, Aparna, Barbara, Beverly, Cathie, Chris, Corrie, Deonna, Dot, Georgina, Heather, Hope, Jamie, Jana, Jenn, Jeanette, Jeanne, Jenina, Kerry, Kirby, Leigh, Lois, Marlene, Melanie, Paden, Page, Perri, Rachael, Rena, Rob, Scott, Shermeen, Sheryl, Stacy, and Tova.

Thanks to my nemeses, who taught me life's most important lessons.

A Word from Bonhoeffer Publishing

We hope you enjoyed *The Poppy Field Diary*. The sequel, *Through Dancing Poppies*, is scheduled for publication in 2016. If you would like to receive an announcement upon its release, sign up with your e-mail address at www.bonhoefferpublishing.com. We promise we won't put you on an intrusive mailing list and we will not sell or give your e-mail address to anyone. Bonhoeffer Publishing is a values-based publishing company. Our vision is to promote and distribute quality, thought-provoking, entertaining material that enriches lives. If this book did not meet your expectations, please contact us through www.bonhoefferpublishing. com. We will do our best to make it right.

Endnotes

1 Allie Malloy, "Married nearly 66 years, Ohio couple dies on same day." CNN, August 27, 2013.

2 Maddy Sauer, "Family of couple who died holding hands: 'They were always together.'" TODAY, October 17, 2013.

3 Thomas Keneally, *American Scoundrel: The Life of the Notorious Civil War General Dan Sickles* (New York: Nan A. Talese/Doubleday, 2002).

4 Kristen P. Mark, Erick Janssen, Robin R. Milhausen, *Infidelity in Heterosexual Couples: Demographic, Interpersonal, and Personality-Related Predictors of Extradyadic Sex*, Received: 4 September 2009 / Revised: 10 December 2010 / Accepted: 12 February 2011 Ó Springer Science+Business Media, LLC 2011.

5 Shirley P. Glass, Ph.D., *NOT "Just Friends"* (New York: Free Press, 2002).

6 U.S. Department of Health and Human Services. National Center for Health Statistics, Survey on Child Health, Washington, D.C., 1993.

7   Jean Bethke Elshtain, *Family Matters: The Plight of America's Children* (The Christian Century: July 1993), 14–21.

8   U.S. Department of Health and Human Services. National Center for Health Statistics, National Health Interview Survey, Hyattsville, MD, 1988.

9   Karen Hemer, "Gender, Interaction, and Delinquency: Testing a Theory of Differential Social Control," *Social Psychology Quarterly* 59 (1996): 39–61.

10 U.S. Department of Health and Human Services. National Center for Health Statistics, Survey on Child Health, Washington, D.C.; GPO, 1993.

11 C. C. Harper, and S. S. McLanahan, (2004), "Father Absence and Youth Incarceration." *Journal of Research on Adolescence,* 14: 369–397.

12 The words of Socrates as represented in Plato's work, *Phaedo.*

13 Mimi Alford, *Once Upon a Secret* (New York: Random House, 2012).

14 Nick Squires, "99-year-old divorces wife after he discovered 1940s affair," The Telegraph Media Group, December 29, 2011.

15 Matthew Kelly, *The Seven Levels of Intimacy* (New York: Fireside, 2007).

16 Lewis B. Smedes, *The Art of Forgiving* (New York: Ballantine Books, 1997).

17   O. Henry, *The Gift of the Magi*, first published in *The New York Sunday World*, December 10, 1906.

18   "The Dancing Boys of Afghanistan," PBS *Frontline*, http://www.pbs.org/wgbh/pages/frontline/dancing-boys.